JAN 19

OUR YEAR OF MAYBE

ALSO BY
RACHEL LYNN SOLOMON

You'll Miss Me When I'm Gone

OUR YEAR OF
MAYBE

RACHEL LYNN SOLOMON

SIMON PULSE

NEW YORK LONDON TORONTO SYDNEY NEW DELHI

SIMON PULSE

An imprint of Simon & Schuster Children's Publishing Division
1230 Avenue of the Americas, New York, New York 10020
First Simon Pulse hardcover edition January 2019
Text copyright © 2019 by Rachel Lynn Solomon
Jacket design and illustration by Sarah Creech copyright © 2019 by Simon & Schuster, Inc.
All rights reserved, including the right of reproduction in whole or in part in any form.
SIMON PULSE and colophon are registered trademarks of Simon & Schuster, Inc.
For information about special discounts for bulk purchases, please contact Simon & Schuster Special Sales at 1-866-506-1949 or business@simonandschuster.com.
The Simon & Schuster Speakers Bureau can bring authors to your live event.
For more information or to book an event contact the Simon & Schuster Speakers Bureau at 1-866-248-3049 or visit our website at www.simonspeakers.com.
Interior designed by Tom Daly
The text of this book was set in Palatino.
Manufactured in the United States of America
2 4 6 8 10 9 7 5 3 1
Library of Congress Cataloging-in-Publication Data
Names: Solomon, Rachel Lynn, author.
Title: Our year of maybe / by Rachel Lynn Solomon.
Description: First Simon Pulse hardcover edition. | New York : Simon Pulse, 2019. |
Summary: Aspiring choreographer Sophie Orenstein, eighteen, wonders if seventeen-year-old Peter Rosenthal-Porter, gifted pianist, best friend, and secret crush, will love her back after receiving her kidney.
Identifiers: LCCN 2018010507 | ISBN 9781481497763 (hardcover)
Subjects: | CYAC: Best friends—Fiction. | Friendship—Fiction. | Transplantation of organs, tissues, etc.—Fiction. | Musicians—Fiction. | Love—Fiction. | Jews—United States—Fiction. | Seattle (Wash.)—Fiction.
Classification: LCC PZ7.1.S6695 Our 2019 | DDC [Fic]—dc23
LC record available at https://lccn.loc.gov/2018010507
ISBN 9781481497787 (eBook)

FOR MY PARENTS, JENNY AND BRAD,
for (almost) always letting me bring
a book to the dinner table

I can't have you, but I have dreams.

—Brandi Carlile

OUR YEAR OF
MAYBE

SOMETIMES

PETER AND THE PIANO BELONGED TO EACH other the way I always wanted him to belong to me.

At the baby grand in his living room, he held his hands over the keys, fingers trembling as they waited to launch into a song. The anticipation was my favorite part. He drew his lower lip between his teeth and squinted at his scribbles on the sheet music.

I didn't know how he kept his back so straight. As a dancer, I'd suffered countless teachers critiquing my posture. But Peter at the piano was flawless, as though he'd been carved from the same wood. He and the instrument understood each other, while I sometimes wondered if I tried too hard to make dance love me.

On the floor, I flexed and pointed my feet. My arches were killing me. They always were. We were in the middle of practicing a piece we'd probably never show anyone else. I started dance at the same time Peter started piano lessons, and as kids we performed for each other—showed off, really—which turned into this: I choreographed solo routines set to his original compositions. A long time ago my sister had jokingly called us the Terrible Twosome, and the name had stuck.

"Hey, Peter," I say, trying to sound confident and casual and *cool*. We were alone in his house, a rarity, and I wouldn't have dared ask this question if his parents were hanging around. I let out a deep breath. Eight counts. Sixteen. "Do you . . . ever think about *it*?"

Truthfully, it was something I'd wanted to ask Peter for a long time. I was fifteen and he was fourteen, and we'd been best friends since we were toddlers. We talked about his doctor's appointments and his medications and even the catheter in his belly. But we never talked about this. And, well, I was *curious*. I couldn't help myself.

Slowly his head spun in my direction. He needed a haircut. Peter with his hair a little too long was my favorite Peter. I wondered what it would feel like to drag my fingers through his dark locks. Maybe I'd trace my thumb along the shell of his ear, see if it made him shiver. Thinking about it almost made *me* shiver.

"Do you mean sex?" His voice cracked on the word "sex," and I nodded. I would have laughed if I hadn't been so serious about it all. Peter's vocal cords were stuck in boyhood; it reminded me we weren't as adult as I wished we were. "Yeah . . . I mean, sometimes."

"Me too," I rushed to say. "Sometimes." An understatement. Lately it seemed like the only thing I thought about. This time

I did laugh, as though to show him I was totally comfortable with the conversation. *Ha-ha-ha, I think about sex too! But only sometimes!*

I wondered if "sometimes" was an understatement for Peter, too.

He moved fluidly through some arpeggios, and I returned to my mission: to figure out if Peter's "sometimes" somehow involved me.

"I've been thinking." I tugged the elastic out of my ponytail, which stole a few strands of hair. "So many people talk about how they regret their first time. How they wish it had been with someone else." Right. Like I knew *so many people.* "And I was thinking, um, as I said, that when we, you know, *do it* for the first time . . . that it should be with each other."

His finger landed on a sour key.

"I mean," I said to his shoulders, my cheeks burning, "you're my best friend. You know me better than anyone else in the world. I can't imagine it being with anyone but you."

He'd liked me once—an embarrassing declaration when we were in middle school that went nowhere. At the time I'd been honest, told him I didn't feel the same way, and after a few weeks of awkwardness, we were back to normal. But we were older now. My feelings had changed. Only I was going to be craftier about it than he had been.

Slowly he twisted on the bench, posture still perfect. "Me either. I guess it would be natural for us to—" He waved his hand in a horrifying motion that was maybe supposed to mimic

3

sex. "In the future, though," he added, like he was confirming that it wasn't going to happen tonight.

"Right." God, I hoped it wouldn't be too far in the future. "Like . . . before we graduate from high school?"

A beat. Two. His face scrunched, like he was trying to calculate the possibility of either or both of us liking someone else enough to completely disrobe in front of them in the next three years. Then he nodded, apparently reaching a conclusion, and stuck out his hand like a freaking Boy Scout. "Sophie, I would be honored to lose my virginity to you."

He was serious, too, but one corner of his mouth threatened to yank the whole thing into a smile. We shook on it.

"Maybe . . . ," I said, feeling brave now, wondering how adventurous I could be. "Maybe we should seal it with a kiss?"

His Adam's apple bobbed in his throat as he swallowed once, twice. "I . . . guess we could do that," he whispered. He scooted over on the piano bench, making room for me. I slid in next to him, swatting his arm when he let out a nervous laugh.

"Be serious," I said, and then it was happening—his lips on mine. Warm, gentle, uncertain. Sprite and spearmint gum. I put my hands on his shoulders, gripped him a little, mostly to steady myself, and I wondered if I should open my mouth or move closer or—

Or nothing at all, because it was suddenly over.

"Should we—uh—try this from the second verse?" His hands were back on the keys, where they remained the rest of our practice session. Every so often I'd catch his mouth tip upward or his cheeks redden, and it made me feel oddly victorious.

Though we never talked about the details of the pact, my mind happily filled them in on nights I couldn't fall asleep right away. Because I was in love with him—the kind of love that made my throat ache with all the things I couldn't say. He just hadn't figured out quite yet that he was too.

PART I

CHAPTER 1

SOPHIE

SOME DANCERS ARE GAZELLES. THEIR LEGS SLASH the air like scissors through silk, and their arms beckon the audience closer. They are works of art, pretty things to stare at.

I am no gazelle. On dance team, none of us are.

We are lions.

Montana Huang, fresh off a unanimous vote for captain last week, leads us in rehearsal in the gym—*five, six, seven, eight*—and then we roar to life. We toss our hair, swivel our hips, bare our teeth.

"Sophie!" Montana growls, her brows leaping to her hairline. "The second eight count starts with punch-punch-hip-circle-hair-flip, not hip-circle-punch-punch-hair-flip." She demonstrates.

Admittedly, I'm a little distracted today, but not the kind of school's-almost-out distracted some of the other dancers seem to be. "Sorry," I mumble before Montana restarts the remixed nineties hip-hop song.

Sophomore year, I quit the studio I'd been dancing at since I was a kid. I needed freedom from my teachers squawking, "Back straight!" and "Chin up!" and "Don't forget to *smile*." I didn't want to smile all the time—sometimes I wanted to look angry, because the steps were raw and ferocious, because I *felt* angry. I wasn't delicate, and I didn't want to be.

And I saw the way guys watched the girls on dance team during assemblies and football games.

I wanted Peter to watch me that way.

Once a week I take a jazz class at my old studio to stay on top of my technique for the team. But back when I took competition classes, I was at the studio four days a week, sometimes until ten p.m. It was too much.

Punch-punch-hip-circle-hair-flip. Run, run, run, and grand jeté. Heads down, new formation. Again and again—"Sophie, are you with us?"—and again.

"Great last practice," Montana says when we're all sweat-slick and out of breath. "Check your e-mail for our summer schedule, okay?" A chorus of yeses. A grin from Montana. "We're going to be rock stars next year."

I chew the cap off my water bottle and pin loose strands of red hair back into my ponytail. Junior year is officially over. In the locker room, my teammates trade summer plans. They hope we'll have a real summer this year, the possibility of a tan. They talk about parties I won't be attending despite the "maybe" I marked on all social media invites. "No" has always felt too brash to me, too final. I guess I like having options. Sophie Orenstein: perennial maybe.

"Anyone want to carpool to Grant Gleason's party this weekend?"

"Did you see the finale of *Dance Island*?"

"I need a better smudge-proof eyeliner. Was it dripping down my face all practice and no one told me?"

My summer will be spent first in a hospital room and then recovering from a voluntary surgery my parents are still convinced I shouldn't have volunteered for.

For me, it was never a question of *should* or *shouldn't*.

Only a matter of *when*.

The curtains of his first-floor bedroom window are open when I race across the street to his house. In my life, I have never simply walked to Peter's house. I am always on fast-forward, eager to get to him. A lion, though Peter is not exactly my prey.

His legs are stretched out on the red plaid comforter, one arm triangled behind his head, the other balancing a book on his lap. When Peter's nervous or concentrating hard, he draws his bottom lip into his mouth and keeps it there, like he's doing now.

In Peter's room, each of his hobbies gets its own space. In one corner: his vintage record player and stacks of LPs. Along the wall opposite his bed: an alphabetized bookshelf. In another corner: his pet chinchilla, Mark, the most adorable creature on this earth, and his maze of a cage. Next to his bed: his Yamaha keyboard and pages of sheet music, though we don't play as the Terrible Twosome as much as we used to. School and other commitments got in the way. I'm hoping that will change this fall. And half hidden by his closet: a storage bin for his medical supplies.

I drum my fingers on his window, and Peter glances up from his book and beckons me inside. I shake my head and beckon him over to me instead.

"You look like shit," I say when he opens the window, instead of hello.

He bows, dark hair slipping past his eyebrows. "Thank you. I try."

A long time ago he made me swear to always tell him the truth. Everyone lies when you're sick. They say you look great when you do not, that things are going to get better soon; they just know it. Peter hates those platitudes.

Even when he isn't feeling great, though, he is still beautiful. Full, dark eyebrows, strong jaw, hazel eyes that focus so intently on mine, that make it hard to look away.

And things *are* going to get better soon. That one is true.

"What are you reading?"

He flashes the cover at me: *The Feminine Mystique* by Betty Friedan. "I've got a paper due for my gender studies class." Because he's homeschooled, Peter often opts for advanced classes. They almost always sound more interesting than what I'm taking at North Seattle High.

"Learn anything interesting about me?"

"Oh yeah. I've got your mysteries *allllll* figured out." He feathers his fingers as he says this. "You could always read it and learn for yourself."

12

It's probably Peter's deepest desire for me to love reading like he does. Though I'm not as terrified of it as I was when a diagnosis of dyslexia illuminated why I struggled so much in elementary school, I don't read much for fun.

"Maybe I will." Glancing down, I say, "I see you're wearing my favorite pants."

It's this ancient pair of navy sweatpants he basically lived in a few years ago. They're threadbare at the knees, the seams on the sides nearly splitting apart. I don't even think the elastic waistband is still, well, elasticky. But I only tease because I love him.

"Don't pretend you don't want to burn them."

"Oh, I'm burning them. After the surgery. Don't worry." I clear my throat. No more joking around. "Are you okay to go for a walk, or do you have to do an exchange? I wanted to talk."

As I say this, the half-moons under Peter's eyes become more apparent, the sag in his posture a bit deeper. "I'm fine for another couple hours. I could do a short walk."

He tosses some alfalfa into Mark's cage and zips a North Face fleece over his plaid button-down. This boy is so Seattle it hurts. Then he climbs out the window and into the evening with me. I'm practically chasséing into his backyard, tugging on the silver chain of the tiny Star of David necklace I wear every day, my heart a wild thing inside my chest.

"Everything okay?" he asks.

It's Wednesday, and we may not have a chance to talk like this until after the transplant Friday morning.

"Extra energy from practice. You'll come see us perform in the fall, right?"

"Definitely. Hopefully I can go to every game." The uncertainty hangs in the air. *Hopefully* the transplant will go smoothly. *Hopefully* no complications. *Hopefully* it will work. We are optimism soup. "Where are we going?" he asks as I lead him through the greenbelt behind his house and into the woods. We wind around trees that have been here longer than either of our families.

"Patience, ratty-sweatpanted one."

He makes a *tsk*ing sound and pats the thighs of his pants. "I like these pants. I'm gonna be sad when you burn them."

If Peter and I were together, we'd hold hands on this walk. I'd trace the knobs of his knuckles, lean in close, bury my face where his neck meets his shoulder. He'd press me up against a tree, kiss me until we both were dizzy with desire.

Sometimes being around him is agony, the gap between what we have and what I want too wide to ever cross.

After about ten minutes, we reach a clearing with a pond. We played here all the time as kids. In his portal fantasy phase, Peter was convinced that if we found the right rotting tree trunk or patch of grass, we'd tumble into another world. But we haven't been here in years. The pond is an unhealthy gray-green, and the ground is decorated with crushed beer cans. It used to be the place we'd go to hide from our families, back when our parents said more to each other than "good evening" when they happened to take the trash out at the same time.

14

I hug my sweatshirt tighter around me, wishing I'd changed into something warmer than gym shorts after practice.

"Are you having second thoughts?" Peter asks suddenly, his voice threaded with panic.

"No!" I say quickly. It's true—I'm not. It's just that I've been anticipating our surgery for so long that it's become impossible to imagine our lives on the other side of it.

His shoulders soften, and he lets out a long sigh. "Okay. Because. You know you don't have to do this, right? I mean, of course I'm thrilled you're doing it, and my parents are thrilled you're doing it. But you don't have to. You know that."

I do. But I love Peter more than the world. More than my parents, more than dance, more than my sister, Tabitha, and my niece, Luna. It's easy to fall in love with someone who's a master of their craft. Peter at the piano has an intensity I've always admired. An electricity, like if I touched him in the middle of a Rufus Wainwright song, he'd burn my hand. Lower lip between his teeth, dark hair in his face, shoulder blades rolling beneath his T-shirt as he moves up and down the keys. I can never help imagining if he'll ever touch me with the same kind of gentle desperation.

Performance art has always connected us. Our music tastes overlap but aren't identical, and when we play together, we feed off each other's energy. My heart never feels closer to his than at the end of a song, when we're both out of breath, grinning at each other like we've created something only the two of us will ever understand.

Aside from that, Peter is a certified Good Person. A good friend, even before my feelings for him turned romantic. When I had to repeat fourth grade because my reading comprehension was below grade level and my report cards were abysmal, Peter read aloud with me at home. I was still a grade ahead of him, but he was patient while I made my mouth form unfamiliar words like "chronological" and "tangible" and "eclipse." I remember whispering a word to myself first, worried I'd mispronounce it if I said it out loud. The letters were always jumping around. "It's just me," Peter would say. "Try it." It was only after I'd been held back and continued to struggle that my parents brought me to a specialist. Girls are often diagnosed with dyslexia later than boys. It explained so much, though it didn't excuse the teasing I'd endured, the kids who'd called me stupid. I wasn't, my specialist said. I just learned differently.

"You have a bigger brain than they do," Peter said. "They're jealous." I snorted, but then he told me he'd been reading up on it—a very Peter thing to do—and there was scientific evidence: usually the left hemisphere of a dyslexic person's brain is larger than the brain of someone who doesn't have dyslexia. Plus, he said, John Lennon was dyslexic.

When he started homeschooling, a mix of online courses and a couple at a local homeschool center, I spent my afternoons and weekends with him, ignored other kids' invitations to parties and sleepovers until they eventually stopped coming.

He is solid and constant. The moon and the stars.

I would do anything for this boy, and I'd have done it sooner if I could, but I had to wait until I turned eighteen a couple months ago to see if I was a match. Sometimes I wonder if the reverse is true—if Peter would do anything for me. Deep in my bones I know that if Peter were healthy, if my kidneys had failed instead of his, he would. He's just never had a chance to prove it like I have.

I unzip my backpack and spread a blanket over the ground. "I wanted to give you something," I say as we sit down. "Before the surgery."

"You're already giving me something kind of huge."

"Fine, something you can actually hold." Making my face super serious, I pull Operation out of my backpack.

He bursts out laughing. I adore Peter's laugh. It's like your favorite song played on repeat. "Stop. You're the best. You're already the best, and then you do this? There isn't even a word for what you are."

His words swim through my veins and try to convince my heart he feels what I feel.

"Fantastic, brilliant, wonderful, perfect."

"All of those. You are all the adjectives. You and your big brain." Every so often, that joke pops back up.

Beautiful, intriguing, irresistible—those, too? I don't say.

We scoot closer to each other on the blanket, Peter's thigh against my thigh, Peter's hip against my hip. My entire left side hums with electricity, but I'm careful not to press myself into him the way I want to. I am constantly pretending that Peter touching me is not the most incredible feeling in the world. I've trained my breath not to catch in my throat, willed my heart to slow down. I am more aware of my body when I'm with him than when I'm onstage.

"Why are you doing this, Soph?" he asks, idly brushing a thumb across my knee, a gesture that nearly splits me open on the forest floor.

He's asked this question so many times. A voluntary surgery like this is no small thing. The only thing in my life that comes close, four stubborn baby teeth when I was eleven, can't exactly compare.

I've gotten so used to sick Peter that I wonder what a healthier Peter will be like. He won't be on dialysis anymore. He won't sleep so much, eat so little, throw up the small amount of food he's able to get down. He won't hurt.

"You are my best friend and favorite person," I say. "And you really, really need to start wearing jeans again."

He doesn't laugh. "Are you scared?" He whispers it, though we are the only people around. Like he wants to keep our conversation a secret from the trees and sky. He reaches over and squeezes my hand.

"Yes," I say simply, squeezing back. I can't be dishonest with him, not about this. Even though there is no way I'm changing my mind, I'm terrified of what will happen when I am unconscious. When they cut me open and put part of me into Peter.

On the blanket, my phone lights up with a message from my dad.

Where are you? Luna's party starts at 6.

18

It's five till. "I completely spaced," I say with a groan, smacking my forehead. "It's Luna's birthday."

"Wait. Before you go." He reaches over and pulls up the hem of my sweatshirt. His hand fumbles between the sweatshirt and my tank top for a second, like he's searching for where, exactly, the kidney I'm giving him is located, and then he strokes my back. Slowly I exhale. Through the thin cotton fabric, his fingers are warm.

There are a thousand other reasons I'm doing this, but still, this gesture makes me think what I have only allowed myself to think about on the rarest occasions: that maybe, after the transplant, Peter will want me, too.

"Don't worry, Soph," he says, replacing my nerves with something even scarier. "I'll take good care of it."

CHAPTER 2

PETER

WE CAN SEE SOPHIE'S HOUSE OUT OUR KITCHEN window, so it's almost like her family's having dinner with mine.

"A lot of cars over there," my mom muses, aiming her fork at the window.

"Her sister's having a thing," I say to my plate.

"A *Thing*, you say?" my dad says in the most dadlike way. He could open up a school to train fathers-to-be in the art of bad jokes and gentle sarcasm, but his sense of humor suits him as a dentist, too. "That explains it! I've heard Things are very popular these days. Especially with the young people."

Years ago, my family would've been invited to the party Sophie forgot about. But somewhere in between hospital visits and mortgage payments and Sophie's younger sister's pregnancy, our parents slipped away from each other. What initially brought them together—proximity and religion, my dad being

Jewish along with both of Sophie's parents—was no long
enough. They keep to their separate homes, pinballing Sopl
and me back and forth between them.

"How was your day, Peter?" my mom asks. A commun
college writing professor, she's always been tremendous
empathetic, more sensitive than my dad. If I was having an esp
cially difficult day, she'd hold a hand to her heart like it caus
her physical pain too. For the past ten years, she's been workii
on a novel. I'm not sure she dreams of publication, necessarily
she just wants to finish it. After dinner, like she does every nigl
she'll retreat to the couch with a glass of wine, her laptop, and
furrow between her brows.

"Not bad." I spear a hunk of stuffed eggplant. On our fridg
is a list of kidney-friendly foods. "One more paper due tonigl
and then I'm free for the summer—well, after the recove
period."

"Overprotective" doesn't even begin to describe Benjamin I
Rosenthal, DDS, and Holly Porter. Until I begged her to stop la
year, my mom tracked the times of all my exchanges on a sprea
sheet. Strict bedtimes, which I never questioned because I w
always exhausted anyway. No long vacations, which meant
travel beyond the state's borders. No driver's ed. No driving w
Sophie until she had her license a full year and was accident-fr
I wasn't even allowed to take the city bus until last year becau
what if an infection stunned my body the exact moment I
down, as infections are known to do? No trips anywhere tl
didn't approve first, which didn't make sense because how v

21

I supposed to get there if I couldn't drive, take the bus, or ride with Sophie? Shockingly, I didn't own a bike, either.

My parents trade a look, and after several seconds that send me into only a mild panic, they make some kind of silent agreement to allow my mom to speak first.

She stretches across the table to cover my hand with hers. Her nails are pale blue and filed into claws. It's the one luxury she allows herself: a different color and design each month. "Baby, we're all crossing our fingers for the best. But we don't want you to be devastated if we don't get the outcome we're hoping for."

"I—I know." The reality wraps its cold fingers around me. There are never any guarantees. Sophie's kidney could fail. My body could reject it. I know all the risks, everything from infection to death.

But, God, it could also be a whole new life for me.

My mom smiles tightly, thinly. We all have sparkling teeth; my dad has us go to the dentist every four months instead of the typical six. "We have to be cautiously optimistic."

Those words could define my entire life. A new expression appeared on my parents' faces after Sophie and I went through all the tests, and they're wearing it tonight. Extreme hopefulness tempered by realism, like they won't give in to joy because there's always a chance something could go wrong.

We've been through it before—when the major thing that could go wrong, did. I had one transplant when I was five, from a nonliving donor, but my body rejected the kidney. That failure made it a thousand times harder to find another match. Made it

something of a miracle that the perfect person was living across the street from me this whole time.

I came to terms with my life, however short it might end up being, a long time ago, after periods of both anger and depression that I worked on with a therapist. There was dialysis. Constant fatigue. Doctor's appointments. Blue pills and pink pills and green pills, pills so large I worried they'd never slide down my esophagus. Iron pills after I developed anemia. Pills I choked down when I couldn't eat anything else, pills that made me even sicker with side effects.

Sometimes I wonder if Sophie's parents wish she'd latched on to a healthier friend. Someone whose idea of a wild Friday night involved more than a Star Wars marathon and the weird salad my dad used to make all the time, a combination of foods good for the kidneys: cabbage and red bell pepper and cranberries and garlic, drizzled with olive oil. Sophie claimed to love it, but I wonder if she said so just to make me feel better about it. Especially when it gave us both garlic breath.

Truthfully, Sophie with garlic breath could never bother me.

"You promise you'll check Mark's water every day while I'm in the hospital?" I ask my parents. "And you'll give him a dust bath at least twice a week?"

"We raised a teenage boy," my mom says. "I'm pretty sure we can handle a chinchilla."

"Though it's hard to tell who's hairier," my dad dad-jokes.

My mom laughs and I groan, but the moment of levity won't last long. In our family, it never does.

Apparently, I'm a medical marvel. I was born with renal dysplasia, which means one of my kidneys wasn't working. Sometimes the normal kidney can do the work of both kidneys, the same way someone healthy can live with one kidney. But my working kidney wasn't normal. I should have died before I was born.

My condition progressed to chronic kidney disease before I even started kindergarten. A kid suffering from an old-person illness. Doctors explained to me in the most basic terms how kidneys functioned: like little trash collectors that removed waste and extra water from the blood, which was then sent to the bladder as urine. After my good kidney and then my first donor kidney failed, I went back on dialysis. The kind of dialysis most people are familiar with involves being hooked up to a machine for hours at a time, multiple times a week. But I hated going in for it. Being surrounded by machines only made me feel sicker. I was surviving—but not actually living.

Now I'm on peritoneal dialysis. A few years ago, a surgeon placed a soft tube called a catheter in my belly, and I do "exchanges" five times a day. I pour dialysis solution into a bag that flows through the catheter. The solution soaks up extra fluid and waste, and after a few hours, I drain it and begin the process again. Each exchange takes about fifteen minutes. At the beginning, my parents did it for me, but as I got older and my body fell into a prolonged awkward stage, I grew embarrassed. A milestone in any young boy's life: learning to clean his catheter site.

You can still have a normal life, all my doctors said. But some days it felt impossible. I played baseball for a year, but I missed too many practices and the coach was too freaked by my condition to let me play in the games, even after my mom yelled at him. Instead, I lifted weights to keep up my strength. Dialysis was supposed to be painless, but sometimes it made me nauseous and stole my appetite. Food could taste metallic. Occasionally my legs would swell. If I didn't get twelve hours of sleep, I couldn't function.

My parents kept me on a tight leash after an infection landed me in the hospital the summer after sixth grade. They suggested homeschooling. It made sense, and I was too tired to fight it.

The transplant list never sounded entirely real to me. As a kid who read too many fantasy novels, I imagined an actual list scribbled on parchment. A wizard who used a quill to cross off names would get to mine and twirl his mustache. "Peter Rosenthal-Porter? I don't think so," he'd say, and move on to the next name. He was like the Dumbledore of organ donation.

Until we learned Sophie was a match, I'd given up hope that I'd get lucky twice.

Sophie and dialysis have been the two constants in my life. We performed for our families and for ourselves as the Terrible Twosome. She told me stories when I was bored and made up games for us to play, new worlds for us to live in. Sometimes she just sat next to me and watched movies. So many goddamn movies. On days I couldn't stay awake, she took naps next to me, her body warm against mine.

I liked waking up when she was still asleep, her chest rising and falling with her steady breaths.

Later that evening my mom buries herself in what must be the twelfth revision of chapter eight hundred of her book and my dad scrolls through Netflix, spending an inordinate amount of time deciding what to add to his queue. I'm down the hall in my room, in the middle of my post-dinner exchange. It's then that I'm struck with a sudden thought: After the transplant, I won't have to do this anymore. All these medical supplies, which make my room feel more like a hospital than I'd like, will be *gone*, a revelation that nearly chokes me up.

If it's successful.

I shake that thought away. No pessimism. Not after all these years on the list when a match was right across the street.

Optimism only, I remind myself. Okay. I allow myself to imagine September. While I like homeschooling, I've thought about returning to school for a while, and summer will give both Sophie and me enough time to recover before school starts. Mainly, homeschooling was just . . . easier. Easier not to explain my exchanges and unusual diet, bodily functions most people find embarrassing, my entire medical history when someone asked what they thought was an innocuous, curious question. At North Seattle High, I can be an entirely new person.

After I finish the exchange and clean up, I thumb through my record collection. Normally I'd put on my headphones and play keyboard, but I'm exhausted and still have to submit that final paper. When I realized I didn't only have to play classics on piano, I started learning as much modern, piano-centric music as I could: Rufus Wainwright, Ben Folds, Regina Spektor. I put on *Soviet Kitsch*, one of Regina's older albums, filled with clunky piano melodies and irreverent lyrics. Years ago I started writing my own music, which at first borrowed chord progressions from my favorite songs before I endeavored to create something of my very own.

When Sophie and I played together, sometimes she offered suggestions. "Try going lower on that part, instead of higher?" or "Can you slow down the beginning?" There was something about our collaboration, about watching her move to my music, that messed with the tempo of my heart.

My parents tend to go all out for my birthdays: baby grand piano, keyboard, top-of-the-line speaker system. I got a vintage record player off eBay when I turned fifteen. And then there's Mark.

For the longest time, I wanted a sister or brother. When I was nine and my parents made it clear a sibling wasn't going to happen, they said I could have a pet instead.

"Anything I want?" I asked.

"Anything you want," my dad said.

"Except for a dog," my mom added quickly, because we all knew who'd end up walking a dog. So we went to the pet store that weekend, and I picked Mark.

He's nocturnal, so he's waking up now. Chinchillas can't get wet—they come from desert climates and their fur can be slow to dry—so they take dust baths to get clean. Mark gets really into it, rolling and flopping around. Sophie and I used to film videos and put them on YouTube for all our literal dozens of subscribers.

I get what my parents were trying to do. They wanted my home to make me happy—not just because they felt sorry for me, but because they wanted me to have a reason to stay here. If I had everything I could possibly want in my house, I'd never want to leave and risk one of those freak accidents they were always worrying about.

I accepted it. It was easy to curl up in here with Sophie and hide away. Easy to get complacent.

I dump dust into Mark's dust house, unlatch his cage, and reach a hand in.

"Hey, you," I say to him now. His tiny black nose twitches, and I bury my fingers in his soft fur. "I'm going to miss you when I'm in the hospital. I want to think that you're going to miss me too, but . . . that might be giving you too much credit." I pull him out of the cage, holding him against my chest before I let him into the dust bath and he loses his little mind.

Then I do what I always do when I'm lonely and Sophie isn't here: I message her.

How's the party?

She sends back a picture of herself in a party hat, a finger drawn across her throat. As usual, her hair is spilling out of its ponytail. She's always wanted to grow it long, but she's never had the patience. So many times I've stopped short of telling her I like it the length it is. That I always like her hair, whether it's damp from the shower or untamed in the morning or curling softly onto her shoulders.

But I've never been very good at giving Sophie compliments, and even if I did, I worry she'd laugh them off. Assume I was just being nice.

That good? I write back.

I stare at my phone for two, four, eight minutes, until it becomes apparent she's gotten wrapped up in party festivities. Sighing, I drop the phone onto the bed and flop backward, frustrated for more than a few reasons. At the top of the list is my complete inability to articulate my feelings to Sophie. The one and only time I tried, it was disastrous.

Sometimes I feel so utterly trapped by these four walls, by this house. I've never done anything to lose my parents' trust. It was my body that betrayed them. My illness isn't what's prevented me from fully participating—it's everything that goes along with it, my overprotective parents and my perpetual exhaustion and how easy it was to say thank you for the flat-screen TV instead of "Could I take driver's ed next semester?"

No matter how much stuff I have, I'm almost always alone in here.

Complacency.

It's suffocating.

Sometimes my body feels more like a medical experiment than something that belongs to me. If the transplant isn't successful—I let the thought back in for a moment—well, I've already lived that life. But if everything goes smoothly . . .

Optimism. I imagine myself back at school, taking AP courses and playing piano in band. Sitting next to Sophie in class, if we're lucky enough to have any together. Parties on the weekend. Making other friends who could hang out with me here when Sophie's not answering her phone.

No. Not here. We'd be anywhere but my room.

Music and Mark and everything else in this room are only such good company. They can't hold conversations with me. They can't laugh. And when Sophie's not here, they can't tell me how much I mean to them, even if they mean a hell of a lot to me.

CHAPTER 3

SOPHIE

A BIRTHDAY PARTY FOR A ONE-YEAR-OLD IS
pretty pointless. Luna obviously has no concept of the passage of
time, despite how cute she looks in a hat too big for her head. That
didn't stop my sister, Tabby, from decorating the backyard and
inviting over a dozen friends. Any excuse for a big production.

If the yard is a stage, I'm merely an usher. I offer smiles to
Tabby's friends as they arrive, tell them where to place their gifts.
Then I escape to a lawn chair in the corner with my earbuds and
a cup of punch.

Most of Tabby's friends are theater kids too. Though we're
both involved in the performing arts, our interests have never
exactly overlapped. Tabby loves musicals but can't dance, and
the idea of memorizing a script makes me sweat. We're only a
year and a half apart and she's a junior like Peter, but her friends
have always very clearly been Her Friends, while he has always

been mine. It's not that she doesn't like Peter, but this party is for her—well, for her kid—and his family didn't make the guest list.

While the party people coo over the spectacle that is Luna playing with a bubble wand, I scroll through my phone until I find my current favorite song. It's a remix of a nearly century-old jazz piece—when you are on dance team, you listen to a *lot* of remixes—with horns and bass and a catchy chorus. I envision the choreography as anachronistic too, vintage Fosse moves mixed with modern and hip-hop. Over and over, I play the first eight bars, trying to visualize how I'd position our dancers. My favorite choreographer, Twyla Tharp, mashed up music and dances that weren't supposed to go together all the time: a ballet choreographed to a Beach Boys song in the 1970s, for example. I'd love to create something unexpected like that, something risky and new.

Every so often my mind drifts to the woods behind Peter's house, his side warm against mine as we sat on the blanket. I crave physical contact between us, but it's also a special kind of torture, one I analyze and reanalyze after every time I see him. The rare moments that seem to dip beyond friendship, like when he slid his hand beneath my sweatshirt and my tank top, are just that: *moments*. Fleeting. Agonizing.

"Sophie?" Dad's voice cuts through my song. I pause it and whip my head around. He's standing on the porch, hands jammed in his pockets, shoulders hunched in an I'm-not-sure-what-I'm-doing-here-even-though-I-live-here kind of way. My dad and I are the kind of people who are okay one-on-one but disasters in large groups. He's a sound engineer at an NPR station in Seattle, and he spends most of his time dealing with knobs and wires instead of people. "Could you come help with the cake?"

"O-kay," I say tentatively, unsure how a dessert has bested my father.

"You looked lonely out there," he says in the kitchen as he starts slicing the carrot cake, confirming he did not, in fact, need that much help—maybe he just wanted to talk to me.

"You know me." I hold out a plate so he can place a cube of cake onto it. "Not exactly a party person."

"It's a little much," he agrees, gazing out into the backyard. "But you only turn one once, I suppose."

He and my mom never expected to be grandparents so young, I'm sure. But when Tabby told us that she was pregnant and she and Josh Cho, whom she'd been dating since eighth grade, had decided to have the baby, Mom and Dad seemed to skip the judgmental phase and climbed right aboard the supportive-parents train. Now seventeen, Tabby's taking classes online, waitressing at a diner in the evenings, and living across the hall with her baby. Josh, who goes to North Seattle High with me, spends so much time here he might as well move in.

Most of the time it feels too crowded. Like there isn't enough space for quiet people like my dad and me to simply *be*.

Mom slides open the door and joins us in the kitchen. "Phil! I saw that," she exclaims as my dad licks buttercream frosting off a finger.

"Guilty," he says, and she laughs, swatting his arm.

"Soph, where have you been all night?" Mom says. "I've barely seen you."

My mom, who's high up at Starbucks corporate, has always been the alpha of our family. She and my dad met in Israel on a Birthright trip, and a couple years later, she was the one who proposed to him.

"I've been here."

"Did you have a good last practice?"

"Pretty good. Not sure how I feel about our new captain yet. She's . . . a little intimidating."

"I'm sure you'll get used to her." She reaches into the fridge for more sodas. "I wonder if Tabby and Josh will sign Luna up for dance classes when she's older. Can you imagine how cute she'd be in a toddler tutu?"

"So cute," I agree.

When Tabby got pregnant before she turned sixteen, it seemed like an opportunity for me to step into her "good daughter" shoes. I could be the easy kid. But nothing in my sister's life changed that dramatically. Her schedule shifted around and she couldn't do as many plays, but she and Josh stayed together. She kept her friends.

And yet, when I told my parents I wanted to get tested to see if I'd be a match for Peter, they lost it. "There are so many health risks," Dad said. "What if something happens to your friendship and you regret donating?" Mom asked.

The only regrets I have when it comes to Peter are things I don't do. Things I don't say.

It felt like fate that I was a match when even his parents weren't. When I reminded my parents it could take years for him to find a match on the transplant list—years he might not have—they didn't know how to respond. I am eighteen and my body is mine, and I will make any and all choices for it as long as I can.

"You know, I was thinking," Mom says as she closes the fridge. This is how she's begun all conversations about the transplant ever since my test results came back and a slim possibility became a reality.

"Mom. I'm doing it. A day and a half from now, in fact."

She sighs. "I know you are," she says quietly, gently touching my arm. "All I was going to say is that it's a very noble thing you're doing. I hope you know that."

I give her slight nod, though "noble" doesn't seem like the right word.

She fixes sad eyes on me, looking like she wants to add something but isn't sure if she should. I head back outside before she can.

We stick a single candle onto Luna's piece of cake and sing "Happy Birthday," which seems to both amaze and confound her. When it's over, Tabby blows out the candle, and Luna destroys the cake.

It's not long before the sky deepens to a dusky blue and Luna gets cranky. Tabby and Josh put her to bed, their friends leave, and I linger outside to help them clean up the backyard so my parents can relax with a bottle of wine and a show about British royalty on Netflix.

"They grow up so fast," Josh says as he and Tabby collect Luna's toys.

Tabby flicks short auburn bangs out of her eyes. "Don't even joke about that. I want her to be this small and sweet forever! Though I wouldn't mind getting more sleep."

"Me too," I mumble. One of the hazards of living with a baby. I tip food scraps and paper plates into our compost bin.

"I can't believe she's *one*," Tabby says. "This whole thing is still unbelievable to me. Amazing in a lot of ways, terrifying in plenty of others."

It's strange, my younger sister growing this family of her own. While Tabby and Josh have been together since they were fourteen, I didn't know they were having sex until Tabby told us she was pregnant. She'd advanced to level forty, and I was still trying to beat level one. Most of the time I try not to think about how at eighteen and with an actual baby in the house, I feel like the baby of my family.

"Working on any new dances?" Josh asks.

"Starting one," I say. "Not sure how much time I'll have this summer, though."

"You'll bounce back fast. I'm sure of it." He checks the time on his phone. "Yikes, I should head home."

"You don't want to spend the night?" After Tabby got pregnant, my parents decided it didn't matter if Josh stayed over. The thing that wasn't supposed to happen had already happened.

"My parents miss me, weirdos that they are," he says. He hugs her, a hand sliding effortlessly through her short hair as he pulls her to his chest. Until recently I didn't know watching two people hug could make me ache. That clear fondness they have for each other: It's impossible not to see. "I'll be back tomorrow for Sophie's Last Meal."

I groan. "Don't call it that!" I have to fast for eight hours before the surgery, which isn't a big deal since I'll be asleep for most of them. But no breakfast Friday before I go to the hospital, where they'll do final tests before the surgery.

We say our good-byes, and then my sister and I are alone in the backyard.

"I should take this compost out to the curb," I say before the silence between us gets awkward.

"And I should check on Luna."

Sometimes Josh feels like a buffer between us, helping us forget we aren't actually that close. We've never been enemies or had fights that ended in tears or slammed doors. But we've never bonded the way some sisters do.

"Wait," I say when she's halfway to the door. "Do you . . . want to hang out tonight? Watch a movie or grab food somewhere or . . . something?"

A pause. Then: "You know, I am exhausted, Soph."

I'm almost relieved by her non-excuse because—what would my sister and I even talk about?

"Right. Right. Another time."

"I'm sure I'll see you around," she jokes, and I press my mouth into a firm line, hoping it resembles a smile.

The next time I see Peter, it's officially summer vacation and the doctors have finished their final tests and we are both in hospital gowns. This is really happening.

"I love you," I whisper to him before we're taken into the operating room.

"Me too," he whispers back, and my last thought before I surrender to the anesthesia is: *You have no idea how much.*

CHAPTER 4

PETER

I'M DEAD. THE PAIN IS SO SEVERE, SO WHITE-HOT, that that's the only explanation. But I can't tell where it's coming from. Can't tell where I am.

Huh. I was hoping heaven would smell less like a hospital room and more like espresso beans. Latkes with applesauce. The perfume Sophie wore the night we stayed home and had what we dubbed "fauxcoming" because I didn't have the energy for the real dance. She probably didn't think I noticed because I didn't say anything. Didn't know what to say, because "you smell good" sounded like it might mean something I wasn't sure I meant. But I noticed.

Maybe . . . maybe this isn't heaven. The thought hits me hard. Obviously hell would stink like a hospital. Now that I think about it, I'm not sure if what I've done with my life would earn me salvation or eternal damnation. Given the circumstances, I've been as good as I can be. I listen to my parents and try not to complain and always do my homework. But I've also never done anything daring, and I don't know if people who play it safe deserve to go to heaven. I want to believe, though, in heaven and hell. From what I understand of it—which, admittedly, is very little—my Jewish side views those concepts differently, more complexly. But when you've been sick your whole life, you have a lot of time to read. A lot of time to philosophize. I've read Dante's *Inferno* and Albert Camus and Zhuang Zhou, who said that when we die, we simply become something else.

It's reassuring to think that after you've spent nearly seventeen years feeling like shit, the afterlife, or whatever comes next, might be better.

At least, that's what I tell myself on my bad days.

The pain twists around my abdomen. Climbs up my back. A jolt straight to my brain. *No.* I'm not ready to die. Who will take care of Mark? I've never even left Washington State. And I'm still a virgin. I'm sure my philosophers would agree that it would be cosmically unfair to die a virgin. I bet they all got laid a lot.

"Peter?" My mom's voice. A hand on my shoulder—and *nails*.

If I can feel my mom's claws, hear my mom's voice, then I must still be alive. . . .

My eyes blink open, and I squint at the bright hospital fluorescents. Machines are beeping. In the corner of my vision, I spot a single GET WELL SOON balloon that must be from my parents.

It takes a while to find my voice. "Did it—am I—"

40

"The operation was successful," my dad says, grinning his I'm-a-nice-dentist-not-a-scary-dentist grin. "No complications for you."

I scrabble under the sheets with the hand that doesn't have a needle sticking out of it. The bandage on my abdomen is thick and wide. Suddenly what my dad said takes on new meaning. No complications for *you*.

"Sophie?" I say, unable to form a complete sentence.

"She's doing fine," my mom says, and my body relaxes into the hard hospital bed. "She's in the room next door."

"Can I see her?" The question doesn't come out right. I need to see her. Need to know she's okay. That's what it feels like: a deep, coursing need that goes all the way down to my toes. My toes, ankles, elbows all need to see her.

"You should rest," my mom says.

"Dr. Paulson still has a lot to discuss with us," my dad says.

"I need to see her." It comes out right this time, and there must be some conviction in my voice, because my parents buzz the nurse and everyone agrees to let this reunion happen.

They wheel me to the adjoining room. Sophie is lying down, but I can tell she's awake. Freckles cover her cheeks, forehead, nose, chin—she must have hundreds of them. I like every single one.

Sophie smiles when she sees me—or tries to. Her lips move, but they don't really curve upward. "How's my kidney?" she asks in a groggy voice. It's strange seeing her in a hospital gown. Her love for dance usually radiates off her; even when she isn't dancing, she's tapping her foot to a song only she can hear or clacking her nails against her phone case. Piano isn't static, but unless you're in a band, you're sitting down.

"It's, you know. Doing its kidney thing." Suddenly my brain is so fuzzy that I can't for the life of me remember what a kidney actually does. Just that I needed one. Really badly. Bad enough that they sliced us both open to fix me. "You look like . . . like shit."

"Peter!" my mom exclaims. She doesn't get it. But Sophie's parents, who are sitting in chairs next to her bed, scrounge up a couple pity laughs.

"It's a joke they have, Holly," Sophie's mom says to mine.

But Sophie doesn't have the energy to laugh. I don't have the energy to energy. I close my eyes

only

for

a

minute.

"You both need more rest," the nurse says, and I fall into darkness again.

Then there are more doctors. So many doctors over the next couple weeks that I can't keep their names straight. They're optimistic. They talk about the anti-rejection medication that I'll have to take for as long as I have the "donor kidney." As though at some point I'll give it back to her.

That's what they keep calling it. The "donor kidney." They remind me a kidney transplant is not a permanent fix. I know that. That one day I'll probably be back on dialysis, back on the transplant list. The "donor kidney" has an expiration date, an average of fifteen years.

Sophie's kidney, I mentally correct.

Part of Sophie, inside me.

Patchy stubble covers my face, and the hair on my chest and stomach starts to grow back, too. I had to shave it before the surgery. The nurses ask if I want them to shave my uneven beard for me, or if they should bring me a razor. I tell them no because I feel weirdly proud of it. Part man, part beast, one functioning kidney. When I get home, I'll take it all off. If my life were a piece of classic literature, shaving my beard would be a symbol of a fresh start.

"Excited to go home?" asks Dr. Paulson, the doctor I've had for years, on my last day in the hospital. A kidney doctor is a nephrologist. I learned that word when I was six.

"I can't wait." There are more weeks of recovery ahead of me, and I'll be back soon for a follow-up, but getting discharged is a huge step, like my body has finally aced a test it spent years studying for.

Dr. Paulson smiles. He's large and blond and built like a Viking.

When I was younger, I thought all kids admired their doctors the way I did. After all, they were saving our lives. But then I realized I didn't think about his lifesaving abilities as much as the intriguing sharpness of his features. His broad chest. I had crushes on girls, too, and other guys. Sometimes they overlapped.

Sometimes they didn't. For a year when I was twelve, I seemed to fall in love with anyone who spoke more than a sentence to me. Then, of course, there's Sophie herself and the spiderweb of feelings I've had for her for the past half decade. The ones I used to think were love that I forced back into friendship. Still, they occasionally flared back into crush territory. Made me wonder what a relationship between us might be like. How would it feel to hold Sophie's hand or kiss her again—for real this time?

When I found the word "bisexuality," it fit. I liked that I had a word to describe myself besides "chronically ill" or "transplant list candidate." It was a word that didn't care what my body could or couldn't do. It was sure of itself and unapologetic about that sureness.

"I think I'm bisexual," I told my parents when I was fourteen, even though it was more than a thought at that point. I was someone who told his parents everything, because I'd always had to. When they didn't respond right away, I explained, "I mean—I've had crushes on both girls and guys. And in the future, I might want to date a girl . . . or a guy."

Talking about dating also made me feel less sick. It helped to imagine a future in which I could go on a date and not have to worry about my next exchange.

My mom actually smiled. "Peter. We know what bisexual means. Your aunt Kerri is bi."

Hearing my mom abbreviate it was both oddly embarrassing and a tremendous relief.

"Oh—she is?"

My dad nodded. "Whoever you date, Peter, all that matters to us is that they're good to you."

Somehow, though, I couldn't tell Sophie. Maybe because she'd been one of the many people I'd crushed on. Mostly, though, I think it was this: that when it came to Sophie, not talking about dating and relationships was safer.

"A couple final checks and you should be good to go," Dr. Paulson says now.

I clench my teeth, waiting for him to find something wrong as he peers at my charts. But there's nothing wrong. Sophie's kidney is functioning like a champ, and I really am good to go. No more exchanges. No more dialysis.

My parents and I wait for the elevator, both of them too giddy to stop smiling. My stomach twinges as we get inside. It drops us down, down, down, closer to the start of my new life. I wonder if it'll be a good summer, a warm summer. I wonder how much closer my mom is to finishing her book. I wonder what classes I'll take in the fall.

Sophie already went home, but I saw her nearly every day she was in the hospital. Our conversations were mostly silly and superficial, our medications making us loopy. Every night she was on the other side of the wall from me, which somehow felt farther away than across the street.

Sometimes I wanted to sneak into her room and talk without a dozen people in scrubs nearby. But I worried what I'd say to her when we were alone. If "thank you" could ever be enough.

If this means things between us are different now.

OTHER TIMES

I WAS IN LOVE WITH HER ONCE. FIVE YEARS AGO, sixth grade for me and seventh for her, my last year of public school.

I would express my love through song, I decided. I wrote about her hair and her freckles and the way she kept me company on my worst days. It was called "Dancing through My Heart," and honestly, I should have stopped right there.

We both took music appreciation as an elective that year, though we obnoxiously joked to each other that we were already pretty good at appreciating it. Making it. When I was confident the song was ready, I told her to meet me in the music room at lunch. I got there early, claiming my spot at the upright piano and flexing my fingers. In my head, I rehearsed the lyrics.

When she pushed the door open, she looked, somehow,

cuter than she usually did, her red hair tumbling from a barrette, bangs swept to one side.

"Did you want to play something?" she asked. We'd been playing as the Terrible Twosome for about a year at that point. The way Sophie devoted herself to dance, pushed herself daily— it was impossible not to admire.

It was also impossible not to admire the shapes her body made when she was doing it.

"Yeah," I said. "But just, uh, listen first, okay?"

She clutched her binder to her chest. Sophie was always so much shyer in real life than onstage, or even on the mock stages we set up in our living rooms. It was like she let her arms and legs express through dance what they couldn't the rest of the time.

I struck the first chord, a G major. And then I opened my mouth.

They were the first lyrics I'd ever written, and I realized pretty quickly that they should probably be the last. Puberty mangled my voice. I grimaced as I heard it, hoping she could hear how heartfelt it was even though I couldn't do it justice.

When it was over, she stared for a few solid moments. The silence felt like it lasted longer than the longest song, longer than "Bohemian Rhapsody" and "American Pie" and "Stairway to Heaven" all put together.

Finally she laughed. "You're so weird," she said, moving closer so she could palm my shoulder.

"Oh," I said, not understanding. "I am?"

She sat down next to me, pushing me over with her hip, a gesture that was both annoying and distracting. "This was a joke, right? You're always saying you could never play in a real band because you can't write lyrics and you can't sing. So . . . you proved it to me."

It was true; I'd often joked about that. All the pianists I could name who played modern music sang, too.

"It's not a joke," I mumbled.

"What?"

I chewed on my lower lip. It would have been so easy, then, to take it back. Instead, I cleared my throat. "It . . . wasn't a joke, Soph. I . . . think I like you? As . . . more than a friend."

A silence gaped between us.

"I love you," I elaborated. As though my previous statement had been unclear.

"I. Um. Wow," Sophie said. Her cheeks turned pink, and I would have found it adorable if I weren't so embarrassed myself. *Say something else*, I willed her. *Something other than "wow."* "Wow," she said again, and I wished I could vanish. I wished someone else would come inside, save us from each other and this new awkwardness that had never existed between us before.

Had my hormones ruined nearly a decade of friendship?

"I'm sorry," I said quietly.

"Don't be sorry!" She wouldn't make eye contact. "I—I've only ever thought of you as a friend. *I'm* sorry."

My face was hot. We were eleven and twelve. What did I think would happen? That we'd shyly hold hands at the movies but ignore each other in the halls, the way other "couples" our age did? Yes, I'd been imagining doing exactly that for months. Stupid, stupid, stupid.

And what was I supposed to do now? Suddenly stop liking her, as though it were a song I could simply switch off?

She tried to smile. "I'm really flattered, Peter," she continued.

Somehow that made it worse. "I'm going to disappear now." I held my hands over my face.

"Nooooo!" She peeled my hands away. "Don't be embarrassed. We're okay. I promise I won't be weird about it."

"Sure. Okay."

"Do you want to get pizza?"

I didn't want to get pizza.

"Yeah. Let's get pizza."

Maybe I didn't know what love meant back then, but it felt real to me. In the years since, that love, or whatever it was, stretched and thinned. Sophie poked holes in it, and then she sewed them back up. Sometimes I was convinced I'd gotten over the crush. But other times I wondered how I could stand to be in the same room with her without touching her.

Those other times were the hardest.

PART II

CHAPTER 5

SOPHIE

BEFORE MY SISTER BECAME A MOTHER, OUR morning routines were a tug-of-war. I'd use up the hot water; she'd eat the last bagel. She'd insist on leaving way too early; I'd make her late. When we finally got into the car, she'd belt show tunes and I'd beg her to stop.

"Happy first day of senior year!" Tabby sings as she gets Luna settled with some yogurt and Cheerios. "Excited?"

We've had a year to rehearse this new routine, the one where my sister the mom is front and center, but I haven't memorized the steps yet.

"Actually, yes." I slot my empty cereal bowl into the dishwasher. Our parents go to work early so one or both of them can watch Luna when Tabby waitresses in the evenings, so I try to be good and clean up after myself.

My last first day of high school doesn't feel momentous in the traditional sense. I've always planned to go to community college, where I'll wait for Peter to graduate, then transfer wherever he picks. Since I have no idea what I want to study, it makes sense to stay at home for another year and save money. But right now all I can focus on is Peter heading back to school with me. And that feels pretty spectacular.

In the months since the surgery, I slept and popped pain pills and went to checkups and watched all of *Gilmore Girls* and played board games and *rested*, something I've never been very good at. Peter recovered more slowly, even had to be on dialysis for a few weeks right after the transplant. I was slow to start exercising again, but my doctor cleared me to start dance team practice, and I'm itching for it. I even miss my weekly jazz technique class.

"Does it feel weird?" Tabby asks, brushing bangs off her forehead. Her hair used to hit her waist, but she chopped it when Luna started sticking strands in her mouth. She pours herself a glass of orange juice and leans against the counter next to me. We're the same height, just shy of five feet. We both grew up scrawny, though dance gave me muscles and pregnancy filled out Tabby's curves. Even standing side by side, she *looks* more adult than I do. I can't believe she's only seventeen.

"It doesn't feel like something's missing, or anything like that. But . . . it hurts sometimes, if I move a certain way. I'll have to take it easy at practice."

"Are you sure it's smart to go back to dance so soon?"

"The doctor said it was okay as long as I don't overdo it." And I won't. I know my body.

But my body is different now.

Maybe Tabby and I were born out of order. I used to beg her to order for me in restaurants. Before I knew I was dyslexic, I worried I'd mispronounce what was on the menu. It got to the point where my parents asked Tabby not to, told me if I wanted to eat, I had to order for myself. They thought it was run-of-the-mill shyness, so they felt pretty bad after my diagnosis.

"Okay," she says, but she doesn't sound convinced.

Putting my back to her, I open a box of organic granola bars and slip a couple in my bag for later. "I've already missed a whole summer of workouts. It's a miracle they're even keeping me on the team. And last time I checked, you were Luna's mom, not mine."

"Let's forget it," she says, shrugging it off. "Do you know what fall show they're doing this year yet?"

"As soon as I know, I'll tell you."

Her shoulders sag, and an odd emotion, one I'm not sure I can name, crosses my sister's face. But before she can say anything else, Luna lets out a wail from her high chair.

"Ladybug, what's wrong?" Tabby coos at her, and her face twists into something I definitely recognize. "Diaper change."

As she scoops up Luna and races down the hall, I pocket my keys and wonder if she misses our old morning rituals: fighting about nothing instead of fussing over a baby.

Honestly, sometimes I do.

I make a big show of opening my car's passenger door for Peter as he heads down the front walk. Tabby and I share this sensible sedan; since she works nights, our general agreement is that I get the car during the day unless she needs it to take Luna somewhere. Weekends are always a negotiation.

"You see these?" he says, gesturing to his jeans. "These are for you."

I clasp my hands together. "You're too good to me."

It's not just the jeans, though. It's how he looks so ridiculously, wonderfully *collegiate* with his blue plaid shirt and tan jacket and backpack slung over one shoulder. It's his hair damp from a morning shower. It's how clean boy is the best smell in the world, how I hope we can have a hundred more mornings like this.

My outfit is similarly casual, a striped shirt tucked into high-waisted skinny jeans, my Star of David necklace slipping in and out of the neckline of my shirt no matter how many times I tug it into view.

Once I turn on the car, I swipe through the Spotify playlists on my phone. Peter leans over, as though he thinks he has a say in the matter.

"My car," I say, holding the phone closer so he can't see the screen. "My music."

He groans. He doesn't have his license yet; his parents have been too overprotective to let him even take driver's ed. I might struggle with reading, but—this isn't the case for all dyslexic people—my spatial skills and hand-eye coordination are excellent, and I turned out to be a naturally good driver. Sure, I had to take the written test twice, but who doesn't?

I settle on something he'll like anyway, a Rufus Wainwright album he introduced me to a few years ago. I tend to prefer more upbeat music, but there's something soothing about his voice.

If there's a chance to make Peter happy, even if it's small, I usually take it. It's a side effect of having a sick best friend. You tend to give up things you like that you realize don't matter that much: pizza toppings, what TV series to marathon, what music to listen to. It used to bother me that I didn't get my way as much as Peter did, but I got used to it. He deserved to get his way. I was convinced of that.

He relaxes into the seat, silently satisfied, a smile nestling into one corner of his mouth. He fiddles with something on his wrist.

"What is that?"

He rolls up his sleeve and shows it to me. "Medical ID bracelet. All transplant recipients are supposed to wear them in case of an emergency. And . . . so are donors." With that, he unzips his backpack and takes out a similar silver bracelet. "I told your parents I wanted to help pick it out. Do . . . you like it?" He sounds nervous.

Peter bought me jewelry. A medically necessary piece of jewelry, but still. The steel plate at the center is inscribed with the words

DONATED LEFT KIDNEY, along with my parents' phone numbers and my blood type. Peter's bracelet is simple, but two charms hang off mine: a music note and a ballet slipper.

"I couldn't find anything that clearly symbolized 'dance team,'" he says.

"Peter." My heart is stuck in my throat. Slowly I slip the bracelet onto my wrist. "Thank you."

He exhales, as though he'd been waiting for me to indicate I liked it. "Think of it as a super-intense friendship bracelet." And I have to laugh at that.

"This might be the best gift you've given me," I say as I pull out of our Wallingford neighborhood. "And yes, I'm including the calendar in that." Four years ago, for Hanukkah, Peter gave me a wall calendar with the most stunning photos of Twyla Tharp's choreography I'd ever seen. He knows I prefer physical calendars to anything on my phone, so in theory, the gift was extremely sweet. But—

"I didn't realize it was for the wrong year! I was so excited when I found it." He grimaces, gives me a guilty look. "That's . . . probably why it was on sale."

I turn onto Forty-Fifth, Wallingford's main drag, which is lined with restaurants and bars and cafés, including my and Peter's favorite ice-cream shop, which, in true Seattle fashion, uses locally sourced ingredients and serves odd flavors like cardamom and white cheddar blackberry.

"So . . . how are you feeling?" I ask.

"That's the first time in probably ten years that I haven't

hated that question. I feel all right today. Not amazing, but . . . all right. And my appetite is ridiculous. I haven't been this hungry in a while."

"All right is good! Hungry is good!" I chirp. This is strange, driving Peter and me to school. It's too normal. "God. I can't believe you're finally coming back to school."

"Me either. If there was ever going to be a right time, though . . ." He drums his fingers on the dashboard, tugs on the zipper of his coat. He can't stay still. "Are you sure I look okay? I haven't missed some major fashion trend? People aren't wearing neon onesies or velour jumpsuits or anything now, are they?"

I glance at him out of the corner of my eye. His lower lip is between his teeth, that adorable nervous habit I hope he never outgrows. If I answered truthfully, I'd tell him that not only does he look okay, he looks beautiful, and maybe he should use unscented soap because whatever he did use is seriously distracting. "Only on Thursdays," I say instead.

His nerves are contagious. As much as I'm sure people will be happy to see Peter after all his years of homeschooling, I wonder if anyone is going to be happy to see me after an entire summer. It's a stupid, jealous thought. But I don't love the person I am in school. I'm constantly anxious, behind on my homework, unsure what to say when a teacher calls on me. At dance team practice, I am closer to myself, but I'm only *Sophie* with Peter. Over the summer I dutifully liked Instagram posts to remind people I still existed. I wonder if anyone will have missed me. The reality is, probably not.

While we're stopped at a red light, my hand on the gear-shift, Peter reaches out and grazes my knuckles with his finger-tips, as though each little knob is a piano key and he could play an entire song on my skin. I hold my breath.

"It's going to be okay," he says, like he knows I need the reassurance as much as he does.

As we turn into the parking lot of North Seattle High, Peter's mouth falls open. He stares at the enormous gray build-ing, the trees lining the walkway, the solar panels on the roof.

"I don't remember it being so . . . huge," he says, then adds quietly, "I wonder if anyone will remember me." The fear and insecurity in his voice nearly break me in half.

"Even if they don't, they'll love you soon enough." How could they not? Peter is someone who survived against all odds. We love a good comeback story, a story about someone fighting the evil inside their body and winning. Peter won, and I made the invisible assist.

"I hope so. I hope I didn't wear these jeans for nothing." He starts to unbuckle his seat belt.

"Wait," I say. "Before we go in. I wanted to see—" I glance around, make sure no one can see inside the car. Then I lift the hem of my shirt and twist in my seat, showing Peter the scar below my navel. The doctors told me that a year from now I'll barely be able to see it.

Peter copies me. The slash starts beneath his belly button and runs along the side of his abdomen. The evidence of his first transplant is still there, a ghost of a scar. The physical proof of what we did pins me to my seat.

"We match," he says softly. Then jingles his bracelet. "In more ways than one."

I like that a little too much.

CHAPTER 6

PETER

"AT LEAST WE HAVE THE SAME LUNCH?" SOPHIE says as we stand in the front office, peering at our very different schedules. When I imagined returning to school, I assumed I'd sit next to her, share notes, partner on class assignments. Sophie and public school seemed inextricably linked.

My eyes flick over the printout the school secretary gave me. AP Lit, AP US History, trig, chemistry, Latin II, band. I knew Sophie wasn't taking any APs, but I still hoped we'd have an elective in common. I rub the bracelet on my wrist. My sleeve covers it, but I'll have to get used to how foreign it feels. I guess if I could get used to dialysis, I can get used to anything.

"Lunch seems so far away," I say, because *I'll miss you* and *I don't want to be alone* would have sounded pathetic. A knot of nerves twists tight in my stomach. I pocket the schedule, positive I'll consult it at least a dozen more times.

I know the transplant wasn't a magical instant cure. That I will live with this disease for the rest of my life. That there are hurdles ahead, that even my immunosuppressants have side effects associated with them. That I'll have to go through life as a Very Careful Person, limiting sun exposure, going back to the doctor for follow-ups, monitoring my caloric and sugar intakes.

But it all seems so much more manageable. I feel . . . free.

Sophie pushes her shoulder against mine. "You just had surgery and you're scared of public school?"

"Yes."

Despite her teasing, Sophie's never judged me, though she's had plenty of opportunities. Back when our parents still let us have sleepovers—as long as we left the door open and one of us slept on the floor—one night when I was eleven and she was twelve, she crawled into bed with me around two a.m. "I can't sleep," she whispered, tugging the blanket off me to cover her. When I woke up, I realized I'd wet the bed. That was the most embarrassing part: that I couldn't control my own bladder.

But if Sophie was pissed (ha) or revolted, she didn't say anything about it. She just hugged me, told me it was going to be okay, and helped me strip the dirty sheets off the bed.

I'm still not exactly sure how she felt about it. If our bond transcends things like bed-wetting. Maybe it does. Maybe it's another reason I'm lucky to have her.

"You'll be fine," she says, emphasizing the last word. "Most kids aren't feral." She mimes swiping a paw at me.

When she hugs me, it lasts a few seconds longer than usual.

Her hair smells like citrus, fresh and clean. It makes me even more reluctant to let go. Makes me wonder if my mercurial crush is back again or if I just like the scent of citrus.

After I declared my love for Sophie, we navigated a period of awkwardness that lasted a few months. Her rejection made me terrified of complimenting her, touching her. Slowly we found our way back to who we used to be. These days we're generous with our displays of affection, especially post-transplant.

"Learn a bunch," Sophie says, a hand lingering on my shoulder, right above my heartbeat. "If you don't know it all already."

"I'll see if there's any space left in my brain. Even though it's not as big as yours."

The joke usually never fails to cheer her up, but now her smile wavers. A Sophie smile is one of the purest expressions of joy—probably because I only see her do it around me. When she's with her family, she's only half smiling, hiding her teeth.

"See you in a few hours," she says, and we take off for opposite sides of the building.

On my way to first period, I'm stopped exactly three times.

Tim Ochoa, who sat next to me during a fifth-grade science unit on volcanoes, says, "Peter . . . Rosenberg? No fuckin' way! Good to see you, man!" and then slaps my shoulder. I'm so stunned I don't correct him on my last name.

Annabeth Nguyen, who shyly asked me to the sixth-grade dance, which I wound up spending in the hospital, says, "Wow.

Peter, is that you? You look . . . You look *good*." And then turns five shades of red.

Vivek Patel, whom I shared a locker with in seventh grade, stares at me like he's just seen a ghost and says, "Whoa. I thought you died." Cue eerie silence during which it becomes apparent that I am not, in fact, dead.

I'm not really on social media except for Tumblr, where I mostly reblog things, so it makes sense, I guess, that they're surprised to see me. Sophie made sure we were early so I had time to get everything done—locker assignment, brief school tour, devastation upon learning our schedules didn't overlap. Still, I get to AP Lit seven minutes before the bell.

Slowly students trickle in, exchanging hellos and compliments about hair that's either grown out or been chopped off over the summer. I sit silently at the end of a middle row, clutching my backpack to my chest before finally letting it drop to the floor.

The bell rings and Mr. Lozano, a youngish guy in a Shakespeare T-shirt, passes out the syllabus. There are only about twenty of us in class, so he asks us to introduce ourselves along with one thing we like that starts with the first letter of our name.

When it's my turn, I mumble, "Peter, and, uh . . . pizza," which is both stupid and unmemorable, but for some reason it's the first thing that popped into my head.

Oh my God. Why didn't I say freaking *piano*?

As I feel my face warm, Mr. Lozano wraps it up with "And

I'm Mr. Lozano, and I love literature!" This sparks a few groans. "Sorry, guys, I had to." He puts a medieval poem up on the screen. "Since I'm sure everyone did the summer reading, which included *The Canterbury Tales*, this language shouldn't be too alien. At least for those of you who read the book and not the SparkNotes version. Which I'm sure none of you did. Any brave souls want to try reciting it?"

Middle English isn't too foreign to me, but I'm not about to volunteer on my first day, especially after the whole pizza situation. The girl next to me raises her hand, stands up, and clears her throat:

> *Whan the turuf is thy tour,*
> *And thy pit is thy bour,*
> *Thy fel and thy whitë throtë*
> *Shullen wormës to notë.*
> *What helpëth thee thennë*
> *Al the worildë wennë?*

"Great pronunciation, Abby," Mr. Lozano says. "Spend the next few minutes discussing your interpretation of the poem with the person next to you. Then we'll talk about it as a group."

I shift toward Abby, but she's already moving her desk so she can partner with the girl to her right. I'm next to the window, so there's no one on my other side.

Partners. When I thought about going back to school, I never once considered the anxiety that comes with picking partners because I stupidly assumed Sophie would be there next to me. More specifically: the anxiety of realizing no one wants to be your partner. The back of my neck grows warm as I glance around the room, trying to catch the eye of any other loners. But everyone's already deep in conversation.

Then the guy in front of me twists around. "Partner?" he asks. The seat next to him is empty, and I nod, trying not to let on exactly how relieved I am. He gets up so can he sit backward in his chair, which is attached to the desk. "Are you new? I don't think I've seen you before."

"Sort of. I'm Peter."

"Chase. So what language is this poem in again?" His hair's a golden brown, his skin a light olive. His glasses aren't the massive thick-framed ones most kids are wearing; they're thin and oval-shaped with wire frames. Old-man glasses, really. Earlier, he said, "I'm Chase, and I like challenging teachers who make us play getting-to-know-you activities."

"Middle English."

"And that has nothing in common with our kind of English because . . . ?"

"Did you not read *The Canterbury Tales*?"

Behind his grandpa glasses, his dark eyes shift left. Right. Back to me. "Shh. I was one of the people who read the SparkNotes version," he says conspiratorially.

My first day, and I'm helping someone else instead of the other way around. I used to do it with Sophie all the time. "Middle English is really inflected, and it's actually a Germanic language. The grammar is more similar to German than to English."

"Interesting. What does this poem mean, then?"

"Well," I start, because while I'm not one hundred percent sure, I have a guess. "I think it's a reflection on mortality. A memento mori. We can translate it to, 'when the turf is your tower/and the pit is your bower/your skin—'fel' is skin—and white throat/shall be food for worms/what will help you then' . . . and then I'm not entirely sure of the last line."

Chase is staring. "How . . . did you get all that?"

"I . . . read a lot." The mahogany bookshelves in my room. All those first editions. A warmth flows to my cheeks for the twelfth time this morning, though Chase obviously has no idea what my room is filled with.

"So it's about the passage of time? Like, this is what's gonna happen when you die?"

"Yeah, I think so. Oh! It could be that all of this is going to happen when you die, so what will the good things in the world matter to you then? So take advantage of all of this while you're alive?"

"I can appreciate that." He pushes the sleeves of his plaid shirt to his elbows. It occurs to me that at least forty percent of the male population is wearing plaid. "A little depressing, though." He actually looks sad, like he was expecting the poem to have a deeper, possibly more upbeat message.

"Maybe it was less depressing a thousand years ago?"

Mr. Lozano calls the class back together, and when he asks

us what we thought of the poem, I get brave and raise my hand, explaining the analysis Chase and I came up with.

"Fantastic insight, Peter who likes pizza," Mr. Lozano says.

Someone pumps their fist. "Yeah! Pizza!"

Public school is weird.

Mr. Lozano continues: "This might shock you, but this poem was once used romantically. A man might have sung this to a woman to seduce her."

"Because what's hotter than worms?" a girl in the back row says.

I find myself laughing along with everyone else. Relaxing, even. I think I'm going to like this class.

"Thanks for helping me, sort-of-new Peter," Chase says when the bell rings. "Partners next time?"

Something springs to life in my chest. "Sure," I say. First period of my first day and I already have a potential new friend. Someone who knows nothing about who I am or who I used to be, and that feels even better—the idea that though I'm not a complete stranger here, in a way I'm starting fresh.

Sort-of-new Peter. It fits.

CHAPTER 7

SOPHIE

AFTER THE LAST BELL, I CHANGE FOR DANCE team in the privacy of a bathroom stall, which I've never done before. Most dancers I've met don't get easily embarrassed about their bodies. But today when I put on my black spandex shorts and swap my striped shirt for a sports bra and tank top, I want to keep my scar secret. I'm not embarrassed by it; I just want it to remain solely mine.

The first few weeks after the surgery, I stared at it for a long time in the bathroom mirror after I showered. Now it's as much a part of me as my freckles.

When my feelings for Peter changed, I began looking at myself in a different way, wondering which parts of my face, my body, he might possibly like. Wondering if he thought I had too many freckles, or if my eyes were too far apart, or if my hair wasn't soft enough. I craved compliments he wasn't in the habit of giving out. "I'm not sure about this shirt," I'd say, waiting for him to tell me I looked amazing in it.

But my dancing—he praised that all the time, told me he couldn't believe I could do a switch leap, though mine were far from flawless. Those compliments I held close to my heart.

I shove my hair into a stubby ponytail and peer at my reflection. This is the time in our lives we're supposed to have complicated relationships with our bodies, but I've never had a reason to dislike mine. I'm small, pear-shaped, muscular. My body does what I ask it to. I respect it, push it far enough but never too far, and it rewards me with art.

"Sophie, hey," says sophomore Neeti Chadha as her face appears in the mirror next to mine. I scoot out of the way as she winds black curls into a cute bun. "You weren't here this summer, were you?"

"No, I wasn't." I stare down at the bracelet on my wrist. "I had . . . some health stuff." Since I was going to be missing practice, I only told Montana.

"Oh no, are you okay?" Neeti asks. I can't tell if it's genuine. Neeti and I have never spoken much. I nod. "That's good. How's Tabby? I keep seeing her baby pics on Instagram. So adorable."

"She's good."

"Cool. See you out there." With sparkly teeth, she grins one last time at her reflection and then bounces out of the locker room. Not once does she say she is happy to see me or she's glad I'm back.

"Welcome back, Tigers!" Montana Huang says when we're

all in the gym. Her black hair's up in its usual ballet bun. She has a dance background like a lot of our teammates do, though others have experience with gymnastics and cheer. Our school's cheer squad was cut a couple years back after the team got wasted and trashed the gym, so now we're the ones who dance at football games in the fall and basketball games in the winter. Coach Carson basically lets Montana do what she wants. She spends the beginning of practice on the bleachers, half watching us, before retreating to her office.

We start a routine Montana taught over the summer, and I'm slow to catch up at first. I also don't want to bend my torso too much, so I keep my movements as soft and fluid as possible.

Dance is a language to me, one that sometimes feels easier than English and relies on my entire body to communicate. I can string together axels and leaps and pirouettes, make them mean something. Dance may not always be beautiful, and in my opinion it shouldn't have to be. It has the power to make people *feel*, and I crave being completely in control of that. As a kid I loved watching the older dancers at my studio, the way they played and pushed and sometimes even fought onstage grabbed on to my heart and never let go. I've never known how to do that with words.

By the end of practice I'm sweaty but refreshed, and I linger in the gym for a while, doing a few extra stretches. Sure, I could have marked the steps, but Tabby was wrong. I didn't overdo it, and I feel fine.

"My parents are cool with me having a party after our game against Lincoln next Friday," Montana's saying to her girlfriend, Liz Hollenbeck, another senior. They met on dance team and have been dating since early last year.

"I love your parents. Can we trade?"

"No, because I love them too." Montana's eyes dart to me. She must realize I can hear her because that can only explain what she says next. "Sophie! You're invited too, of course. The whole team is."

I wrap my fingers around my outstretched foot and stare at the floor. Montana has always intimidated me: the severity of her bun, how completely natural and even drill-sergeant-esque she is in front of the team. She gives off this air of effortlessness, confidence in all aspects of her life. I am only like that onstage.

"Maybe," I say. As usual.

"She never goes to parties," Liz says, tucking a short strand of blond hair behind one ear.

I bite the inside of my cheek. I don't go to parties because Peter doesn't go to parties, and when I'm not with Peter, life is different. Duller. *I'm* duller—Peter must have noticed it today at lunch, when we sat with some of the dance team. A couple of my teammates asked him a few questions because he was new and therefore intriguing, but I kept quiet, and no one asked me anything. Now that he's in school with me, he'll know what I really am when he's not around: a burnt-out light of a person.

But I could take Peter to his first party. Our first party.

"Actually," I say, switching legs. "I think I'll go."

"Great. I'll text you my address," Montana says, which is necessary because, even though I've spent three afternoons a week over the past few years with her and she sits at the far end of the dance team table at lunch, I have never been to her house.

"I'll meet you in the locker room, okay?" Liz says.

"I'll be there soon." Montana waits until Liz disappears and then asks, "Sophie, did practice go okay for you today?"

"Definitely. I missed it . . . over the summer."

"Yeah. Wow. I still can't believe what you did." Her phone vibrates, and she grabs it, sends a quick text. "Are you still working on some choreography for us?"

It was something I mentioned toward the end of last year. Casually, just to put it out there, to see what would happen. Montana had seemed interested, but she was probably just being nice. Of course the goal is for the team to perform it . . . but I thought it wouldn't happen for a while.

I grab at my ponytail, pull it out, retie it. It's like I never know what to do with my hands, and my hair is just *there*. Maybe I should wear it in a ballet bun like Montana does. "Yeah, but . . . I don't know if it's ready."

"I'd love to see what you have. Do you have the song with you?" Montana asks. She slides her phone back into her bag. A diamond stud in her nose glints when it catches the light. She must have gotten it pierced over the summer. I wonder if it hurt. "I could give you some feedback."

I suppose I can't keep it inside forever. . . .

"Feedback. Sure," I relent, scrambling to my feet and finding the song on my phone, syncing it to Montana's portable speakers. "Okay, so it starts with this a cappella clapping sequence at the beginning."

Montana shakes her head. "Show me."

All my choreography, though no one's seen much of it yet, has a story, like all good dances should. This one, the jazz remix, sets up a competition between the dancers. Some are trying to prove this more modern style of dancing is better, while others insist the classic steps are timeless. Eventually everyone comes together and performs a mix of old and new. I try my best to show both parts, and by the end of it, I'm out of breath.

"I like it," Montana says. "It's really playful. But it might look better if you did a series of pirouettes instead of piqué turns in that second section? More graceful, yeah?" With flawless technique, she demonstrates.

At first her feedback stings, but dance is always a collaboration: among dancers, between dancer and choreographer and audience.

"I like that a lot." I take a swig of water. "I'll keep working on it."

"We could start learning it before basketball season."

I cap my water bottle. "Really?"

"Why not? The song is super fun and high-energy. You'd have to teach it to us, though. You're the one who knows it best."

"I'm . . . not great in front of big groups of people." It's the part of being a choreographer I'll have to overcome eventually. Eventually, as in not this year.

"We could work on it together." Montana packs up her speakers. "Are you free this weekend?"

This weekend. Peter and I haven't made plans yet, but I'm sure we'll come up with something. A Star Wars movie marathon maybe, or if he's feeling up to it, a Terrible Twosome rehearsal. Besides, a few hours with Montana is a few hours I'm not with Peter. It's part of why I quit the studio: to spend more time with him.

Montana is a thousand times more elegant and confident than I am. What would we talk about? How would we fill the silences?

"I can't this weekend," I say. *Come up with an excuse. Anything.* "I . . . have to babysit. Rain check?"

Montana looks unsurprised, but not hurt. "Sure," she says. "Rain check."

Immediately I feel bad. It was sweet of her to offer to help. And it could have been fun, but weekends are for Peter and me. That's how it's always been.

"I'll definitely be at that party, though," I call as she slings her bag over her shoulder and heads out of the gym. A consolation. She waves good-bye and smiles, like she doesn't fully believe me.

CHAPTER 8

PETER

OUR FAMILIES USED TO HAVE DINNER TOGETHER at least once a month. We'd rotate houses and cuisines, our dads would swap terrible jokes, and Sophie and I would roll our eyes. But I loved that our families were close. My own family feels microscopic sometimes. My mom's sister, Kerri, lives in Maryland with her wife, but my dad's an only child. The three of us have stared at each other through so many lonely holidays.

Tonight Sophie's entire family is packed into my dining room, and my dad had to hunt down a leaf for the table we hadn't used in years.

I've missed them.

"Another dumpling?" my mom asks Sophie's mom.

"Yes, please, Holly," Becki replies. "This is absolutely decadent."

What I can't help wondering, though, is whether my parents offered to host and to cook as some way to balance out what Sophie did for me. As though it's a debt that can be repaid in dumplings and chocolate lava cake, which my mother made for dessert. They went all out: nice plates, cloth napkins, candles. Soft jazz music plays from the speakers. I've never been able to tolerate music that's so unsure of itself, but I don't say anything.

"It's a shame we don't do this more often," Sophie's dad, Phil, says.

Sophie rolls her eyes at me. They say this every time they do manage to get together. If they really wanted to see each other, they'd find a way to make it happen.

"Life gets in the way," Sophie says.

My dad points at her like *bingo*. "Exactly. It's a real shame, though. A real shame . . ."

At one end of the table, Tabby and Josh are trying to get Luna, installed in a high chair they brought over, to eat some rice.

"How are you feeling, Peter?" Sophie's mom asks.

"Really good today," I answer truthfully. My doctor warned about side effects from the immunosuppressants, but my body seems to have fully adjusted at this point.

Overall, I've managed to get into a new rhythm. School, homework, checkups, piano, though I haven't started lessons back up and am not yet sure I will. Classes are mostly interesting, though in band I'm just the substitute pianist. I sit behind Eleanor Kang, who is never absent. The major post-transplant difference is my energy level. I'm still on a diet, one that is low salt and low fat and low carb and devoid of a handful of odd foods like grapefruit and alfalfa sprouts and raw eggs. And, of course, I'll be taking the anti-rejection meds as long as I have Sophie's kidney.

"How's your book going?" Josh asks my mom.

Her eyebrows pinch together, and she groans. "Agonizingly slow, but it's going."

Sophie's mom shakes her head. "If it brings you so much agony, Holly, why don't you put it aside for a while? Work on something else?"

"I have to finish it first. Besides, it's more agony *not* to be working on it."

"Have you read any of it?" Sophie's dad asks mine.

"Not a word," he says.

My mom asks Josh about his classes, and he brightens. "I'm taking a film analysis class, which should be fun."

"His homework is watching movies," Tabby says as she spoons rice into Luna's mouth.

"And I'm very good at it."

"What about you, Tabby?" my dad asks her. "Classes and work going well?"

"Busy, but good! Can't really complain about free diner fries."

"Good," my dad says.

"Good," my mom agrees.

"Good!" Sophie says emphatically, but I'm the only one who

laughs at this. If we got together more than once a year, maybe our families would be able to do more than small-talk.

By the time my mom serves the chocolate lava cake, the conversation has turned to the favorite topic of three-fourths of our parents: being Jewish.

"Do you have plans for Rosh Hashanah?" my dad asks Sophie's parents.

"We'll go to Temple De Hirsch Sinai for services," Becki says. "Probably a small get-together at our house afterward." After a brief hesitation, she adds: "You're welcome to come, of course!"

Sophie groans, mashing a palm into her forehead. "With Rabbi Edelstein? Mom, he mumbles! There's almost no point in even going."

"Soph, it's the one time a year we actually go to temple. I think you can handle it. We're High Holidays Jews," her mom explains to mine, who's nodding like she understands, which she would if my family ever discussed religion. "We only come out for Rosh Hashanah and Yom Kippur, but we're terrible the rest of the year."

My mom pokes her cake with a fork. "Right."

We celebrate both Hanukkah and Christmas, but neither has much religious significance for me, and I didn't have a bar mitzvah. My mom hasn't attended church in my lifetime, and my dad wanted me to "find my own way," which I . . . haven't. Yet. Sometimes I wonder if I'm drawn more to

Judaism because of Sophie. I've always liked my Jewish side because it made me feel more unique in somewhat homogeneous Seattle, which is strange because it's not like I had any control over it. But there it is.

Part of the truth is this: I thought I'd die before I ever got a new kidney, so I didn't want to waste what I thought was precious time discovering religion. I've never told that to anyone except the therapist I used to see—that shorter, shittier life was simply the hand I'd been dealt, and I'd accepted that. Everyone else acted like if they dared lapse into pessimism, it might kill me. But in therapy, I yelled, and I cursed, and I cried. I worried aloud about all the things I thought I'd never do, and having a bar mitzvah didn't make the list.

Tonight, as our families talk about Judaism, I'm struck with curiosity.

"You met in Israel, right?" I say to Sophie's parents.

They exchange grins. "We did. On Birthright." Sophie's dad dabs at his mouth with a napkin. "Has Sophie never told you the story?"

I shake my head, and Sophie and Tabby roll their eyes.

"Believe it or not, Peter and I don't usually discuss your love life," Sophie says.

Sophie's mom gently swats her arm from across the table. "He went with a group of friends from his synagogue, and I went with a group from Hillel. He was so shy!"

"And you were scarily outgoing," Phil puts in, and then lets Becki continue the story.

"We sort of flirted on and off the entire trip—as much as I could get from him, at least—but it wasn't until the last night, when we got separated from the group and spent hours wandering through Tel Aviv together, that we really connected. We stayed out all night."

"Oy vey," Tabby jokes. "Scandalous."

It's Becki's turn to roll her eyes . . . but she also doesn't deny Tabby's insinuation, which makes Sophie gasp and cover her ears. "That trip . . . It was incredible," Becki says. "Aside from meeting Sophie's dad, it made me proud to be Jewish."

That tugs at something inside me. Sophie doesn't seem to care, and Tabby and Josh are preoccupied with Luna. But I wonder what it's like to feel that. That sense of pride.

"Anyone want more cake?" my mom asks. A little too loudly.

"Yes, please," Tabby says.

"You didn't have to do all this," Phil says.

My mom waves a hand. Glittery gold nails. "It was no trouble at all. It had been so long, and we wanted to do something special for your family."

Suddenly Becki claps her hands. "Oh! You know what else we haven't had in a while?"

"What's that?" my mom asks.

"A concert from the Terrible Twosome."

Sophie and I lock eyes. "I don't know," she says. "We haven't played together all summer."

"We won't judge," Becki insists. "We love seeing the two of you doing your creative thing."

"We should do it," I say to Sophie.

She twists her mouth to one side of her face, then appears to give in. "We could do that piece you wrote last year. 'Starlight'?"

"Yeah, I love that one."

We move into the living room. Our families take seats on the couch and chairs, and Sophie removes her shoes and socks so she can dance barefoot on our hardwood floor. She's wearing black leggings and an oversize gray sweatshirt, which she also takes off, revealing a blue tank top and freckled shoulders.

I slide onto the piano bench and play a few C scales to warm up.

"Play 'Free Bird'!" Josh calls from the couch. I pivot to see Tabby elbowing him.

"Ready?" Sophie asks.

I give her a brief nod. This song starts at the low end of the piano and slowly works its way up. I wanted it to sound like nighttime, stars gradually appearing and making the dark seem less hopeless. I sink into the first ominous chords, and Sophie takes her place on the floor in a child's pose. Slowly her body comes to life, though I only see her out of the corner of my eye: arms, legs, a flash of red hair.

It probably sounds cliché to say that the rest of the world falls away when I'm playing piano, but I swear that's how it feels. I started piano lessons when I was eight; my parents heard me humming to myself constantly and figured I might be a musical person. My hands know these keys. When I'm at the piano, I have eighty-eight keys and three pedals to create an infinite number of sounds. It's a special kind of power.

And yet—even when I'm inside the song like this, it's hard not to be aware of her presence, her movements, her breaths.

I may not understand dance, but I do understand music, and I've always loved watching Sophie. Not in a gross way like I'm leering at her body or anything. It's deeper: two artists connecting. It's impossible to watch someone do what they love and not feel *something*, and what I feel for Sophie in this moment is pure and true. A familiar longing.

We finish "Starlight," and then I grin at Sophie and start banging out a louder, more animated song. We haven't played this one in a couple years at least, but I've always liked it. Once we hit high school, our art became moodier. Less naive. She laugh-groans, but then, as though remembering the choreography she made up so long ago, busts out hip-hop moves that make her sister double over, cracking up.

After another couple songs leave us sweaty and breathless and smiling from ear to ear, I beckon Sophie over to me and link my hand with hers. Together, we take a bow as our parents give us a standing ovation.

"We really do need to do this more often," Sophie's mom says again. Sophie's eyes meet mine, still blazing with the rush of our performance, her cheeks pink, and I think, *Yes, we do.*

CHAPTER 9

SOPHIE

I'M OPENING THE DOOR TO OUR HOUSE AFTER dinner with Peter's family when a sudden pain bites through my scar. It's so strong and unexpected that I gasp out loud, bracing myself against the door to keep from falling.

"Soph?" Tabby says, passing Luna to Josh as she jogs over to me. Our parents are still crossing the street. "Soph, are you okay?"

My sister's voice is filled with a worry I'm not used to hearing. I've activated Mom Mode.

"Yeah. Just—a second." I breathe deeply, clutching my abdomen.

Tabby moves my hair out of the way to rub the back of my neck. If I weren't in pain, I'd push her away. It's strange for my younger sister to be fussing over me like this.

"Should we go to the hospital?"

"No! No. It—it's not that serious." It *can't* be that serious. We talked through all the risks with the doctors, like how some donors experience new sensitivity to extreme temperatures. I knew occasional pain at the incision site was possible, though rare. What I was doing for Peter felt more important. A few weeks of discomfort and then I'd be fine. That's what I said to convince myself.

My parents have reached us now. "Soph, what's going on?" my dad asks. He and my mom wear twin worried expressions I grew up seeing etched onto Peter's parents' faces.

Tabby motions to Josh to take Luna inside. "She's in pain," Tabby says, continuing to rub my upper back in a way that's oddly comforting. She doesn't have to add but does anyway: "The transplant."

My parents help me inside and park me on the couch with a heating pad, a glass of water, and a bottle of ibuprofen. Tabby sits in the armchair next to me, rocking Luna to sleep. Watching me.

"We should have spent more time discussing it before she went through with it," my mom says to my dad in the kitchen, loud enough for me to hear.

"I'm eighteen," I mumble. "My body . . ." But I trail off, realizing they probably can't hear me. Instead I close my eyes and burrow deeper into the couch.

"Should we take her to the doctor or wait until tomorrow?" my mom continues. "See if she feels better in the morning?"

"Let's see how she feels in the morning," my dad says.

A deep sigh. "This is exactly what I was afraid of. She was much too young to make this kind of decision."

I spring to a sitting position, ignoring the flash of pain that for a split second agrees with my mom. "Are you serious?"

My parents rush into the living room. "Sophie?" my dad says.

I shake my head. "How can you talk about being too young to make this decision after what happened with Tabby? Where was all this concern when she got pregnant?"

At this, my mama-bear sister turns ferocious. Josh, who's been tidying up the hallway, pokes his head into the living room. Sometimes I forget he doesn't live here. Which is something I feel like I shouldn't forget.

"You think they weren't concerned?" Tabby says. "Maybe you were too wrapped up in Peter to realize it was a big deal—"

"Really? Because it seems like it isn't a big deal at all. It seems like you still have a completely normal life."

Tabby spits out a laugh. I haven't seen her like this . . . well, ever. "What Josh and I are doing is *extremely* hard."

He puts a hand on her shoulder. "Tabitha . . ."

"I'm sorry having a baby at sixteen wasn't the stroll through the park you hoped for."

I know it's terrible as soon as I say it. No one ever asked what I wanted. If I wanted to share my space with a newborn who would make studying and sleeping impossible. If I wanted Josh, as much as I like him, to be here all the freaking time. It's incredible how one tiny human can change so much.

My parents act like we're this big wacky family. I'm the one who did a selfless thing, and all they have for me is judgment and, tonight, pity. But as sisters tend to do when they're acting like brats, I said something I thought would shift the attention to Tabby. I needed my parents to stop saying the transplant was a mistake—so the microscopic part of me that wondered if they were right would be quiet.

Tabby's face is red, her eyebrows slanted. Luna lets out a piercing wail. "Shh, shh, ladybug, I'm so sorry," Tabby coos, patting Luna's back the way she patted mine.

"Girls," my dad says softly, barely able to be heard over Luna. "Sophie, Tabby has nothing to do with this."

"Right. Because Tabby can do no wrong."

"That's not what I said."

"I do *not* regret what I did for Peter." I get to my feet. Luna's crying has reached ear-shattering decibels. "God, Tabby, can't you get her to stop?"

"Does it not look like I'm trying?"

"Girls!" Mom says this time, her voice louder than Dad's was. "Please. We're all on edge right now, so if everyone could calm down—"

"I'll calm down in my room," I say, yanking the heating pad from the wall outlet.

Upstairs, I turn on my laptop. According to WebMD, I'm either dying or totally fine. The kidney transplant sites tell me this kind of pain is rare but not entirely unheard of after a transplant, which I know already. Still, it helps me relax a little.

I clutch the bracelet on my wrist, sigh, release my grip. Something about its presence, and those two tiny charms, soothes me. My room is nothing like Peter's, but I wouldn't exactly call it messy. Sure, there are clothes on the floor, draped over the back of my desk chair, under my bed. But my desk area is clutter free—I can't focus if it isn't—with a giant whiteboard mounted on the wall next to cutouts from the Twyla Tharp calendar Peter got me years ago, an array of folders to organize my assignments, the rainbow pens I use to mark up my notes.

My teachers let me record their lectures because I have a lot of trouble listening and taking notes at the same time. I sort the past week's audio files into folders on my computer. Then I download an audiobook for English and curl up in bed with my headphones and heating pad and imagine Peter next to me, warm and solid. His hand on my back, tracing the ridges of my spine. I don't always think about kissing him. Sometimes it's enough to imagine him holding me.

I dance my thumb along his name in my phone, though if I really wanted to see him, I could go across the street. Right now putting on a coat, slipping into shoes, *walking* seems like too much effort. The lights are off in his room anyway.

Playing with him always feels incredible. But tonight was different, maybe because it had been so long or because I was keenly aware of the scars connecting us. This time when we played, we had more in common than we ever had before.

Instead of feeling like the surgeons stole a part of me and gave it to Peter, it feels like that missing piece stitched us closer together.

I wonder if he felt—*feels*—it too.

When my feelings for him changed, it wasn't because of a singular romantic moment between us. It was gradual, a side effect of the music we made and the hours we spent together. I started noticing how cute his smile was, how much I liked his eyes, the warmth that flooded my body when we hugged or leaned against each other while watching a movie. When I made him laugh, something deep inside me rumbled along with him. Something that said, *Do that again*.

After his declaration of love, the one in hindsight I wish I could have returned, Peter went out of his way to ensure I knew he didn't feel that way anymore. I don't think we hugged for a full month. So I decided I'd wait for a sign. The problem is, anything can be a sign if I wish hard enough.

Over the years, it gradually dawned on me that if he didn't get off the transplant list, he might die. And I would lose not only my best friend, but someone I was starting to love in a completely different way. That was when I vowed that if there was any chance I could help him, I had to try.

At dinner, I was surprised by his sudden interest in Judaism. I wear my Star of David necklace every day, the one my parents gave me for my bat mitzvah, but to me it's more a symbol of belonging to something than a statement of religious devotion. Plus, my dyslexia made my Torah portion really freaking hard, so this necklace is sort of a reminder that I did it.

To me, "being Jewish" isn't the same as "practicing Judaism." I'm pretty sure there's a difference, that I can feel part of something, that I can like that it makes me unique even if I don't like going to temple. I'm Sophie Rose Orenstein and I have red hair and freckles and I dance and I'm Jewish. It feels like a defining quality, though it's not the only quality that defines me.

Someone knocks on my door. I'm positive it's one of my parents, so I'm surprised when Tabby enters.

"Luna's asleep," she says quietly, "and Josh went home. Can I come in?"

"You mean he doesn't live here?"

Tabby lifts her eyebrows.

I dial back the bitchiness. "Sorry. That was uncalled for."

"Yeah. It was." She steps inside, fidgeting with her hair. "I can't imagine how hard this is for you."

"You're suddenly so smart?"

"I've always been smart."

It's true. Tabby was seven months pregnant when she took the SAT. She scored in the ninety-eighth percentile.

My bed creaks as Tabby sits down. "I'm sorry," she says.

"Me too," I grit out. If she can be mature, I can too. "I . . . didn't mean to take that out on you. You're a good mom."

"Thanks. What you did was amazing. Complicated, but amazing. And . . . I know the way you look at Peter. I see what's there."

"You don't—" I shake my head. "There's nothing there."

"Remember when I said I've always been smart?" She taps her temple. "Does he know?"

"I don't think so." I take a deep breath—and then I let her in. "I've been hiding it for the past three years. Gahhh, it feels like I've been suffering forever." I mash a pillow over my head and groan into it.

"Oh my God, that long?"

I nod. We are sisters sharing secrets. The kind of sisters we've never really been.

"Why haven't you said anything? Done anything?"

"It never felt like the right time, I guess. And now, with the transplant . . . I don't want him to feel like he owes me, or something." I want him to love me because he wants to, not because he feels like he has to. "I never told you this, but . . . we kissed once."

Tabby's eyes widen. "You did? Shit, when?"

I have to laugh because this new Mama Tabby doesn't swear nearly as much as she used to. As though a one-year-old would pick up on it. "Yeah. A few years ago. We were sort of . . . experimenting."

It was my perfect first kiss with Peter. Tentative and sweet and searching. It was full of curiosity, each of us wanting to know what it felt like to press your mouth to another person's. I've thought about our perfect second kiss a hundred, a thousand times, and all that matters to me is that it lasts longer than the first.

"He might be waiting for you to say something. To make a move. What would be the worst-case scenario?"

"He doesn't like me back."

"And then what? You're still best friends. The awkwardness would go away after a while, right?"

I want to believe that it wouldn't be gutting to learn he doesn't feel the same way. That's why uncertainty is so safe: I can wrap myself in this potentially unrequited love and never risk getting shut down.

And as much as I hate to admit it, Tabby knows significantly more about romantic relationships than I do. I wonder what it would've been like if she'd confided in me about Josh when they started dating. If, when she got pregnant, I'd been a confidante as opposed to a mess of confusion and shock.

"Maybe you're right," I say, and then add: "Thanks."

She yawns. "It's past my bedtime. God, I'm old."

I whack her with a pillow. "Go to sleep, Grandma."

After she leaves, I lift up my shirt and trace the jagged scar on my abdomen. It will fade, maybe one day even disappear, but I'll always know what happened beneath my skin. I wonder how long I'll be nervous about changing in front of other people. Peter is the only one who would understand how I'm feeling, but I can't burden him with this, too.

I mull over what Tabby said, imagining all the different ways I could tell him how I feel. If I could hug him and have him not only hug me back, but bury his lips in my neck and tell me I'm beautiful, amazing, *his*. We could belong to each other, tied together in the most intimate pas de deux.

I have been imagining us together for a long, long time. Sometimes we are sweet and gentle. Sometimes we are wildly acrobatic. Sometimes we reenact scenes from movies I've seen. I don't know exactly what sex is supposed to look like, but it's probably much messier than it is in my mind. Still, it is my fantasy: We can be as skilled as I want.

I slink over to my dresser. I keep the vibrator in the back of a drawer, wrapped inside a too-small sweater with dreidels on it. I bought it at a sex toy shop in Capitol Hill when I turned eighteen in March, one of those places owned by women, with a focus on women. Most of all, I was *curious*. Maybe it's the dancer in me that wanted to know everything my body could do. And tonight I want to prove I control my body, that I can still make myself feel good.

Once I wear out the batteries, I lie in bed for a while, staring up at the ceiling.

Hiding my feelings for Peter kills me sometimes, and the vibrator takes the edge off for only a little while. This time of night is when my feelings are most dangerous. When I ask myself questions like, if he loved me, wouldn't something have happened between us by now? Or is he as scared as I am? Is he in bed across the street thinking of me?

Maybe my sister is right: It's time to take the leap and finally tell him. Not for the first time, I wish I were more in real life like my onstage self. My body has the courage my mind and mouth never seem to have.

I message Peter good night when what I really want to say is *I'm in love with you* and *I want you* and *Is there any chance you want me the same way?*

The pain dulls but never quite goes away.

CHAPTER 10

PETER

TWO WEEKS INTO THE SEMESTER, I STILL HAVEN'T gotten a chance to play piano in band. Eleanor Kang's bound to catch an autumn cold sometime soon, though. I'm hopeful.

I'm in the school library, getting a head start on my homework before tonight's football game. Sophie's performing at halftime, and we're going to a party afterward. I'm sure it has nothing in common with the two-person parties Sophie and I used to have on Friday nights. Movies and records and early bedtimes. For me, at least.

I'm not sure I even know the rules of football. My parents aren't interested in sports, and I've never seen it played. I click out of my Word document and google it—but someone in the carrel across from me is humming. Loudly. Too loudly for a library, and yes, I'm going to be That Person and say something about it. I push out my chair and peer around.

"Excuse me—" I start.

"Hey," says Chase Cabrera from my English class. The hummer. "You're in the Friday-night nerd club too?"

"I—uh—what?"

He leans back in his chair. Flexes his arms above his head. "We're doing homework in the library on a Friday because we're both extremely cool?"

"Yes. That's exactly right."

He taps his laptop. "This Dante essay is slowly sucking the life out of me. Have you finished it yet?"

"Yeah. I actually read the book last year. For, uh—for fun. So you're going to have to let me be president of the Friday-night nerd club."

"I could settle for VP. Seriously, though, you read Dante for fun?"

"I . . . had a lot of free time," I say. "No offense, but why'd you take the class?"

He groans, then rubs at his eyes, jostling his old-man glasses. "My mom wanted me to take as many APs as possible so I have a chance at scholarships. My sister basically got a full ride—thanks, Carlie—so it's a lot of pressure sometimes." He stretches out his legs. "I can't remember the last book I read that wasn't for school. In my family, it's like, get into a good college or else." He runs his hands over his face, like it's all too much.

"I'm sorry," I say, wishing I could understand, even a little, what it feels like for people to want too much from you.

He shrugs. "Nah. It's fine."

"I could help you. With the book." This is how my first non-Sophie friendship starts: with Dante Alighieri. "As nerd club president, it might even be my duty."

One half of his mouth pulls up into a smile. His glasses sit on his nose tilted slightly to the right, and his smile goes slightly to the left. I like the opposite symmetry of it. I like that no one else in our year wears the kind of glasses he does.

"Thank you. Thank you. If you can get one one-hundredth of your knowledge into my head, maybe I won't be totally screwed." He swivels his chair over to my alcove. "You're . . . on the Wikipedia page for football?"

"Oh." My face heats up, and I chew on my bottom lip before explaining: "I've never been to a game. Figured I should proba-bly know how it's played before tonight."

"You've never been to a football game?"

"I . . . haven't done a lot of things." I didn't want to get into this, but he's clearly waiting for an explanation now, one eye-brow raised. If Chase and I are going to be friends, he might as well know why I've been a hermit. "So, when you asked if I was new . . . I've actually lived here my whole life. But I've been homeschooled for the past few years. I have chronic kidney dis-ease, and my parents are really overprotective. I'd been on the transplant list for years. Until a couple months ago. My friend Sophie donated a kidney." I push back my sleeve, showing him the medical ID bracelet.

Chase's dark eyes widen. Clearly, this is not what he was expecting to hear. When he speaks, his voice is softer than usual.

"That's . . . wow. How are you feeling? Is that okay to ask? My mom has a friend with chronic pain who told us to stop asking because she was never going to have a happy answer. So—please ignore me if I shouldn't have asked that."

"I'm kind of the same way, actually. Or—I used to be. But I'm a lot better now. I don't have to—" I break off, realizing I was about to talk about the exchanges I no longer have to do. *Peter. No.* "Anyway. *Inferno.*"

"Only if you're sure I'm not keeping you from your very serious Wikipedia research."

"I'm sure."

Chase rolls up his sleeves, as though we're about to embark on something more strenuous than discussing medieval literature.

"First question, then: Why couldn't a book about hell be more interesting?"

I flip through Chase's copy of the book. "It's an epic poem, an allegory about man's spiritual journey. Dante dies, and in the underworld, each person's sin is punished in a really poetic way. Like, fortune-tellers have to walk with their heads on backward so they can't see what's ahead."

"That's clever. I like that."

"He's guided by this Roman poet, Virgil, through the nine circles of hell, and as they get deeper, the sins people have committed grow worse." I point at the diagram in his book.

Chase examines it. "Where do you think you'd be?"

I consider it. "Anger."

"Fifth circle? You're bad."

Before therapy, I used to be angry all the time—about my first donor kidney failing all those years ago, about my life as a shut-in. I banged out songs on the baby grand that made my parents invest in quality earplugs.

"I'm not nearly as angry as I used to be. Maybe I'd be stuck in limbo. What about you?"

"Hmm. Heresy? I've never been very religious."

For a moment I ponder that. I still have no idea how religious I actually am. Clearing my throat, I decide to trudge onward. "So, Dante descends further and further, ultimately winding up in the ninth circle, where Lucifer is condemned for having committed the ultimate sin against God, treachery. He has three faces, three mouths. They're each chewing on a traitor: Brutus and Cassius, who killed Julius Caesar, and Judas, who betrayed Jesus."

Chase pulls his computer onto his lap and types a few notes. "Aside from the fact that we get to read something about Satan eating people, why do you like it so much?"

"I guess it, like, *spoke* to me or something." I emphasize the word "spoke" like I know what I'm saying must sound ridiculous.

But Chase doesn't seem to think it's stupid. He's watching me intently, waiting for me to say more.

"Part of it is that I like how poetic the punishments are. Gruesome, sure, but it's the ultimate karma. I also like the idea that when you die, things aren't over. Even if you're damned to an eternity of suffering. I'm Jewish, but on some days I'm convinced I'm an atheist, and on others I'm more agnostic, so most of the time I don't really believe in any kind of afterlife. So I guess I wondered, because I was sick . . ." I trail off, because anything else is too deep, too dark for this nascent friendship. Chase probably hasn't had to confront his mortality like I have.

Also: I realize I said "Jewish" as opposed to "half Jewish." It might be the first time. *Well, half Jewish*, I nearly feel compelled to add. But I don't.

He's quiet. I'm worried I've said too much and consider brushing it off when he says, voice serious, "I can understand that. Like I mentioned before, I'm not very religious either, so I have no idea what it feels like, but it . . . it makes sense."

"Have you ever read a book like that?" I ask. "I mean, not about death, necessarily, but something that spoke to you?"

"Not a book," he says. "But music, absolutely. There are some songs I'm positive just had to be written about what I was going through."

I nod vigorously. "I get that. I feel that way about most of Regina Spektor's songs . . . except the really weird ones."

"There are a lot of those."

"You know Regina Spektor?"

"A couple of her more recent albums, yeah."

"You have to listen to *Soviet Kitsch*. And *11:11*—that's her self-released one. What she can do with the piano, it's incredible." I'm rambling. "I, uh, I play piano, so most of what I listen to is pretty piano-centric."

"That's cool," he says, then scrunches his face. "Just don't tell me you're a Coldplay superfan. We'd have to end this friendship right now."

"Definitely not. I mean, Chris Martin's a good pianist, but they've got to be the most overplayed band of the 2000s."

"Agreed. Thank God."

"What are you into?"

He lets out a breath, as though about to begin a very long story. "Some classic rock, some punk, a lot of newer stuff." He lists names of bands, a few I've heard of, many I haven't. "I've been really into this one lately." He opens a music player and quietly, quietly, so the librarians won't hear us, clicks on a song by a band called Shovels & Rope. He glances at me expectantly, waiting for my judgment. Like he's worried I'll hate it and think he has shit taste in music.

"This is good," I say, and I swear he sighs in relief. "Sort of has a Neko Case vibe, but less depressing." When Chase looks blank, I feign shock. "Neko Case? Really?" I lean over and find one of my favorite songs of hers, "This Tornado Loves You."

"I like this," he says, and when the song's over, he types something else into the search bar.

We go back and forth like this for a while, trading songs, Dante nearly forgotten. When Sophie and I do this, we're both judgmental, convinced our taste is better, frustrated when the other doesn't get the brilliance of a particularly brilliant song.

"You like good music," he says, and at that word, "good," a spark of pride runs up my spine. There's nothing like being complimented on your music taste. It feels better than being told you're smart or attractive or funny. "I'm, uh . . ." He blushes. "We only just started, so we're not telling that many people yet, but I'm in a band. Somehow even my mom's on board with it. Thinks it'll look good on my college apps."

I picture Chase onstage, hair slicked back, singing into a microphone. "What do you play?"

"Guitar, but my voice is shit so they won't even let me sing backup. We mostly play covers right now. We're kinda awful, but I love it." There's that smile again, the one at odds with the angle of his glasses.

"You're really selling it." I check my phone. Kickoff is in an hour, and it's an away game. "I didn't realize it was so late. Do you know where the nearest bus stop is?"

Chase raises his eyebrows. "Are you serious? I'll drive you. We're going to the same place."

"That would be great. Thank you."

He waves his hand like it's no big deal. "Thank *you*," he says, and it sounds genuine. He taps the book. "If I can ever repay you . . ."

My stomach twists. Favors are dangerous, and I'm too indebted already. Especially since I still don't know how—*if*—I can ever repay Sophie.

"Don't worry about it," I say, gathering my books and laptop. "You don't owe me anything."

CHAPTER 11

SOPHIE

GLITTER AND SPANDEX AND FALSE EYELASHES—
that's what game nights are made of. I'm not naturally a *rah-rah*,
school-spirit kind of person, but performing—performing, I
love, whether it's in Peter's living room or in a studio or on a
football field in the pouring rain.

We're up 14–7. The dance team and I are shivering in the
first row of the bleachers in our warm-up jackets, and the
Seattle drizzle that's plagued the entire first half is threat-
ening to become a downpour. One of my lashes is coming
unglued. When I try to reattach it, it sticks to my finger, until
finally I let the rain wash it away.

"A few more minutes," Montana says. She has a green ribbon wrapped around her ballet bun, which is slicked back so
tight it must hurt. She paces in front of us, bouncing on the balls
of her feet. "You all ready?" A chorus of yeses. "That's what I like

to hear!" Her gaze lands on mine. "Sophie? You ready? You look a little scared."

I clench my jaw. My teeth are chattering.

"I'm ready," I say. "Just cold."

At this point I've been to dozens of football games, and while I don't actually like the sport, I love the anticipation I feel as I wait for us to perform at halftime. If the team isn't doing well, we cheer people up. If they're winning, we amp up the crowd's energy even more.

Peter is somewhere in the stands, but I can't see him. I took extra painkillers before the game, though the doctors said the pain I experienced last week wasn't extremely common but still within the realm of normal. They asked if I wanted to talk to a counselor. I had a psych evaluation beforehand, but what am I supposed to say to someone now? I gave my best friend a kidney, and now we're not magically both in love the way a part of me secretly hoped?

A whistle blows, and the guys hustle off the field, their cleats splashing in puddles of mud. Halftime.

"The North Seattle High Dance Team!" the announcer yells as we rush onto the field, cheering and pumping our fists.

The song's bassline thumps through my feet. We're all wearing baggy pants. We snap them off halfway into the dance, revealing silver sequined shorts. Rain soaks my hair and mud climbs up my legs, but the adrenaline keeps me going. Montana is right next to me, and she hits everything perfectly, as always. The dance is sexy; I know it is. I thrust my hips, pout my lips. The crowd whoops louder. I love that sound.

I want to be sexy.

I want Peter to think I'm sexy. That has to be the only thing between friendship and something more, right?

The stands roar when we finish our routine. I strike my ending pose, my heart beating fast. I'm drenched and sweaty, and when I look up at the bleachers, despite the weather and the fact that everyone is basically wearing the same REI jacket . . . I spot him. His hood is up, but I'd know the shape of him anywhere. I wave a hand wildly, pushing my wet hair out of my face.

"Amazing job, you guys!" Montana squeals as we head back to the sidelines. "Gabe, your energy was incredible. And, Kunjal, you finally nailed that turn!" Her gaze meets mine. "Sophie, your timing was perfect."

I'm still glowing when I sit back down on the bleachers, thinking about the dance and my perfect timing and Peter, Peter, Peter. I'm tired of waiting—I'm going to kiss him after the game. For real this time, not a kiss to seal a pact. Our perfect second kiss. I will throw my arms around his neck and our wet bodies will collide. Maybe the force of it will knock us both to the ground. We'll get mud in our hair and on our clothes, and I won't even care.

The game goes into overtime, and we end up winning. I am sure it was very tense for everyone who actually cared about the game.

I'm nearly frozen when everyone rushes the field after the final buzzer. I hang back for a second and wave my phone, searching for a signal.

Then two hands land on my shoulders. "Hey! You guys were great!"

I spin around to find Peter wiping rain out of his eyes. His jacket is soaked, but he's grinning, a full Peter smile. He looks really, really hot all wet like this.

"Thanks. I'm so glad you came!" I squeal, and push onto tip-toes to hug him.

And then there's this moment—a moment that could almost be our perfect second kiss. It's raining, and his dark eyes are locked on mine, his arms around my waist, and it's almost too cinematic to be a real thing that is happening to me.

But then he pulls away, ending the hug. It would have been too perfect, that kiss. My arms are heavy as I drop them to my sides. I try not to think how whenever we hug, he is always the one to pull away first.

In my head, I play out the rest of the fantasy, where I tackle him onto the football field. But . . . it's pretty muddy. Dirt isn't exactly sexy. And there are so many people around. That's another thing I want my perfect second kiss with Peter to be: private.

"Seriously," he says. "That one part, with the jumping? I don't even get how you did that."

"Yeah." My voice is soft. I'm suddenly shy, aware of how cold I am. "Um, so the party." I squeeze water from my ponytail. "Still feeling up to it?"

He eyes me strangely, because of course we're going to the party. That was the plan. "Absolutely. I'm kind of excited, actually."

"Right," I say. Maybe part of me was hoping he'd say he'd rather be alone with me. But if Peter wants to go, we'll go. Inside my shoes, my socks are wet. "Let's go home first so I can change, and then we'll go."

It takes us a while to get to my car because every few feet someone wants to scream in our faces and we have to scream back.

Peter pumps his fist into the air. "Go Tigers!" he shouts, and around us, everyone growls it back, roaring like our mascot. It's adorable, the way he's enchanted by it all, by this perfect high school scene. I've experienced this a few times each season, but I have to keep reminding myself that it's all brand-new to him. He grins at me. "This is so great," he says so that only I can hear.

"Yeah," I say, grinning back. Even in the glow of the stadium lights that make most people look slightly alien, Peter is beautiful. The familiar love-ache in my stomach intensifies, and I make a vow: I'll tell him at the party how I feel about him, how I've felt for years. "It is."

CHAPTER 12

PETER

MY FIRST HIGH SCHOOL PARTY FOLLOWING MY first high school football game isn't exactly what I expected. First of all, the host's parents are here, snatching everyone's car keys at the door.

The smell is overpowering. Beer and sweat and several dozen brands of perfume and cologne and body spray mingling together. An earthy sweetness that, having grown up in Seattle, I instantly recognize as weed. Then there's the music, something heavy with bass and beeps and meaningless lyrics.

"What do you think?" Sophie asks after she relinquishes her keys. She's changed into a short black dress, and her hair, still damp from the rain, hangs in loose waves on her shoulders.

I like your hair like that, I could tell her.

The problem is, I don't know what happens after that.

I could find out.

"It's . . . a party," I say.

"Excellent observation." Sophie's standing very close to me, probably because the party intimidates her. It intimidates me a little too, so much that part of me wishes it were just the two of us alone in the comfort of my room. We could lie on my bed while a record softly plays in the background, her red hair spilling across my pillow.

A bigger part of me demands I take advantage of being out of my house with a slightly extended curfew. Demands that I be brave.

"Your hair," I blurt out.

Sophie's eyes grow wide as she buries a hand in her waves. "What about it?" She sounds worried, which makes me realize my half compliment probably didn't sound like one at all.

Before I can respond, Montana, the host of the party and one of Sophie's dance teammates, grabs Sophie's arm. "You came!" she shouts. "Liz and I are playing flip cup in the basement." And she tugs Sophie away and out of sight.

At first I'm all set to follow her downstairs to the basement. See what exactly flip cup is and if I'm any good at it. This is what I wanted, right? A chance to be on my own, make some of my own friends?

Or . . . I could try to navigate this party without my shadow, though a not insignificant part of me longs to be at home with a book instead. At the game, it took me only an instant to spot her when everyone rushed the field. Maybe you can sense someone's presence after knowing them this long. You can glance at a crowd and immediately know where they are, like a special searchlight beamed straight from your heart to theirs. Or maybe the piece of her I now have somehow ties us together.

I guess I'm wondering how tightly those knots are tied.

After I get a cup of water, I peek inside each room, which (a) makes me look like I have a purpose and (b) gives me a chance to search for the few people I've been friendly with in class, like Chase Cabrera or Eleanor Kang. My self-guided tour occupies me for at least twenty minutes. In the kitchen, there are Costco-size bottles of vodka and cranberry juice, plus a cooler full of beer. In the living room, people are dancing or chatting on couches or chairs. In the game room, what I assume is beer pong is in full swing. No one waves me over, says hi, asks me to play.

It hits me that everyone here has had years to cement bonds with their classmates. I'm a random new kid who showed up and expected—what? People to flock to me? Sophie's been mine for so long that I'm not sure how to make friends. How to ask someone if they want to grab a bite to eat or come over and listen to records.

I'm utterly alone in this house full of semi-strangers.

"Hey! Nerd club president!" Chase Cabrera claps me on the back, causing me to splash water down the front of my shirt. "Oh—shit, I'm so sorry!"

"It's okay!" I say, too eager because, though my shirt is now soaked, I finally have someone to talk to.

"I'll get a paper towel."

"No! Really, it's fine." What I mean, though, is *Please don't leave. You've saved me from looking like a friendless loser.* "It's just water."

When we got to the game, I was certain he'd ditch me, but he invited me to sit with him and his friends, a guy named Noah and a girl named Trinity and her boyfriend, Hunter. I've seen Chase at lunch, and sometimes he sits with them and sometimes with other people. I get the sense he's well liked but not attached to any singular group.

"Water?" Alcohol, I imagine, has flushed his cheeks to match his red plastic cup, and his glasses are more crooked than usual. "We gotta get you a beer."

My stomach drops. "I can't drink. Because of, uh, the medications I'm taking." I'm very cool. It's painful how cool I am.

"Ahh, right. I'm sorry." He stares at his own cup, as though wondering whether it would be a dick move to drink it in front of me, and a silence gapes between us.

"You don't have to—" I start, pointing to his cup as he raises it to his mouth. Heat rushes to my face. I'm not normally this awkward. Why am I acting so goddamn awkward? I can't say a single right thing tonight.

"What?"

"Never mind," I mutter, and he takes a swallow of whatever drink vodka and cranberry juice makes. Whatever it is, I'll never know what it tastes like.

It reminds me I haven't been cured. That my health is still a delicate thing.

Chase is staring at me as though unsure what I'm doing here, and, honestly, I don't know either. God, what did I think we were going to talk about if I found him? *Inferno*? I shrink to the size of a red plastic cup.

Music! We could talk about how bad this music is.

But as soon as I open my mouth, someone calls his name.

"Chase! Derek needs you to referee this game of beer pong!" someone yells.

"Duty calls," Chase says. "I'll see you later, okay?"

"Sure. Okay," I say, and he disappears into the crowd.

The next hour is a parade of awkward. I'm awkward in the living room, where I find myself on a couch between two couples making out. I'm awkward on the dance floor as I try to maneuver into the hallway. I'm awkward in the hallway as I wait in line for the bathroom. I'm awkward in the kitchen, where I deny alcohol again and again. I thought I could do this—be on my own. That's why I don't look for Sophie in the basement. I don't want it to be so obvious that I need her.

But when I ask a couple people whether they've seen her—to make sure she's okay—one actually says, "Who?" even when I give her last name.

The idea that other people don't know this girl who's been my entire life for so many years is mind-boggling. It's become clear, though, since school started, that Sophie has been the kind of person who keeps to herself. Whether we sit with the dance team or occasionally with Josh and his friends, she focuses on her lunch or on me. No one asks her questions, invites her into the conversation, and she doesn't make an attempt to join it.

I've given up and am on my way to find the basement when she finally stumbles back to me. Into me, actually, when her heel catches on the carpet, and I have to grab her shoulders to prevent her from falling.

"Having fun?" she asks as I help steady her. The rim of her cup is stained with her lipstick. I can't tell what's in it.

"Oh yeah," I say. "Giant buckets full of it." She raises an eyebrow. "Is . . . it that obvious?"

She links her arm through mine. "I have an idea," she says, and tugs me out of the crowd, upstairs, and into an empty bedroom. She closes the door behind us but doesn't lock it. "It's just us." She gestures for me to sit next to her on someone else's bed. "We only need you and me to have a good time, right?"

"Right," I agree, my heart starting to pound. "What . . . do you want to do?"

Now that she's here, I want to be able to relax. But I'm alone with Sophie in a stranger's bedroom, my heart thumping in anticipation. The opposite of relaxed.

She laughs too loudly. Shoves my arm. "Peter," she says. Like my name is an admonishment. She claws her hands through her hair, her perennial nervous habit.

"Sophie," I say back, which makes her laugh again.

When Sophie and I talked about losing our virginities together, which we've never discussed since, my feelings for her had dimmed back to friendship. This is what stops me every time I nearly compliment her, though: remembering how it felt in that music room in sixth grade after I confessed that I liked her. I don't want to go back to that place. If anything's going to happen, I can't make the first move this time.

"Do you know a guy named Chase?" I ask.

"Chase Cabrera? Glasses?"

I nod.

"I had math with him last year. He was a little loud, but I don't really know him. Anyway, why?"

Loud. I guess it makes sense Sophie would find someone outgoing "a little loud."

"He's in my AP Lit class. We've talked a few times."

"Aww, are you making friends?" With that, she reaches over and smudges my cheek with her thumb. "Baby Peter's growing up." She twirls a strand of her hair around one finger, then takes a sip of her drink. Twirl, sip, repeat.

All of her is a little mesmerizing right now, the red of her hair and the pink of her cheeks and the black of her dress.

"You guys were great out there," I say for about the third time tonight. I'm close enough to count her freckles.

She stares down at her ID bracelet, flicking the charms back and forth across her wrist, and blushes deeper. If I pressed my mouth to her cheeks, would they be warm against my lips? "Thanks." Twirl. Sip. "Do . . . you remember when my mom took me bra shopping for the first time? And I was too embarrassed to tell what we were doing, just that we were going to the mall? But you begged and begged to go along with us because you wanted to go to the bookstore?"

"And so you let me tag along, and I sat in front of the lingerie store for an hour waiting for you and your mom, reading *The Perks of Being a Wallflower* and pretending I wasn't mortified." I laugh, though I'm unsure where she's going with this. "I'd forgotten that."

"Only you would remember exactly what book you were reading. I'd never seen your face that red," she says, then stares up at me from beneath her lashes. "Except for now."

At this I'm sure I blush even deeper. "You—you should probably have some water," I croak out. I hand her the bottle I've been slowly peeling the label off of for the past hour, and her mouth stains it burgundy. The plastic crunches as she sips.

After she swallows, she bounces a fingertip on the end of my nose. "You're too good, Peter. I love you. You know that. I one-hundred-percent adore you." She leans in closer and puts a hand on my arm. Brushes it gently. "You look so good tonight."

My heart can't be controlled. It's manic now.

"You do too." It comes out shaky.

Sophie scoots even closer to me on the bed. The box spring squeals beneath us. She pulls up one of her legs, crosses it. Tugs her dress down. Her knee settles against my thigh, and I can't help grazing it with a few fingertips. "It feels like something's changed between us. Do you feel it?"

"Yes," I say, voice breathier than I'm used to hearing.

Something does change. A shift in temperature. A quickening of my heartbeat. The wind outside bending a tree to tap against the bedroom window, which makes Sophie whip her head toward the window, then quickly back to me. The force of it tugs the silver chain from beneath her neckline. The small Star of David dangles in the space between us.

"Peter. I don't just love you," she says. "I like you. I like you so much."

She leans in first, but I meet her there.

It's not a shy peck like before. Her mouth is warm, sour from the alcohol. Teasing me with a life I'll never have. Kissing Sophie is a strange mix of familiar and foreign, familiar because this is Sophie and foreign because this is *Sophie*.

This time when we break apart to catch our breath, Sophie is grinning wilder than I've ever seen. We wait a few beats before going for each other again, and I capture her Star of David charm between my thumb and index finger.

And it's good. *Great*, even. I move my hands to her hair, which is thick and coarse and feels incredible. No wonder she's always playing with it. But a warning light flashes in my mind. This is Sophie, who made a sacrifice I can never repay. Sophie, whom I love—and maybe more-than-like.

It's the "maybe" that makes me hesitate. It settles against the uncertain thud of my own heart.

Her hands are on my collar, and then they're suddenly fiddling with a shirt button. That mental warning light goes off again. WARNING. WARNING. That's when I wake up, realize what we're doing and that we shouldn't be doing it. I have no idea how much she drank, but she's definitely impaired, and this has to stop.

"Wait," I say, holding a hand between us. I touch my mouth, and my fingers come away stained with her berry lipstick.

"What is it?" Her pale-blue eyes are dreamy, as though still lost in the kiss. The necklace at her throat swings back and forth. Then she giggles a little, a drunken hiccup of a giggle, as though she can't quite believe what happened either.

Before I can start to explain—if I even have the words—the door bangs open, and a guy wearing a backward baseball cap says, "Sorry, kids—wait, hey, you're Peter Rosenthal-Porter, right?"

"Yeah . . ." I glance at Sophie, who looks as puzzled as I am. Her face is flushed, and I can only imagine mine matches.

The guys turns and yells to someone in the hallway. "This is the guy I was telling you about!"

It happens fast—partygoers rush the room, almost like they rushed the field at the game. I spring up from the bed, and Sophie copies me, readjusting her dress and dabbing at her mouth.

A football player in my chem class—I think his name is Ty—grabs my arm and says, "This dude is a fucking miracle! He beat cancer or some shit!" Then he takes Sophie's arm too, holding us up like we are two prizes he won at a county fair. If I look scrawny next to him, Sophie looks like a doll. "And this girl is a fucking hero. She gave this guy a kidney. A fucking *kidney*!"

Apparently, kidneys cure cancer—who knew? I open my mouth to correct him, but it's too loud in here.

Everyone whoops, and someone gives Sophie a shot glass with something blue inside. I'm about to warn her not to drink it because what the hell is it, but before I can, she downs it in one gulp. More cheers. She's wobbly on her feet as she waves, smiles at everyone, basking in this unusual attention.

"Are you serious? That's what you were doing this summer?" one of the dance team girls asks Sophie, who nods and holds up her ID bracelet as proof.

"That's amazing," someone else breathes.

Ty hoists her up onto his shoulders and races out of the room with her, the rest of the party chanting her name like she is the winning team. I'm the miracle, but Sophie . . . Sophie is the hero.

CHAPTER 13

SOPHIE

LAST NIGHT'S DRESS IS BUNCHED UP AROUND my hips and my head is pounding. I roll over in bed and groan, the party coming back to me in flashes. Shots with Montana and the rest of the dance team. Football players who'd never before spoken to me shouting my name. Tugging Peter into a bedroom.

Kissing him.

I told Peter I liked him, and we *kissed*. And it was brief, but it was still something, still *progress*. The attention I got from the rest of the party isn't nearly as groundbreaking as this. Suddenly I am so, so awake, all my nerve endings electrified. I swing my legs out of bed and—

"Ow!"

I draw my legs back up to the bed. "Peter?"

He's sleeping on the floor next to my bed, a blanket tossed haphazardly over him.

"Hey," I whisper, trying to soothe my heartbeat, which starts racing when I notice the stubble on Peter's jaw, his wrinkled shirt, his feet sticking out of the blanket. Morning Peter is too much for me to handle, especially after last night. I resist the urge to touch my lips. "Sorry for kicking you."

He pushes himself to a sitting position, rubs the sleep out of his eyes. "What time is it? I didn't mean to fall asleep here."

More of the night comes back to me. We got home around two a.m. He helped me inside because he wanted to make sure I was okay, I remember him saying. He must have been too tired to walk across the street.

"It is . . . almost eleven."

"Guhhhh . . ." He reaches for his phone, scrolls through his messages. "At least I was lucid enough to tell my parents I might crash here." He stands up, stretches. His shirt lifts up, revealing a slice of his stomach.

"About last night," I start, feeling my face flame.

"Right . . ."

"I wasn't . . . fully myself."

He cracks a small smile. "That's a good euphemism."

In that moment, it strikes me how easy it would be to brush this all away, forget it ever happened. But I want more from this friendship, and I've never been this close to it.

Maybe I was more myself last night than I thought—a version of myself who was unafraid to reach for what she wanted.

"I don't want it to be something that happened that we never talk about again." I force myself to make eye contact with him, needing to know that he knows exactly what I mean. His middle school declaration of love. Our virginity pact. Those mismatched feelings that I thought, last night, were finally happening at the right time. The way he kissed me, I was convinced he felt the same way. "What if . . . ? What if we tried this for real? You and me, I mean."

Peter leans against my dresser, pulling his lower lip between his teeth. I wish he didn't look so perfect in my room, all morning-rumpled, his hair wild. He waits a few moments before responding. Each moment feels like a sudden stop in a song—when your breath hitches and you're waiting for the music to kick back in.

"I . . . I think I need some time to think about it," he says finally.

It's not the worst response.

But it's not the one I wanted.

"I know people say that dating can ruin friendships, and I'm sure it does sometimes, but definitely not all the time, right?" I'm desperate to fill the silence between us, to persuade him. Tip him over the edge so he can fall with me. "And—what if it made our friendship better?"

"How?" He asks it softly, earnestly. It's not a combative question, but one that comes from a place of real curiosity. "What would be different?" His eyes are on his bracelet, his thumb tracing the engraving there. "Aside from, I guess, kissing . . . and . . . other things."

Those would be the main differences.

There's a limit to how much you can love someone as a friend, and Peter and I have hit that limit. The only way I can love him more is by actually making love. That has to be the reason it's called that.

I try to imagine Peter with someone else, a girl with the patience to grow her hair long, one who has no freckles and no scars. They're in college in a tiny dorm room bed, and he's on top of her, and he's whispering to her things he should have whispered to me. Even in my imagination, it's brutal.

"Have you thought about it?" I ask, pulling the sheets around my bare legs. "About . . . *us*?"

"If I'm being completely honest, yeah, I have." He fiddles with the knobs on my dresser drawers, pushing one of them out and then back in. His mouth curves in a sheepish smile. He's blushing, and it gives me a buzz of satisfaction that this conversation is as intense for him as it is for me.

I wonder what we look like in his imagination, if we look any of the ways we do in mine. If we're laughing or if we're serious.

Why he stopped imagining us.

"I mean . . . we made that pact," he continues.

It's the first time either of us has acknowledged it out loud since we made it.

"Right."

"I—I'm sorry. I need some time. To think about it," he repeats.

My room is too small. Too warm. Too disappointing. "Okay."

By now I should know this is what happens when I try to get something I want from Peter.

He shuts my dresser drawer too loudly. "I should, uh, probably go."

"And I have to pick up my car."

I throw on a hoodie and Peter jams his feet into his shoes. I follow him downstairs—where, much to my shock, my parents are calmly eating breakfast with his.

"I hope you like scones," Peter's mom is saying, holding up a big box. "We got these from that new bakery on Stone Way."

My mom takes a bite and lets out a horrifying moan of contentment. "*Mmm, mmm, MMM*. So good."

"What's . . . going on here?" I ask.

"Breakfast," my dad says. I take a scone. "Sophie, Peter, can you take a seat for a moment?"

We slide into chairs at the kitchen table, my heart an increasingly panicky thrum inside my chest.

"We've been talking," my mom says, "and we think you two are probably a little old for sleepovers."

Apparently, I hadn't been embarrassed enough for one day. It's not even noon, and I would definitely like this day to be over, or at the very least for our parents to stop talking. They do not.

"We've been so lax about it," Peter's mom continues, "and of course we're thrilled you two are such close friends, but it can't happen anymore. Okay? You're still welcome to spend as much time together as you want, but you've got to sleep in your own beds, in your own rooms."

I open my mouth to say Peter slept on the floor and not my bed, but that seems beside the point.

Peter's nodding. "Right. Of course. Sorry."

Maybe the strangest part of this is that Peter's parents have always let him get away with just about anything.

We eat quickly, silently, before Peter mumbles something about homework and I follow him to the door.

"So . . . no more sleepovers," I say as we step outside.

"Yeah." He shoves his hands into his pockets. "I'll see you later? Unless . . . unless you want me to take the bus with you to get your car from the party?"

I shake my head. "No. It's okay. You have a lot to do. Homework."

"Yep." He makes this clicking sound with his jaw that he used to do all the time. I found it so annoying, but I never said anything. It's amazing the things that stop bothering you when you're in love with someone.

"Okay," I say, and I *wave* at him, which I cannot recall ever having done in my life. But he returns it, and then he retreats across the street.

Montana and Liz are in the front yard cleaning up stray cups and other party debris. Montana waves when she sees me approach the house. She's wearing pink leggings and a gray hoodie, her dark hair slicked up in its usual ballet bun. Liz, who's as tall as Montana but curvier, is in a puffy black coat and slippers.

"Hey," I say. "I'm picking up my car. I hope I wasn't too embarrassing last night."

"No. You were actually really fun," Montana says. "It was unusual for you."

"Thanks, I think?" I spin my keys around. Drunk Sophie equals fun Sophie. That makes me sad for some reason. The alcohol must have loosened me up, made me more like the shiny lightbulb person I am with Peter.

Liz ties the garbage bag she's carrying into a knot. "That guy you were with, Peter? He's in my Latin class. Is he your boyfriend?"

"Not exactly, but . . ." *I want him to be*, I could say. *And I thought we were finally making some progress.* But now I'm even more confused. Montana and Liz started out as friends, and they must have thought dating was worth risking that friendship. The words dissolve on my tongue. If I were talking to Peter—and not *about* Peter—I'd have no shortage of things to say.

"It's complicated?" Liz says. At practice, she wears her blond bob in a stubby ponytail, but this morning it's pushed back with a yellow headband. Her face is free of its usual winged eyeliner, the kind I've practiced myself but never have been able to get right. It's odd seeing them outside of school like this, even odder than at the party last night. They seem about 150 percent less intimidating than usual.

I let out a breath. "Very."

They must assume I don't want to talk about it, because Montana says, "Do you want to work on your choreography?"

"What?"

"Do you want to come in. Work on your choreography." It's not a question this time. She keys in a code on the side of her

126

garage that opens the door, and she beckons me to come inside with them.

"Oh . . ." I search for an excuse and can't find one. "I don't want to interrupt if you two are hanging out. . . ."

"Just come inside," Montana says with a roll of her eyes. She tosses the garbage into a bin and leads me down into the basement we did shots in last night.

"I can't believe your parents let you throw parties like that. My parents aren't super strict or anything, but I still can't imagine them giving us free rein with alcohol. And Peter's parents are really overprotective. It would never happen."

"They think if we drink in a 'controlled environment' that we'll be smart about it. And hey, I guess it's true. You left your car here last night."

Montana pushes the sofa against the wall. Liz hooks her phone up to the speakers and finds a warm-up song, something by Imogen Heap. The three of us start stretching.

"I'm glad you decided to come," Montana continues. "To the party, and right now." The genuine way she says it makes me wish I hadn't resisted hanging out with them before, although I can't imagine having traded any of my Peter time.

I need some time, he said this morning. And I need to put that out of my mind so it doesn't torture me until that extremely vague length of time has passed.

"You're so good with the team," I tell Montana. "I mean. You're a good captain."

"The best," Liz says.

"Suck-up." Montana smiles, still in her lunge. To me, she says: "Thanks. I try to bring out the best in each dancer. I went to this choreography workshop in San Francisco last summer. It was the best eight weeks of my life." She switches legs. "You should apply."

"I don't know," I say. "I've never been away from home for that long."

"It was incredible. And you have a technical background, so you'd be great. I stayed in a dorm, too. It was basically like college." She rolls her neck. "I can't wait for college. I applied to a bunch of schools in New York for dance. And Liz wants to work in publishing."

"Fingers crossed, we'll end up in NYC together," Liz says.

I feel a flash of something unfamiliar—awe, maybe? I can imagine them there. We're in the same grade, but they seem so much older, more experienced. I've barely thought about what happens after this year. I'll be in community college and Peter will be here, and the year after that, we'll be together again. Somewhere.

I tuck my necklace inside my shirt like I usually do before dancing. "I'll think about it. I'm not sure what Peter's summer plans are yet."

Eight weeks in San Francisco. Eight weeks without Peter—if I even got in. I've only been away from Peter for a week at a time on family vacations. I always worried something awful would happen while I was gone.

"Where are you applying?" Liz asks, and for a second I think she's talking about the workshop too.

"Oh—I'm not. I'm going to go to Seattle Central for a year. I have no idea what I want to study, so I might as well save a few grand." I don't mention waiting for Peter to graduate, though saving money has always felt secondary.

"Smart." Montana gestures to the space in front of her. "Show us what you have."

"It's not much more than last time. . . ."

"Excuses! Come on, Sophie. If you want to be a real choreographer, you need to be more confident about your work. What's the point if no one's going to see it?"

I consider this. That's what dance is—a performing art. It's not something you do alone, and it's not meant to be a secret.

I clear my throat. "Start the music."

We work on my dance all afternoon and evening, until it's dark outside. I'm exhausted when I get home. My mom's sitting on the couch, Luna asleep in her lap.

"Where's Tabby?" I whisper.

"Working late. I'd take her upstairs, but she looks too precious to disturb. Doesn't she?"

Luna's wispy toddler hair is rumpled, and her delicate lashes rest on her cheeks. "She does."

"How are you feeling?" my mom asks.

I shift a hand toward my abdomen, as though needing to confirm I feel okay right now. "Good. Fine."

"And you and Peter, everything's okay there, right?"

"Why wouldn't it be?"

Mom puts on her corporate problem-solver hat. "After what happened this morning—"

"Mom. I get it. No more sleepovers."

"Not just that," she says. "Your dad and I did a lot of research about kidney transplants beforehand, of course. It's not uncommon for the donor or recipient to feel guilty, frustrated, depressed . . ."

"It's not like that with us," I say, and she raises her hands in surrender.

"Okay. But if you need to talk about it, Soph, you can. Even though we disagreed about it, it happened, and we're here for you. Or if you'd prefer to talk to a counselor, or another doctor, we could arrange that, too."

"I get it. Thanks, Mom." I plop next to her on the couch, run my finger along Luna's tiny hands. "God. I can't believe how small they are."

"Incredible, right? That we all start out that tiny."

"Some of us even stay that tiny."

"You'll hit your growth spurt someday."

I groan. "You've been saying that for years. It's time we faced the facts. It's not happening."

"I can't imagine what this must feel like for Peter," Mom says after a few moments of silence. "Can you imagine suddenly having all these opportunities, not being limited by dialysis or constantly worrying about landing back in the hospital? He's always been so bright. Now he has a chance to do something with that."

What about me? I wonder, but she doesn't say anything until I prompt her by repeating the question out loud.

"What do you mean, what about you? You've always had those opportunities."

I burrow deeper into the couch, trying to understand. I've always had those opportunities, but I've never taken them? That I stayed close to home because that's where Peter was? Is that what she's trying to say?

Eight weeks in San Francisco—maybe that's the kind of opportunity she's talking about.

CHAPTER 14

PETER

THE PIANO IN THE MUSIC ROOM AT SCHOOL IS AN upright Baldwin, a deep caramel color. It's probably decades old and decorated with scratches and stains, and the highest C no longer makes an audible sound.

Each piano has its own personality. The baby grand we have at home has always seemed a little arrogant, a little uptight to me. That's how grand pianos are, and they've earned the right to sort of be assholes because they're fucking beautiful. The Yamaha in my room is cool and sleek. Portable. Modern. And this Baldwin: It's a favorite sweater, a mug of hot cocoa. It's home. Over the years it's had so many hands dance along its ivories, and it manages to create the right sound for each of them.

I'll admit it: I'm hiding out here during lunch. It's Halloween and I didn't dress up, and the halls are a literal nightmare. But I'm also hiding from Sophie.

On the ride to school this morning, I attempted normal. "Let's listen to your dance playlist!" I said, and she raised an eyebrow because I've complained on too many occasions that her dance playlists are too peppy for me.

My mouth filled with all the half sentences I couldn't say to her. *I like you, but . . .* and *I love you more than anything, but . . .* and *It wasn't that I didn't like kissing you, but . . .*

Her silver bracelet glinted in the light, and a terrible thought gripped me: What if we broke up and she regretted ever having gone through with the transplant?

I couldn't let that happen. Friends can't hurt each other the way more-than-friends can, and being friends with Sophie is so much safer than being "more."

That terrible thought hasn't left me all day, and it's why I couldn't bear to sit with her at lunch. I have to figure out a way to tell her without hurting her. My mess of feelings for Sophie has been invaded by something else: gratitude. And I'm no longer sure if what I feel is true attraction or love or if I'm just thankful beyond words.

She deserves certainty from me. If anything were to happen between us, I'd want to be all in. I'd want to know it wasn't just my emotions about the transplant warping my feelings.

"More than friends" is such an odd phrase. It seems to suggest there's something beyond friendship that's even better, a bliss that can be achieved only by linking hands and locking lips. It's as though friendship isn't enough—not when there's the potential for "more."

We've never needed "more."

Sophie is driven and talented and soft and understanding. She's confident when she dances, this sureness she doesn't have in any other part of her life. She always smells good, sometimes like citrus and sometimes like lavender and sometimes like vanilla. She's beautiful; I've always thought that. But above all that, she has this reliability to her that's meant so much to me over the years.

I can't lose that, and I want to believe she wouldn't want to either.

The piano keys are worn. They're not the perfect weight of the baby grand in my living room, but they're also not the manufactured weight of the keyboard in my room. It's a good piano. I wish I had a chance to play it more in class. Playing alone is fine, sure. But I've always believed the piano was meant to be more than a solo instrument. It's why I like the Terrible Twosome. I've spent so much of my life alone that I don't want to be alone with the instrument, too.

I warm up with some scales and then start Rufus Wainwright's "Cigarettes and Chocolate Milk," one of my all-time favorite songs, humming the lyrics, stumbling over a tricky part at the bridge until I finally get the fingering right.

Someone sneezes.

I whip my head toward the door, where Chase Cabrera has a hand over his mouth, an expression of pure horror on his face.

"Sorry!" he says. "I didn't want to disturb you."

My face heats up. "It's fine. I was just messing around."

He takes a few steps into the music room. My hands wander

around the keys, and I squint as I remember the notes for a song I learned long ago.

Chase starts laughing a few bars in. "You are *not* playing 'Clocks' right now."

I stop playing the infamous Coldplay song. "It's, like, the first song you learn on piano when you realize you don't have to only play Beethoven. That or 'A Thousand Miles.'"

I slide into that song's agonizingly catchy opening, and Chase groans.

"Seriously, though," he says, "you said you played piano, but I didn't realize you *played piano*. You're really good."

"Thanks," I say, trying to sound solid, like I deserve the compliment.

"What were you playing when I was, uh . . . spying on you?"

"Rufus Wainwright."

"I've heard *of* him, but I haven't *heard* him."

"Start with *Poses*. That's my favorite album. The bonus track is this incredible cover of 'Across the Universe.' It miiiight be better than the original Beatles version."

Chase slides into a chair next to the piano, the place I usually sit when Eleanor Kang, who has a shockingly strong immune system, is in my spot.

It's only then that I notice what he's wearing. At first I'm not sure he's wearing a costume at all. He has on a white T-shirt with the words GO CEILING! inked in blue.

"And you are . . . ?" I ask.

He grins. "A ceiling fan."

I mash a hand into my forehead. "That's so bad. But also so good." I gesture to my lack of costume. "Forgot it was Halloween."

"Nah, you went as a Nirvana fan, circa 1992."

"It's the plaid flannel, isn't it?"

"You wear a lot of it."

"So do you!" I say, but we're both laughing. "It's a daily reminder that neither of us is unique. And that we live in Seattle."

Chase snorts. "I'm actually glad to see you," he says, which makes my heart do this thing in my chest I'm not sure it's ever done before. He drops his voice. "You know, uh, the band I told you about? We snagged a last-minute slot at a Halloween show tonight. We're only, like, the opener for the opener, but . . . it might be cool."

It's clear he's trying to bite back a smile, like he doesn't want to let on how excited he is.

"That's awesome. Good for you guys."

"We'll mostly play covers, but yeah. I can't wait. We learned 'Monster Mash' last night, and we're not terrible at it." He's full-on smiling now, a megawatt smile. "Unless you and your fantastic non-costume have other plans tonight . . . you should come."

I nod, trying not to seem overeager. "I think I can make it." Appropriately casual.

"And. Uh." His eyes flick to the linoleum floor, and then up to the piano, but not quite to my face. "I've been thinking our band needs a keyboardist. I'm not—I mean, we barely know each other, but . . ."

"You want me to play in your band?" I say it incredulously because I am incredulous. Sure, I've toyed with the idea of being part of something like that, but this . . . Music's always felt like it belonged to Sophie and me.

"Come see us play tonight first. See what you think."

"Okay. Yeah. I'll be there."

The bell rings, signaling the end of lunch.

"I'll text you the info," Chase says.

I play a glissando as I hop off the piano bench. "Go ceiling," I say, raising my fist in the air.

That evening, I borrow some of my dad's old wide-legged pants—why do dads never throw out their old clothes? I don't know, but I'm grateful for it now—put a blazer over a T-shirt, and part my hair down the middle. While Mark is taking a dust bath and generally being adorable, I find a pair of round glasses I used as a Halloween costume freshman year. There: John Lennon. Sophie went as Ringo Starr, which turned out not to be a very recognizable costume at all—tragically, a little like Ringo himself.

The only way my parents let me go is by giving me a strict curfew and insisting on driving me there and back. It still feels like a new kind of freedom. Maybe they're beginning to loosen their white-knuckled grip on me.

"Are we picking up Sophie, too?" my dad asks as we get in the car.

"No," I say quickly. "She's not going."

I considered inviting her. I could imagine the two of us having fun at a Halloween show. But . . . a bigger part of me wanted to see if I could do this on my own. What it would be like to just be Peter Rosenthal-Porter at a show on Halloween that a cute boy invited him to—at least until his parents pick him up.

Still, I can't ignore the ribbon of guilt that snakes through me. Sophie and I spent past Halloweens coordinating our costumes, watching *Beetlejuice*, and passing out candy, but we didn't discuss plans for this year. After the party we each need some time away from the other.

My dad's quiet for a while as we pull out of our neighborhood. I remain still, hoping Sophie doesn't spot us. I stop short of sinking into the seat to fully hide my face.

"I hope you don't feel too uncomfortable after that conversation about the sleepovers."

"*Dad*." My face ignites.

He clears his throat. Turns on the blinker. His key chain has a tooth with a smiley face on it. It's always looked demonic to me, especially as it swings back and forth. "You know, er, if you ever . . . if you ever feel as though you need to talk about . . ."

"Are you trying to have a sex talk with me?"

"I'm not doing a very good job, am I?"

"We're both embarrassed, so I'd say it's right on track."

"Well. Good?"

I watch the sadistic tooth swing back and forth. More silence. More traffic. More time for this awkward conversation.

"I'm not sure I need—" I start, right as my dad says, "You

know, it's always best when it's good for both people."

Uh, I was definitely not expecting that.

"Whoever you're with, Peter—whether you're with a girl or a boy—it's never just about you," he continues, eyes planted firmly on the car in front of us. "You want to be safe, of course—that's number one. But you also want to check in with the other person. Intimacy is a partnership. It should be about mutual satisfaction."

I could have gone the rest of my life without hearing my dad say the words "mutual satisfaction."

"OkayIgetit," I say in one breath. "Partnership. Absolutely. I'll remember that."

He asks me about school and I ask him about work and we sit in more traffic, cutting it close to the time Chase's band goes on. By the time I tell my dad good-bye and he offers to pick me up anytime before my extremely generous curfew of ten thirty and I make it into the venue just as the band is about to play, my face is still hot.

It's an all-ages community center in Sand Point adorned with pumpkins and spiderwebs for Halloween. Not exactly the coolest place for a show, but considering I've never been to one, I probably shouldn't pass judgment. I wade through various demons and witches and superheroes, but no one's near the stage. So I linger in the back, unwilling to get too close.

The lights dim and the background music stops, and the band heads onstage, Chase in his ceiling fan costume with a mint-green guitar slung over his chest.

"Happy Halloween," the drummer says into the mic. She's dressed as a *Game of Thrones* character I can't remember the name of. "Thanks for coming out tonight. I know you're all here to see Laserdog, but hopefully you'll put up with us for a few songs."

A few people in the crowd whoop. I don't recognize anyone from school. In fact, I don't recognize anyone in the band, either. I guess I assumed they'd be other kids from North Seattle High moonlighting as wannabe rock stars.

"So, uh, we're Diamonds Are for Never," the lead singer says. "And you might know this one."

Diamonds Are for Never launches into a cover of a Clash song. The audience continues to hang back—judging instead of dancing.

It's immediately apparent that Chase was one-hundred-percent right: They're not good at all. Somehow that makes them more interesting to watch. They're battling with their instruments, each person trying to be the loudest. It makes me wonder if a piano is exactly what they need to tie them together.

Most of the time, I watch Chase. He's unsure of himself onstage. He glances between his bandmates, waiting for a cue from the drummer or vocalist. It's significantly less confidence than he has in his daily life, and I like that a lot. His uncertainty. His humility. His apologetic shrug when they don't finish the song at the same time.

I like *him*.

140

"This is Peter," Chase says in the community center lobby after their set. The entire band is sweaty but smiling. The walls are covered with posters for upcoming events: a craft fair, a knit-a-thon, a senior swing dancing night. "Peter, this is Aziza, Dylan, and Kat."

Dylan, the bassist, wears white glasses and has platinum-blond hair and appears to be dressed as some kind of mad scientist. Aziza, the drummer, has wild spiral curls and, in her warrior costume, the most impressive biceps I've ever seen. Kat is a four-foot-ten girl—approximately Sophie's size—who sings lead.

"This is the piano guy?" Dylan says as he buckles his bass guitar into its case.

"You told them?" I ask Chase, who gives a sheepish shrug. "Yeah. I'm the piano guy."

Dylan grins, exposing a train track of braces. "What'd you think?"

"Don't put him on the spot," Aziza says. But she blinks at me with large dark eyes and then contorts her face as though bracing for bad news. "Buuuut I do kinda really wanna know."

At this all of them lean forward. I lean back against the wall. "You guys had great energy," I say, which I hope sounds like a compliment.

They let out sighs of relief. "We were so fucking nervous," Kat says.

"What exactly are you, by the way?"

"I'm Picasso's blue period," she says, gesturing to the

blue-painted tampons glued to her shirt. "And you're John Lennon? Nice."

"How did you all meet?" I ask.

"We were in this queer youth group a few summers ago." Chase nestles his guitar in its case. "Kat is a freshman at Seattle U, and Dylan and Aziza go to the same high school."

"Queer youth group?"

Chase nods. "Sort of half support group, half activities. I came out as gay to my parents when I was fourteen."

Chase is gay. Up until this point, I was unsure whether we were just friends or if there was potential for something more. Now *more* seems like an exciting and realistic possibility, one that makes me stumble over my next words.

"I'm, uh—me too," I say, because I'm still figuring out how to verbalize it. "I mean—I came out to my parents a few years ago too. I'm—I'm bi."

As soon as I say it, I sense my shoulders relaxing—not necessarily in relief, but more like I didn't realize I'd been clenched up about this for so long. This is the first time I've been around other queer kids. The first time I feel, automatically, that I have some common ground with other people.

My religion connects me to Sophie, sure—but that feels so much larger, less individual, at least to me. My sexuality is *mine*.

It feels kind of like I already belong, and I didn't even have to try.

"Me too!" Kat says, and holds out her fist, as though I've

now been inducted into a club with some kind of bisexual fist bump.

So I bump it. And I grin.

"And I am still figuring things out," Dylan says.

Chase and these near-strangers know a secret about me. Sophie, who sacrificed so much for me, doesn't.

I try to push the guilt away.

"We should take these to the van," Kat says, gesturing to the instruments.

Chase glances at me. "I'll be out in a minute."

"I'm so glad we have a *fan*," I hear Aziza say as the three of them head out into the parking lot before Laserdog takes the stage.

"So. What did you *really* think?" Chase asks. He's sitting on a couch across from me, and he leans closer, balancing his elbows on his knees. Before the lights cut out for Laserdog, I see the nerves painted on his face, the worry line between his brows, the set of his jaw. Then he's thrown into a soft blue darkness.

"You're putting me in a terrible situation. You realize that, right?" I shout to be heard over the music, some kind of electro-funk that's not really my thing.

"Yes. But you know music. You know Laserdog is garbage."

"The audience loves them."

"I value your opinion."

I scoot to the edge of my couch so I don't have to yell nearly as loudly. Chase values my opinion. I'm touched by that.

"You're all good at your instruments. It seemed like . . . you

143

weren't as cohesive as you could be. Like . . . you were all battling for attention."

He's quiet for a few moments, staring at his sneakers. I wish I could take it all back. That clearly wasn't what he wanted to hear. He wanted me to tell him they were brilliant.

"That's actually really helpful," he says finally. "It was hard to hear up there, with the monitors and everything. So thanks. I mean it."

I still feel like I should have bent the truth.

He taps my shoe with his, which sends a bolt of lightning from my ankle to my hip. "You think you might want to try it out? Playing with us? If we're not too shitty, that is."

"Only marginally shitty. I can handle that."

My phone buzzes in my pocket—fifteen minutes before my curfew, and my dad's on his way.

"I'm getting picked up soon," I say, standing. "My parents . . . I told you they're overprotective."

He nods, getting up from the couch. "Got it."

"I had a good time. I mean it." I dust off my dad's pants. I'm sure they were outdated even when he wore them.

"I'm glad."

We're facing each other now, a foot and a half of space between our bodies. The tug in my chest is magnetic, nearly impossible to ignore.

We're not close enough friends yet to hug, are we? Or should we fist-bump, the way Kat and I did? Give a two-fingered salute like a too-cool love interest in a YA novel?

144

In my panic, what I do is stick out my hand.

For a *handshake*.

The socially awkward police better come arrest me now, lock me up before I vomit on someone's shoes or make a dad joke.

I must look horrified by what my hand has done, but Chase just stares down at it and laughs.

"You crack me up. Pleasure doing business with you, John Lennon," he says as he shakes my hand, his olive skin warm against mine.

CHAPTER 15

SOPHIE

WHEN SOMEONE TELLS YOU THEY "NEED SOME time," they should give you an exact date they'll be ready to talk about whatever difficult thing they can't talk about right now. *I need some time, but let's reconvene next Thursday at four p.m.*, they should say.

I've been trying to give Peter space to think about the kiss. Yes, it's been only a couple days, but it's all I can think about.

"Sophie, you're not spotting," my teacher says in my weekly jazz technique class. I've been falling out of my double and triple pirouettes all afternoon.

"I know. I know," I mumble.

I make it home in time to go trick-or-treating with Tabby, who got the night off from her waitressing job. Still, my mind's somewhere else.

"Sophie, you're dawdling," Tabby calls from a few paces ahead, and I rush to catch up with them.

Tabby and Josh are really into graphic novels and dressed a little more elaborately than I did, as characters from *Saga*. Tabby's Alana, an army deserter on the run with her baby (Luna) during an intergalactic war. Josh, with horns on his head, is Marko, Alana's husband. They lose their minds when someone actually recognizes who they are.

On past Halloweens, Peter and I made our own Star Wars or Harry Potter costumes, or something related to whatever obscure book Peter was into that year. Once we went as half of the Beatles. Always what Peter wanted, but I was happy to defer to him, happy to see him happy. I loved seeing him get into it, even if we never trick-or-treated more than a few blocks and he couldn't eat too much candy.

This year I painted whiskers on my cheeks and wore all black. I didn't see Peter at lunch, and I didn't mention Halloween to him earlier because I was too wrapped up in everything else. I didn't think it was something I had to mention—I've never had to before.

We go along Forty-Fifth Street first, where a lot of the Wallingford businesses are handing out candy, then back up into our neighborhood. I'm past the age to be excited about candy and too young and not yet jaded enough to trick-or-treat ironically like some of the college kids toting around pillowcases, so most of the time, I hang back while Luna collects her goodies.

Okay, sometimes I collect a few goodies of my own. I have not yet outgrown sugar rushes. Plus, I'm on my period, and I'm fiercely craving a Reese's.

"Your sister is so cute," a woman says before dropping a Hershey's Kiss into Luna's outstretched bag, though her face is a little uncertain. Josh is Korean, so I'm not sure whose sister she assumes Luna is.

It can't be the first time someone's assumed this, though, and it probably won't be the last. I feel a strange pang of discomfort for the two of them.

Tabby opens her mouth, but Josh beats her to it. "Yes, she is," he says quickly. "Happy Halloween."

We retreat down the block. My bag is half full, because I am usually an optimist, and when it's candy, it's hard not to be.

Tabby sighs loudly and adjusts her wings. "I don't know why you have to do that," she mutters to Josh, "let people think she isn't actually our kid."

"Isn't it easier this way?"

"It's a lie." Tabby grips Luna's hand as we cross the street. She started walking quickly, and now, at sixteen months, she rarely needs help.

"What good does it do if I tell a little old lady the truth? We're seventeen, and this is our daughter. We don't need her judgment. She doesn't know us."

I stay quiet, unsure what to say. It's strange to observe this very adult conversation between my younger sister and her boyfriend.

I turn to my niece instead. "What do you think, Luna? Did you get a good haul?"

She grins a toothy toddler grin. "Yes!"

"Do you have any idea what you're dressed as?"

Luna's face furrows, as though she's considering this. "Yes?" she ventures.

"Luna's happy," Josh says, scratching at where his horns dig into his scalp. "That's the most important thing."

Tabby sighs again. "Sure. Fine."

While the trio approaches another house, I hang back and text Peter. **Beetlejuice later?** We used to watch it all the time on Halloween—maybe this will remind him how much fun this holiday used to be for us.

But half an hour passes without a response. I sigh too loudly, dragging my feet.

"What is it?" Tabby says.

"Peter. Things have been weird since Saturday."

Tabby gasps, a theatrical gasp I've heard her utter in more than one production. "Did something *happen*?"

I'm fully aware that Josh is listening too, but I figure Tabby tells him everything anyway. And maybe he and my sister will have some sage advice that can only be gleaned from years of confidence in knowing another person is deeply attracted to you.

"I . . . sort of kissed him and then told him I thought we should try dating." I don't mention that I was drunk when I kissed him—we still kissed, and I was perfectly sober during our awkward morning conversation.

149

"Wow. And?"

"And nothing. He said he didn't want to risk ruining the friendship." I roll my shoulders in an exaggerated shrug. "What I can't understand is if he's so intent on keeping our friendship perfectly intact, why he isn't responding to my messages."

"Peter's an introspective kind of guy," Josh says. "Maybe he needs some time to think about what it would mean to be a couple."

"Do you feel like . . . ?" Tabby trails off, chews her bottom lip. "I almost don't want to say it, but *if* Peter happens to not feel the same way, do you feel like you could stay friends?"

I stop in my tracks. "Yes! Are you serious? I—we'll always be friends." Truthfully, it's never crossed my mind. We will *always* be Peter-and-Sophie—that's not up for debate.

Except the ideal version of Peter-and-Sophie is handing out candy together tonight. That version planned costumes together and laughed while they painted each other's faces. That version doesn't need to text because they're together right now.

That ideal version has already talked about being boyfriend and girlfriend.

And in that ideal world, Peter is always, always texting Sophie back.

My sister holds up her hands. "Okay, okay. I'm sorry for saying it."

"He needs time." I echo Josh, saying it with a conviction I'm not sure I feel.

When we get back to our neighborhood, we stop at Peter's last. I'm half expecting him to open the door—wishful thinking, I'm sure—but his mom does.

"Aren't you the cutest?" she squeals when she sees Luna. "What exactly is she?"

Josh scratches at his horns again. "Too hard to explain."

"Hi, Holly," I say. Her long nails are orange, with tiny spiderwebs. "Is Peter home? I'm having trouble reaching him."

"Sorry, Sophie. He's actually out tonight. His dad dropped him off in Sand Point for some kind of concert."

A concert? What kind of concert? While we were trick-or-treating, I convinced myself he fell asleep or turned his phone off—and didn't let myself think of the scariest possibility: that there'd been some kind of emergency. Peter loves music, of course he does, but he doesn't go to spur-of-the-moment concerts. We saw Rufus Wainwright years ago, but that was planned months in advance. Plus, his parents came with us. They were worried about what might happen to him at a concert, despite the fact that I cannot imagine Rufus Wainwright fans being anything but tame.

I never considered he'd be *out*. Without me. Without telling me.

I force my voice to sound less wrecked than I feel. "Oh . . . okay. Do you know when he'll be back?"

"His curfew's in a couple hours. He really didn't tell you he was going out?"

I smile tightly. "No. I'm sure I'll talk to him tomorrow. Thanks."

"Sorry, sweetheart," she says before closing the door.

151

Hi, you've reached Peter. Uh, Rosenthal-Porter. I guess you know that if you called me. So, uh, leave a message and I'll call you back when I can. Or text me. Okay. Bye. BEEP.

I hang up without leaving a voice mail. Until tonight I didn't know Peter had a voice-mail greeting, didn't know it was so awkward and stilted and yet one-hundred-percent Peter. Every other time I've called, he's always picked up.

"Still not answering?" Josh asks. He's in the living room chair with Luna and a bottle. Tabby's already asleep, but Luna is apparently on a little-kid sugar high because she wouldn't go down right away. Not even the *Mean Girls* musical soundtrack, her current favorite, would do the trick. Tabby's on a mission to turn her into a theater kid.

I drop my phone onto the couch as I sink into a cushion. "Nope." Josh is still wearing Marko's long jacket and yellow shirt, but the horns lie abandoned on the coffee table. "What was that weirdness with you and Tabby earlier?" I'm not trying to be forward, but I'm curious.

"Agh . . . that." With a sigh, he adjusts Luna in his arms. "It's so hard, you know? There are so many things we never anticipated."

"Like people thinking Luna's your sister."

"Like that."

A pain rips through my abdomen. I can't help it—my face pinches, and Josh regards me strangely.

"You okay?"

"Yeah. Just cramps. I'm on my period." It's only half a lie.

But he looks at me a little longer than he should.

Truth is, the pain hasn't gone away, not completely. The doctors said again that occasional pain is relatively normal for living donors, but chronic pain is rare. Living donor. That's what they call me. When I think "donor," I think of some rich person who gave tons of money to a museum. Even now I can't replace that definition with what I did: giving a physical piece of myself to Peter.

I can't understand, after what we've done, that he doesn't feel the same undeniable tug toward me that I feel for him.

Why he still needs *time*.

"I'm sorry about that lady," I tell Josh, returning to our original conversation topic.

"Thanks." He strokes Luna's hair. "We love this kid, of course. We're head over heels for her. And I love your sister more than anything. But she's exhausted all the time. I feel guilty that she's exhausted all the time. I wish this were easier." He laughs, a this-isn't-actually-funny laugh. "What a shock— being teen parents is hard."

"I could babysit for you guys sometime. If you wanted to go out on, like, a date night or something."

Josh's entire face changes. "Are you serious? Your parents watch her so much that we always feel guilty asking for time for ourselves. That would be incredible."

I smile, though I'm a bit uneasy about it. I've never been alone with Luna, and she's still so small. "Yeah," I say.

"Definitely. I should get to know my niece, right?"

He's grinning now too. "Thank you, thank you. Tab'll be so thrilled. I know you guys aren't best friends or anything. But . . . it's not too late. You two probably have more in common than you realize."

I shake my head. "Parenting has made both of you way too deep."

We sit in silence for a couple minutes, until he asks, "You want to watch *Beetlejuice*? You and Peter always do that on Halloween, right?"

I'm both touched that he remembered and shattered, once again, that Peter isn't here to watch it with me. It's amazing how many times a single thing can break your heart. "Sure," I say. "That would be fun."

We watch the movie and trade candy until Luna falls asleep and my parents gently urge us to do the same since it's a school night.

But what he said sticks with me as I take off my sad cat makeup and steal a few of my favorite candies from Luna's stash. I guess I've always thought my life had room for closeness with only one person.

Peter texts me at eleven thirty, when I'm on the brink of sleep.

Can you talk?

Yes, I type back right away.

Woods behind my house?

I'll be there in 6 minutes.

I spring out of bed, brush my teeth again though I already did an hour ago, and throw a coat over my pajamas. Slowly I creep downstairs and across the dark street. Someone smashed a pumpkin, and the ground is littered with candy wrappers.

Peter's waiting for me, bundled in a plaid scarf his mom gave him for his birthday a few years ago and his REI coat. Normally I'd hug him, bug him to share his scarf with me. Tonight I don't.

"I'm so, so sorry," he says. Peter. Apologizing to me. "I didn't know we had plans."

"I shouldn't have assumed," I say quickly. A pause. "What, um, concert did you go to?"

"Oh. A local band. Some friends from school."

"Oh." I jam my hands into my pockets, gritting my teeth against the cold.

"Are . . . we okay?" he asks, and it's such a strange question. Our relationship isn't something we discuss—not until lately, at least. I guess because we've always been okay, never needed to confirm it.

"Why wouldn't we be?"

"I've . . . been thinking. About what happened on Saturday."

"Yeah?" I ask, daring to feel hopeful.

"I love you so much," he says, but in those words, I can tell: It's not the kind of love I've been craving. "And with the transplant, I can't imagine that becoming more than friends wouldn't complicate things more than they already are."

I try to untangle his words, all the negatives in his sentence, hoping they cancel each other out, giving me a solution I could be happy with.

They don't.

"What if . . . ? What if it made our friendship better?" My voice is tiny, my heart already sunk.

"It's just . . . we know each other so well already. I mean, I have a part of you inside me."

I wish those words—"inside me"—didn't sound sexual.

"I don't want to risk ruining this," he continues. "It would kill me if you ever regretted what you did."

"I wouldn't," I say quickly, touching his shoulder in reassurance. I draw my hand back quickly, though, worried he'll misinterpret the gesture. He doesn't even blink at it, like me touching him is the same as petting a cat or accidentally brushing up against a wall. "I could never."

And that's the horrible truth of it all, isn't it? Peter could slash me open and steal my other kidney, and I would let him. If it would keep him alive, I'd dig it out for him myself.

"You're okay with this, then?"

"Super okay," I say, forcing a smile. "You're my best friend, and the party . . . I was drunk. It didn't mean anything, right? We were probably both just curious." I have to bite out each word.

He hugs me, though I am stiff with cold and disappointment. Still, I don't want him to let go. "Nothing's going to change," he says in a tone that he probably means to sound reassuring. "We're going to stay exactly like we've always been."

CHAPTER 16

PETER

MY FIRST BAND PRACTICE IS PROBABLY THE MOST Seattle thing that's ever happened to me. We're in Aziza's basement, Dylan is wearing a Mudhoney T-shirt, and Kat's singing about a girl who only leaves her house when it's raining and never carries an umbrella.

I stand frozen behind my Yamaha keyboard, fingers perched on the keys. The basement's small and dark and low-ceilinged, our instruments crowded in one corner while Aziza's girlfriend, Bette, watches us from a patchy gray couch.

"Just play around on the keys," Chase told me before practice started. "See what you come up with."

This song, "Precipitation," is like Amy Winehouse crashed a Ramones show, crunchy punk guitar chords with Kat's powerful vocals. When they get to the first chorus, I add some crunchy chords of my own. Chase glances up from his mint guitar, lifting his brows in encouragement. So I keep going, banging out chord progressions that complement his guitar. During the bridge, I slow it down, my sounds low and smooth, but I bring the piano back during the final chorus. Loud. Unforgiving.

We don't all end in the right place. When Aziza gives her cymbals a final smash, I quickly pull my fingers off the keys, but Chase and Dylan are still playing. Kat taps her foot impatiently, and while Dylan stops after one last bass lick, Chase is still going, fingers racing around the frets of his guitar.

"We get it; you play guitar," Aziza says.

Chase grins sheepishly, as though so lost in the music he didn't realize we'd all stopped. It's a grin that does something pleasant to my stomach. Halloween was a week ago, and I'm still daydreaming about Chase's handshake. It's probably the most a person has ever thought about another person's hand.

"Sorry. I got really into it," he says. He flicks his longish bangs, which drooped into his face during the solo, out of his eyes. Today he's wearing a striped button-down, open over a vintage band tee. The Rolling Stones.

"You guys are getting better!" says Aziza's girlfriend from the couch. Bette is a tall blonde with skin so pale it's nearly translucent. She's wearing a Diamonds Are for Never T-shirt she screen-printed herself. "Or maybe that's Peter."

"Definitely Peter," Chase says, dragging the back of his hand across his damp forehead. "The keyboard sounded great."

Aziza nods. "I liked it."

"Yeah?" I say. Their words coax my mouth into an easy smile.

"I think your style fits the sound we're going for," Dylan says.

"No one wants to hear my opinion?" Bette asks.

Aziza shakes her head, tossing around her spiral curls. "Sweets, no offense, but your favorite band is Journey."

"What's wrong with Journey?"

They all laugh as though liking Journey is exactly what's wrong with Journey, and I make a mental note to never admit that I don't hate "Don't Stop Believin'." I mean, there's a reason everyone knows the lyrics—they're damn catchy and fun to sing along to. These are Music People, even more so than I've ever considered myself a Music Person, and they clearly take it seriously.

We take the song from the top again, but halfway through, Kat sighs into her mic and says, "Stop, stop. This is all wrong."

Aziza thumps her bass drum in a frustrated fashion. "I thought it sounded fine."

"'You know that band Diamonds Are for Never? Yeah, they're *fine*.'" Kat shakes her head. "We should strive for better than fine."

"Not 'Closer to Fine'?" Bette says, and Aziza groans at the Indigo Girls reference.

"What are you thinking, Kat?" Dylan asks.

"Backing vocals. This song is in desperate need of them. Peter, is there any chance you can sing, too? None of these jerks can."

"I *can*, but you guys said I *shouldn't*. There's a difference," Chase says.

Sophie's always made fun of my voice, so I only ever sing when I'm playing piano alone. "I'm . . . not sure."

"You know the chorus with the 'whoa uh-oh' part?" Kat says. "If you could harmonize with me, that would sound super cool."

"I'll try."

This time I'm not afraid of the keyboard. I smash my fingers down on the chords, experiment with a few flourishes. And when it's time for me to sing backup vocals, I follow Kat's instructions, and it doesn't sound awful. We try it again, and it sounds a lot better. Again, and it's more intricate. Again, and we end at almost exactly the same time.

"Whoa," Dylan says. "We've never sounded like that before."

"You have a nice voice," Chase says softly, not quite meeting my gaze. "A little uncertain, but nice. I like it."

That stomach flip again—both because of the music we made, and his compliment. *You have a nice voice. You have a nice voice.* It'll reverberate in my mind the rest of the day.

"We're keeping you," Kat decides, and I don't dare argue with that.

Five songs later, each played at least three times through, we're exhausted, Bette's bored, and we're all ready for a break.

"Diner food," Kat declares, and the rest of the band cheers

their agreement. To me, she explains: "It's a band practice tradition."

We cram into Aziza's van, which boasts a bumper sticker that says MUSICIANS DUET BETTER. In the back seat, Chase's thigh touches mine for a full fifteen minutes. It's very distracting. Aziza pulls into the parking lot of the Early Bird Diner—where Sophie's sister works.

Sophie and I have been here plenty of times, though not recently. We usually get waffles and pancakes and split them both. She drenches everything in syrup, I make fun of her, and she says since she's miraculously never had a cavity, she's living on the edge.

Aziza, Bette, Kat, and Dylan skip inside, but Chase hangs back in the parking lot, grazing my arm with a fingertip as though asking me to hang back with him. It isn't a handshake, but somehow the tentative uncertainty of it is better.

"Hey. Is this all . . . okay?" He pushes his old-man glasses higher on his nose. "I don't want it to feel like I'm throwing you into something that you're not into."

"Seriously?" I raise my eyebrows. "I'm so into this."

He visibly relaxes, blowing out a long breath. "Good, because I don't think the rest of them are going to let you go."

"I like them." *I like you,* I want to say. "I sort of always wanted to be in a band. I never thought I'd get the chance. And . . . this might sound weird, but I've never had other queer friends."

"Not weird at all," he says. "I know the feeling. Maybe—"

162

he starts, and then sort of awkwardly stares at the ground, rubbing the back of his neck. "Maybe we could . . . hang out just the two of us sometime?"

"That would . . . Yeah. Okay." In my attempt to not sound as excited as I actually am, what comes out is a statement devoid of emotion. I clear my throat. "I mean—yes. Let's definitely do that."

There's a rapping on the window of the diner. "Come on, losers, it's grease time!" Kat shouts.

The Early Bird is a fifties-style diner with red vinyl booths and black-and-white-checked floors. Aziza and Bette rush over to the jukebox to fight over songs. I scan the restaurant, unreasonably anxious about the possibility of seeing Tabby here.

I slide into a booth next to Dylan, across from Chase. Beneath the table, his shoe bumps mine.

"Sorry," he says. "Small booth."

But it's not that small. And the next time it happens, he doesn't say sorry.

"What can I get you—oh! Peter," Tabby says, standing in front of our table with a notepad in her hand and a very confused expression on her face.

I feel my face flame. "Hi."

"Where's Sophie?"

"I—um—I'm not sure," I say quietly, which doesn't feel like the right answer.

Tabby's eyebrows rise, and I give her what must be a pained expression. I'm not sure what I'm worried about—that Tabby will tell her sister I was having dinner with people who aren't her? Sophie and I didn't have plans. I'm not doing anything wrong, being here.

"You two know each other?" Dylan says, wagging a finger between Tabby and me. "Is there any chance of getting some free food here?"

We order too much of everything, and Tabby throws in a free order of pancakes.

"We should change our name," Kat says thoughtfully between slurps of milkshake.

Dylan catapults a fry at her. "You say that every week."

"You can't change your name. Then I'd have to make a new T-shirt," Bette says.

"What does our new keyboardist think of the name?" Kat asks.

"I like it."

Aziza thumps the table. "The name stays!"

This entire afternoon is so strange and fantastic. In the past, I always envied groups like this, who were loud in public and laughed too much.

Now I'm too loud. I laugh too much.

My phone buzzes with a text from Sophie, and for a second I'm convinced Tabby told her I was here and she's going to demand to know why I'm at the Early Bird and who I'm with.

God I'm so nervous. I'm teaching my song to the team tomorrow. Say something to reassure me I won't make a tremendous ass of myself?

"So, tell us more about you, Peter," Aziza says before I can answer Sophie's text. My fingers itch for my phone's keyboard. Sophie needs me right now, but everyone's waiting for an answer.

It occurs to me I could mention my medical history, that before this year, that would have felt like my primary defining feature. But it isn't now, and really, it wasn't back then, either. "Well . . . I'm a huge book nerd. I have a pet chinchilla. And . . . I can't roll my tongue?"

Dylan asks to see a picture of Mark—of course I have at least a hundred on my phone—and the others prove to me how unusual it is not to be able to roll your tongue by doing exactly that.

"I'm majoring in English," Kat says. "Who's your favorite author?"

"You realize that's like asking someone who their favorite musician is."

"Hole." Kat doesn't miss a beat. "And Janet Fitch."

"Rufus Wainwright. And . . . is it cliché to say Salinger?"

Kat pinches her forehead and groans. "Oh God, you and every other teenage guy who thinks they're Holden Caulfield."

"I am *not* Holden Caulfield. Besides, I like his short stories a lot better than—"

"Yeah, yeah, sure," Kat says with a wave of her hand.

When everyone's immersed in a conversation about whether Pearl Jam is overrated or not, I surreptitiously pull out my phone to text Sophie back.

God I'm so nervous. I'm teaching my song to the team tomorrow. Say something to reassure me I won't make a tremendous ass of myself?

Like, literally anything.

Peter??

The desperation of those double question marks is what gets me. I should have told the band I had to go to the bathroom, given Sophie the reassurance she needed. She gave me a kidney, and I couldn't text her back? Feeling guilty, I thumb back a few messages, one after the other:

I am SO sorry.

Phone was off ☹

You'll be GREAT. I have zero doubts.

The band feels too new to tell her about yet. I want them to be solely mine for a while longer.

Her reply comes back right away. Thanks.

There's something about the finality of that period. There's a sadness to it. Maybe my response isn't what Sophie wanted, or it didn't sound genuine, even though I meant it. Or it wasn't enough to make up for my silence. Punctuation is really messing with me today.

Beneath the table, Chase's shoe taps mine again.

And stays there.

A spark shoots up my spine, and my entire body feels warm. I take a huge sip of ice water in an attempt to cool down.

"Something wrong?" Chase asks me, grinning. Subtly he runs his shoe along mine.

I shake my head. "Nope. Everything's great."

Kat and Dylan are dramatically singing along to the Bowie song Aziza picked on the jukebox. I'm trying not to make eye contact with Tabby, who's fortunately busy enough with her other tables that she doesn't come by ours very often.

"Have you all been playing your instruments for forever?" I ask.

"Playing our instruments," Kat says with a snicker.

"Kat." Dylan shakes his head. "You're the oldest. Be mature."

With her fingertip, Kat draws a circle on the tabletop. "Gutter." She points inside it. "My mind."

"I've been playing bass since I was thirteen," Dylan says. "So only a few years. Basically, I wanted to be Kim Deal. I imagine that's how approximately eighty-five percent of people decide they want to start playing bass."

"And I wanted to be Meg White," Aziza says. "Minus whatever messed-up relationship she had with Jack White."

"Weren't they siblings?"

"No. Husband and wife, I think? And he took her last name?"

"How long have you been playing?" Dylan asks me as Kat and Chase debate the White Stripes.

I squint, as though it'll help me remember. "About ten years?" I say, and Dylan whistles. "But it took a while for me to realize I didn't have to just play the classics, and then I was forever changed. I bought a book of Rufus Wainwright's music and never looked back."

"*Love* him," Dylan says.

"Guys, where's Bette?" Aziza says.

The Bowie song stops, and the familiar opening notes of Journey's "Separate Ways" come through the diner's speakers. Bette stands at the jukebox with a victorious fist thrust in the air.

CHAPTER 17

SOPHIE

I CLOSE MY DANCE TEAM LOCKER AND TIGHTEN my ponytail, letting out a long, shaky breath. Montana lays her hands on my shoulders.

"You've got this," she says, dark eyes boring into mine. She's so close to my face; no one but my family and Peter has ever been close enough to see all my pores and imperfections like this. A few months ago it would have intimidated me, but now her closeness is a comfort. "We've been over it at least fifty times."

I've spent a couple days a week at Montana's and sometimes Liz's—not mine, since a screaming baby makes it hard to concentrate. It makes my life feel oddly off-kilter. Carpooling to school should be normal after Peter's insistence that we're going to be "exactly like we've always been," but it's been marked by strange silences and Peter's desperation to fill them with random facts about books and obscure musicians.

"What if no one likes it?" I ask Montana, who's lifted her hands from my shoulders and is now jamming a few pins into her bun.

"Then they're off the team." She breaks into a smile. "Kidding, but I'm positive they will. And Liz and I will be here to back you up—if Liz can part with her fictional characters for an hour."

On the other side of the aisle of lockers, Liz is sitting cross-legged, eyes glued to a thick book. She holds up a finger. "Five more pages."

"*Two*." Montana pauses, then adds, "And I love you."

"Love you too," Liz grumbles as she turns the page.

"What are you reading?" I ask, and Montana groans.

"Don't get her started or she won't be satisfied until you've read all four books in the series—"

"Five books, with at least two more on the way," Liz says without looking up.

"Yay, there's more."

Liz snaps the book shut. "Queens of Night is a groundbreaking fantasy series. The main character is queer and a badass, but she's also sensitive and soft when she needs to be. And the villain—oh my God, don't even get me started on the villain. She's incredible. This *world* is incredible." Liz slips the book into her locker. "Anyway, this was book five, which came out last week. I'm hoping Emi Miyoshi does a tour stop in Seattle." Rummaging in her backpack, she pulls out a worn copy of a different book. "This is book one. Want to try it?"

I open it up to the tiniest font I've ever seen. "I'm, um . . ." I'm not embarrassed by my dyslexia, but I'm not sure Montana and Liz and I are at this stage of friendship yet.

"You're what?" Montana finishes her bun with hairspray.

"Dyslexic," I finish. "Peter loves to read, but . . . it can be really hard for me."

"They have audiobooks!" Liz says. "I've listened to them, and the narrator is brilliant."

When I assure her I'll get the first book on audio, she beams, and a warmth blooms in my chest.

With one final smoothing of her bun, Montana says, "Dance team practice?"

"Yeah, I guess that's something we could do." Liz winks at her, and Montana rolls her eyes. Their relationship has an effortlessness to it. Their teasing, I can tell, comes from a place of true affection.

Before the transplant, Peter and I teased each other like that.

We meet the rest of the team in the gym. Over and over, Montana has told me to be commanding, but that's easy for her to say. Maybe it's easier for tall people to be leaders. Right now I'm mainly terrified of the judgment: of someone telling me what I've poured my soul into isn't good. There has to be nothing worse as an artist.

"Today we're going to learn a piece Sophie's been choreographing," Montana says after leading us in a warm-up, and while the team doesn't exactly look ecstatic, they don't look horrified, either. I take this as a good sign. "Sophie, take it away."

We swap places and I'm in front of the group now. My ponytail got mussed during the warm-up, so I tug out the elastic. Retie it. Breathe. Breathe. Breathe. "Hey, guys. Um. How is everyone?"

Someone coughs. Montana raises her eyebrows.

There are so many people watching me.

If I can't conquer this, I'll be the quiet girl dancing in the back forever, choreographing pieces for no one but the walls of my room. And dances—my dances—are meant to be seen. I have to believe that.

"I've been working on this new choreography, and I'm excited for us to learn it. So, um, the piece is about two groups that are trying to prove which style of dance is best?" I don't know why I phrase it as a question. My voice keeps rising at the end of my sentences. "We could form two groups? Taylor, you could stand over there next to Gabe? And, Liz, if you could scoot forward so you're next to Kunjal?"

"Could we learn it first before we start blocking it?" Taylor calls out.

Of course. That's what we always do. I was jumping ahead. "Right. Um, I'll play the music and do a few bars so you guys can get the idea. It starts out—" I cut myself off when I catch Montana's gaze. She's shaking her head: *Don't tell. Do.* So I let the sentence vanish.

We don't really have solos on the team, so I haven't performed in front of a bunch of people like this in a while. I start the first section, the one with the more graceful, classic steps.

172

Then the second section, which is a little more hip-hop, a little rawer.

"I like it," says Brenna, a junior who can kick higher than anyone else on the team. Brenna becomes my favorite person. "The different styles of music and dance—you've blended them in such a cool way."

"She has," Liz agrees, smiling at me. I give her a quick smile back, but then make my face serious for the rest of the team.

"Let's break down the first four-count," I say. "This will be the first group, but let's all learn it for now and I'll divide you up later." Solid. Not a question this time.

"Can you go through it slower?" Jonah asks. "I'm not getting the rhythm."

"Definitely!" I do it slower. Then a little faster. Repeat. Repeat. "Five, six, seven, eight . . ."

We do the first four-count over and over, then add the next few, and then I split the team into two groups. And—they're getting it. The dance breathed to life like this is completely unlike what I imagined in the best possible way. Everyone brings their own flair to it. It isn't just mine—it's ours.

"It's looking great!" I exclaim at the end of practice, pulling up my shirt to wipe my sweat-slicked face.

"This was fun," Neeti says. "I love the song."

"Isn't it fantastic?" I'm glowing with this attention, this praise. My desperate texts to Peter the other day—I didn't need his support, not really. Not for this. I did this on my own.

Montana returns to the front. "Thanks, Sophie! I think we're all pumped about this new piece. I wanted to wrap up practice with an interesting opportunity. Our team's been invited to attend a weekend dance intensive in Spokane in a couple weeks. There will be dancers there from all over the state, and the workshops will be taught by college dance professors."

A chorus of excited chatter moves through the crowd.

"It's optional, of course, but it's not too pricey and seems like a great experience." Montana opens her bag. "I've got permission slips! We need your parents to sign to make sure the school's not liable if someone does something stupid. Which *none of you are going to do*." She raises her eyebrows at this, and everyone shakes their heads no.

A weekend away from Peter. It shouldn't be a huge deal, especially since I've been dancing so much with Montana and Liz lately, and he's been hanging out with a couple of new mysterious friends, who I'm sure I'll meet soon. In fact, I'll ask him about them tonight when I see him.

If I can't handle a weekend, how could I handle eight weeks?

As the team disperses, Montana and Liz congratulate me on today's practice. Honestly, they are both still a bit of a mystery to me. Last year I thought they were intimidating, these cool girls who were somehow actually my age but so much more put together. The worry that churns in my stomach is this: I'm not sure what they get out of our relationship. The satisfaction of mentoring a shy choreographer? That cannot be it. They've given me so much, but I've given them absolutely nothing in return.

"What are you doing this weekend?" I ask in the locker room. Practice loosened me up.

Montana and Liz exchange a sweet look. "It's our one-year anniversary," Liz says. "We're going to this Italian restaurant downtown that has acrobats perform while you eat."

"Wow. Happy anniversary!"

"Hard to believe she's put up with my bossiness for this long." Montana slings her arm around Liz.

"I love your bossiness. I love all of you."

My heart twinges. Their declaration of love is so clear, so confident.

"What about you?" Montana asks. "Any plans with your love interest?"

"Love interest," I repeat. It would be funny if it weren't heartbreaking. "Yeah, I mean, we're neighbors. It would be weird if we didn't spend the weekend together."

"Have fun," Liz says. And then she ropes me in for a hug. It's so surprising that at first I flinch, unsure what's happening. "I'm hugging you! Christ, you're skittish."

So I hug her back. And then I hug Montana, which is equally strange—they're both so much taller than I am that it feels a little like hugging my mom—and yet I can't stop smiling as I head for my car.

"Okay, so I have a million things to tell you," I say to Peter, all in one breath. I drop my bag next to me in the booth at a divey Mexican restaurant called Dos Sombreros.

"Me too." He dunks a chip into tomatillo salsa. "Their salsa is the best."

"I have dreams about this salsa. Why would anyone have red salsa when green salsa is a thing that exists in this world?"

We're quiet for a minute as we shove chips into our mouths. Then Peter says, "Tell me your news first, because you look a little like you might explode if not."

"Okay. Okay. Well, first of all, I taught my song to the dance team today and . . . da-da-da, it didn't suck! They actually really liked it."

Peter claps. Like, actually claps. It's adorable. I notice he must have gotten a haircut this week. It makes him look older.

"That's so great, Soph. I'm happy for you."

A server comes by, and we order tacos. Then we both reach for the last chip, and our hands tangle in the basket. I'm not sure who pulls back faster.

It's this kind of thing that makes me anxious we might not be able to get back what we used to have, makes me wonder if this is what we are now: two people uncomfortable with even an accidental touch. We used to knock shoulders and brush arms constantly. We didn't think twice about it. But now every touch feels like it means something. I worry he'll read into it when all I want is for him to stop looking at me like he's worried I'm going to spill my emotions at any moment.

He loved me once, though, the middle school version of love.

"Sorry," I say, though I'm not sure I am.

"It's fine," he mumbles. He pushes the basket toward me. "Take it."

"They'll bring more," I say as I swipe the last chip, dip it in salsa, and chew it slowly. Peter waits.

"So that was thing one out of a million?" he asks.

I swallow, wash down the spicy salsa with a gulp of water. "I have two more." I mention the upcoming weekend dance intensive, building up to my biggest announcement: the workshop I haven't told him about yet. "Montana told me about this choreography workshop this summer. It's . . . it's eight weeks long, though." *Eight weeks I'd be away from you*, I think, and hope he hears the subtext.

"Eight weeks. Wow. In Seattle?"

"No . . . in San Francisco."

I watch his face closely, trying to gauge his reaction. Our server swaps our empty chip basket for a new one. Peter's brow furrows. He doesn't even grab a chip.

"Wow. You should do it. You think you want to do that, like, professionally?"

"Maybe? If I'm any good at it."

"You clearly are."

I smile, but his reaction has thrown me. It's not that I was hoping for him to cling to my legs and beg me to stay, but I expected he'd say he'd miss me, at least. I was hoping for more than *Wow* and *You should do it*.

I shake these feelings off. "Tell me your news."

He grins. "I. Uh. Sort of joined a band?"

"Wait . . . what?"

"You know I've been hanging out with Chase Cabrera? He's in a band, Diamonds Are for Never—"

"Diamonds Are for what?"

"Never," he finishes, and a flush creeps onto his cheeks. "It's cheesy, I know, and they just started out, so they're not amazing or anything, but . . ." He trails off. He's trying to downplay this, trying to make it seem like he isn't bubbling over with excitement. "They wanted a keyboard, and, well . . ."

"That's you."

"That's me."

Peter is in a band called Diamonds Are for Never. I should be happy for him, but my features feel frozen.

"Tabby said you were at her diner yesterday," I say slowly. I found it odd when she told me last night after her shift, but I was too distracted by my impending dance practice to mention it. "You were with them—the band?"

He nods. "Sophie," he says. "Are you . . . okay about this?"

"Why wouldn't I be?" My voice is too high-pitched, too very-clearly-not-okay-about-it. "It's not like music was our thing or anything."

He picks up a chip but doesn't eat it, just crushes it to yellow crumbs on his napkin. "So . . . I can't play music with anyone else because of some dumb thing we did as kids?"

Some. Dumb. Thing.

The chips aren't sitting right in my stomach.

He must realize this affects me because he reaches across the table and, ever so lightly, grazes my wrist with his fingertip. This touch—because he initiates it, it's okay somehow. It's a touch that communicates his apology but nothing else. It doesn't linger long, as though he's worried I'll misinterpret it. As though a real gesture of affection would be too much.

"I—I'm sorry," he says. "The Terrible Twosome wasn't dumb. I didn't mean that. I just meant it was something we did as kids, you know?"

Past tense. The Terrible Twosome *was*.

"I know."

"And you have dance team," he says. "That's music."

I've always had that, though. I've had dance team and dance class and I don't know why it feels different that Peter's off doing something without me when I've been doing this without him—but Peter was never going to join dance team. And Peter and I already have a band.

"I know," I say again. I yank out my ponytail, wincing when the elastic pulls out a few hairs. As best I can, I wrangle it into a bun. It'll never look as sleek as Montana's.

"I mean, the Terrible Twosome couldn't exactly play shows or anything."

"We could," I say in a small voice.

Our parents used to encourage us to enter talent shows, but Peter and I were used to living in our own world. The Terrible Twosome was for *us*, not anyone else.

"Sophie."

Our food arrives, and while Peter digs in, I stab at my taco with a fork.

"You joined a band. Okay. That's awesome. That's really cool." I force a smile. I am a robot learning how to express human emotions. "Do you . . . have any shows anytime soon? Can I hear you?"

"I mean, we're still rehearsing," he says between bites. "As soon as we book a gig, you'll be the first to know."

Gig. Peter is not someone who plays *gigs*.

Is he?

"Great."

While Peter eats, I stare at my plate, fist clenched tight around my fork. I try to take a deep breath, but my lungs are tight.

"We're okay, right?" he says after wiping his mouth with a napkin. "I mean, after—"

That strikes a nerve—no, it doesn't strike it. It fucking smashes a nerve with a hammer.

I drop my fork on the table with a clatter. "I'm not silently pining for you or anything!" I say quickly, my voice jumping up to an even higher pitch again. I can't control it. "God, Peter. I'm *fine*. I'm not still thinking about it. I just want things to be normal, okay?"

I've said this too loudly. Everyone's staring at us. I'm shaking, even. It's true: I want normal back, since it's clear what I really want has to become a secret again.

But . . . I also want him to feel a little guilty that once again he's gotten exactly what he wanted.

"We could play when we get home," he says softly. An olive branch. He's approaching me like I'm a lion he doesn't want to pounce, quietly backing away from this strange conflict. "Or you could show me the piece from dance today."

As calmly as I can, I pick up my taco, then finally meet his gaze. "It really looks better with more people."

CHAPTER 18

PETER

WHEN CHASE TOLD ME HE WANTED TO HANG OUT "just the two of us," I wasn't expecting it would happen so soon. The following Saturday night, though, he picks me up and drives us to the Laser Dome downtown. It's connected to the science center, which I've been to only once, on an elementary school field trip. We played with bubbles and touched sea anemones underwater. For a solid three months afterward, I wanted to be a marine biologist.

"Laser Beatles," Chase explains when I ask him what we're doing at the science center. "Tonight they're playing *Revolver* all the way through, and they project lasers on the ceiling in time with the music. . . . Trust me, it's cool."

"I love *Revolver*."

"It's criminally underrated. 'Tomorrow Never Knows' is a masterpiece."

We get our tickets and head inside. It's much warmer, and Chase's glasses fog up. He wipes at them with his sleeve as he hums. There are a few rows of seats inside the auditorium, but Chase shakes his head and points to a stack of pillows. We each grab one and stretch out on the floor so we can stare up at the ceiling.

"I've never been here before," I say as we're waiting for the show to start. "I've been trying to decide what I want to do now that I have a more . . . freeing life than I used to, and clearly this should have been on the list."

Chase rolls his body to the side, propping up his head with one hand. "What else is on the list?"

I turn to face him. Even in the almost-dark, his eyes are bright. "Nothing like skydiving or cliff-jumping. It's not nearly that thrilling. It's more like . . . Don't judge me, okay?"

"I swear I won't."

I let out a sigh. "I'm sort of . . . exploring more of who I am? Like, I'm Jewish. Well, half, I guess. But I never had a bar mitzvah, and I don't know very much about the religion. I . . . I think I might want to."

"What does it mean, exactly, to be half Jewish?"

"My dad's Jewish, but Judaism is passed down through the mother's side, so if my mom were Jewish, I'd be, well, fully Jewish." It's definitely the most times I've said the word "Jewish" in a single sentence.

It hits me that I've never had to explain all this about myself to anyone before. Sophie has always *known*.

"In elementary school," I continue, "we were doing this unit on world religions. And when we started talking about Judaism, the teacher asked what we knew about it. One kid raised his hand and said, 'My dad told me Jews are kind of greedy.'"

"You're fucking kidding."

I shake my head. "And then another kid said, 'They have bigger noses than other religions, right?' and the teacher was absolutely mortified at this point. But I called out that those were stereotypes and they weren't true, and the first kid told me, 'Peter, you're only *half*.' As though it meant I should have been offended half as much or something. Or I didn't have the right to be offended."

That was when I realized some people didn't like people like my dad or me just because of what we are. There were people who'd hate me despite never having met me. A crash course in anti-Semitism for a nine-year-old.

"You have the right, trust me. Those kids sound like assholes."

"Do I, though? I'm still trying to figure that out. Do I have the right even though I haven't had a bar mitzvah? And what does it say about me that I've known about those stereotypes for as long as I can remember, but I don't know a word of Hebrew besides 'shalom'? Isn't that messed up, that that's all I know? I've even spent more time in churches than in synagogues. All my piano recitals took place in churches." They were nice places, sure, but it felt like I wasn't entirely supposed to be there. Like I wasn't welcome, though my mom was raised Christian. There was something about being half Jewish in a church that felt wrong. I had a strange inkling it would've felt different in a synagogue.

Chase is quiet for a moment. Then: "Being half of something can be kind of a mindfuck. My dad was from Argentina, but he moved to the US when he was a kid. He grew up speaking more English than Spanish, so I don't know the language."

I'm stuck on the "was," though.

"My dad passed away when I was nine," he continues. "Stage-four lung cancer. He wasn't a smoker—life was just cruel."

"Chase. I had no idea." My sympathy compels me to reach a hand out, to graze his sleeve. "I'm so sorry."

"Thank you," he says graciously. "We're okay, though. They caught it so late, and he didn't suffer for very long. We've had a lot of time to cope. And therapy, too. People say it's not something you ever get over—and yeah, I'd love to have my dad come to one of our shows, but my mom and sisters and I are doing fine."

"How many sisters do you have?"

"Three. Two older, and one younger. So it's my super-white mom, her three half-Argentinian daughters, and me. That was the worst part. Of—of losing my dad." He rubs a hand over his face. "There's this whole side I don't know at all. I want to go to Córdoba one day—that's where he was born. I feel like if I could get there, I'd have this sudden epiphany. . . . That probably sounds stupid."

"It doesn't."

A sad smile. "You don't have siblings, do you?"

"I used to want one," I say, shaking my head. "My parents got me a chinchilla instead."

Chase laughs. He's unselfconscious about his laughs, surrendering completely to them. "Right. You mentioned that at the diner last week. I hope this isn't too personal of a question," he continues, "and tell me if it is. But—are you basically cured now? Now that you've had the transplant? 'Cured' is the wrong word, I know. I've been doing some research, but I'm still not sure I understand."

He did research.

To learn more about me, my condition, my *history*.

For a few moments I'm so overwhelmed I can't speak. "I can't believe you did research," I finally manage to say.

He shrugs it off. "I was curious, and I would have felt like a jerk asking a hundred questions."

"It's not a cure, no. I still have kidney disease. I have to take immunosuppressants—anti-rejection meds—for as long as I have this kidney. They trick my body into believing the new organ isn't foreign so it doesn't attack Sophie's kidney."

"It's yours now, though. Not Sophie's."

"Right," I say, though I haven't been able to think of it that way yet. "Right. And a donor kidney . . . Sometimes it only functions for ten or fifteen years. Twenty if I'm lucky."

"That's what I was reading," he says softly. "Shit."

I nod. "I've already lived so much of my life convinced I was going to die young. So I can't think about that now. My . . . mortality or anything. I can't think about being back on the transplant list one day, being back on dialysis. I can only think about *now*."

He scoots closer to me on the floor, so close that his shoe settles against mine. Our shoes have gotten very well acquainted lately. "I still can't believe what you went through. I'm not even fully sure what a kidney does. I'm picturing this bean-shaped . . . thing. That does . . . something."

"Well, as nerd club president, I can tell you exactly what they do. They're basically like trash collectors. That's how my doctors explained it to me when I was younger and was having trouble understanding what was going on. They process blood and sort out waste products and water . . . which become urine." I wince. I've become so desensitized that I forget sometimes that pee is not a normal conversation topic.

But Chase doesn't flinch. "I was such a little nightmare whenever I had a cold. I'd throw tantrums about not wanting to go to school."

"If I had so much as a 98.7-degree temperature, we were probably already on our way to the hospital."

"I'm glad you're better now," he says, his eyes heavy on mine.

The words linger between us as the lights go dark, and I shift my attention to the ceiling, my heart hammering in my chest. My mind turns over his words, trying to figure out if they mean something beyond the fact that he's happy I'm not dead. There are a lot of reasons you can be happy someone isn't dead, like that you're a decent human being.

Or those words, his gaze, his shoe against mine mean something else entirely.

The brightly colored lasers dance along the ceiling. I can hear Chase humming the guitar licks along with the album and softly singing some of the lyrics off-key. The music is alternately experimental and peaceful, and sometimes quiet and full of longing. It's so easy to lose myself in it. At some point during the evening, one or maybe both of us shift so our legs, not just our shoes, are touching, which ignites a very pleasant fire in my belly.

I loved the Beatles before, but now I *love* the Beatles.

It's nearly midnight when Chase drives me home. We're in the middle of this game where we play a song and then hard-core judge the other person if they don't know the band. He gets me on Pink Floyd.

"You're a musician and you don't know Pink Floyd?" he asks, incredulous, spiking the volume of his car speakers. "This is unacceptable."

"I know *of* them," I insist. "I just . . . wouldn't be able to name any of their songs."

He scoffs. "Doesn't count. Listen. They're so inventive. No one was doing this kind of stuff back then."

We drive for a while, over bridges and beneath trees, Pink Floyd serenading us.

"I'd never done anything like this before tonight," I tell him when the song changes. "I think I missed out on a lot. And not just because I was sick—or maybe I used that as a crutch, because I was sick and my parents were overprotective. Until a few weeks ago, I'd never been to a party. I've never gone to a high school dance, and I've never gone on a date."

"Poor, stunted Peter," he says, shaking his head. His golden-brown hair falls in his face, and he shoves it away. "Wait. You and Sophie haven't ever dated?"

"We're best friends," I say, which doesn't answer his question. "Friends" barely seems to encompass what we are. There has to be a word deeper than "friend" and more personal than "donor" to describe someone who has given you a kidney. "But, uh, no. We haven't dated."

"I guess I don't really know her. We had a class together last year, and I think I heard her talk once."

"She . . . she takes a while to open up. But I've known her forever, and she's—she's amazing."

The way I feel about Chase isn't at all how I felt about Sophie. My attraction to Chase is stronger—because I'm older now, because I understand what that attraction can lead to. Chase is newness, excitement. A band with a catalog of albums I haven't listened to yet. Sophie, when I liked her, was all comfort. Warm blankets and a TV show you've seen a hundred times. In a way, though, Sophie's the reason I'm even in the car with Chase right now.

"Okay, so you've never been on a date. Have you ever . . . kissed anyone?" He doesn't say it cruelly. It's almost like he wants to make sure I haven't missed out on the greatness that is kissing someone who wants to kiss you back.

The question brings heat to my cheeks. "Only Sophie," I say, and he turns in his seat to lift his brows at me, like maybe I was lying about not having dated her. "A few years ago. We weren't dating, though. It just sort of happened." I don't tell him about the kiss at the party—those feelings are still too raw, especially after Sophie's outburst at dinner earlier this week. A brief silence follows, so I punt the question back. "Have you?"

"I had a boyfriend last year. I met Jeff at a show last summer. He lived in Olympia, but he'd come up to see this band he was into. We flirted all night, and then when he said he went to high school in Olympia, we sort of tried to date long-distance. But . . . it didn't work. And we only really hooked up once."

My throat goes dry. *Hooked up.* It can mean a hundred different things. It can mean just kissing, or it can mean *everything.*

"Hooked up?" I repeat, before I can rein myself in. I'm too hot in my coat. I fiddle with the zipper, dragging it down halfway so I don't feel like I'm suffocating.

"Made out, fooled around a little. No clothes came off or anything. Is this making you uncomfortable?"

Oh no. Something's giving me away. Is it all the sweating? I shake my head. Too fast.

"No, no, I'm just . . ." *Curious.* I don't bother to finish the sentence. Chase doesn't seem to mind.

"He was the first guy I did anything with. The only guy, actually."

"Uh-huh," I say, still playing with my stupid zipper. Now it's stuck. Excellent.

Made out. Fooled around a little.

I try to stop myself from picturing Chase and this mystery boy. On top of this mystery boy. Underneath him. Chase pinning Mystery Boy up against a wall, his mouth on Mystery Boy's neck.

Yeah, I can't really stop.

"I'm sorry," I say, but Chase shrugs, slowing down as he turns into my neighborhood.

"It's okay. Your first boyfriend—or girlfriend—is supposed to break your heart. That's what my mom said. But mine's completely repaired now. No sympathy needed."

Chase parks in front of my house.

"This was fun," I say, unclicking my seat belt. I'm both eager to get out of the stuffy car and into the cold and wishing the night weren't over yet. "Thanks."

Before I get out, he leans over the console. My entire body tenses as he says low into my ear, "You know, now that you're sure you're gonna be alive for a while, you should try kissing more people."

Then, as quickly as he leaned over, he's back in the driver's seat.

I can still feel his breath on my ear. My neck.

I'm too stunned to reply. I open the door, and I think—God, I *hope*—I say good-bye. I hope I wave. Dazed, I walk up to my house, fumbling with my keys. It takes a few tries to actually fit them in the lock.

I'm surprised to find my mom not on the couch with her laptop, but in the kitchen with Sophie's mom, a bottle of wine between them.

"Peter!" my mom calls out, and then bursts into giggles. "We were just talking about you!"

Giggles. I can't remember the last time I heard my mother giggle.

My mom is drunk with Sophie's mom. Oh my God.

"Did you have a good time?" Becki asks, and then it's her turn to start laughing. Her cheeks are tomato red.

"Clearly not as good a time as you two. What's so funny?"

My mom waves a hand. I notice Becki's nails match hers, wonder if they got them done together. "Nothing you'd be interested in."

"Great. I'll be upstairs."

Becki flings an arm out as though to grab for me. "No, Peter. Stay with us! We're fun!"

They break down laughing again, and while it's mortifying, I'm also happy to see my mom enjoying herself like this. Has the transplant given my parents permission to have fun again? Have they deprived themselves for all these years because of me?

I race to my room, where I shut and lock the door. Then I wipe the mothers from my mind.

Hooked up. Made out. Fooled around a little. Those words, in Chase's voice, are on an infinite loop inside my mind. *You should try kissing more people. Alive. Alive. Alive.*

Lying next to Chase in the dark earlier, it felt like all my cells were on high alert. I wanted to tug him close to me. Line my body up against his, or on top of his, or under his. I'm not picky.

I turn on some music. Pink Floyd. My coat zipper might be stuck, but my jeans zipper goes down easily.

It's not that I never got turned on when I was sick, but whenever I tried to jerk off, I could rarely finish. I couldn't do this most basic thing my body desperately wanted me to do. I was too embarrassed to talk about it with my parents, so I googled it and learned kidney failure could cause "sexual dysfunction" in addition to the 4,268,314 other things it affected.

Things seem to be functioning pretty well right now.

Later, when I drift off to sleep, I dream about the Beatles and Pink Floyd and lights on the ceiling. Chase's eyes. Chase's hands. Chase's mouth.

CHAPTER 19

SOPHIE

ANOTHER FRIDAY NIGHT, ANOTHER RAINY FOOTBALL game. I squint up at the stands, but everyone's REI parkas blur together in one big swatch of bluish gray, and I can't find Peter.

We're not supposed to bring our phones onto the field—Montana thinks it looks bad for people in the bleachers to see us staring at our screens—but I tucked mine into the waistband of my skirt, and I steal peeks at it when the rest of the team is distracted by the game.

Mostly, I'm staring at the message Peter sent two hours ago and trying to figure out how to respond.

Can't make the game tonight. Band practice ☹

I must have sat through at least a dozen of his piano recitals. So far this year, he's seen me dance at one game. He missed my dance recitals all the time when he wasn't feeling up to it. Sure, I danced when we Terrible Twosomed, but that was different. The rest of the time his health came first. It had to.

"Everything okay?" Liz asks, nudging my shoulder.

I wrap my phone in my sleeve, trying to hide it. "Fine."

Next week? I finally text back, staring at the screen for a reply, as though if I blink, I'll miss something.

For the past couple weeks, I've been wrestling with an ugly thought. I thought the transplant would make us better than best friends, that I'd somehow graduate to a new level of importance in his life. It's not why I did it, but at the same time, I couldn't fathom a future in which the transplant didn't connect us even more deeply. But our present is not that future. I don't understand why he's so adamant about our relationship staying the same when he's the one changing it.

He has a small part of me, and I'm the one with a gaping hole that can't be fixed.

By the following week, the team nearly has my piece memorized, and I'm feeling pretty fantastic about it. When I get home after practice Thursday, I'm humming the song under my breath, still bouncing with energy. I'm not ready for homework, but I'm too tired to go back out. I drop my backpack in the hall and wander into the kitchen. Tabby's standing at the counter, dipping a spoon into a jar of Nutella.

She waves at me with the spoon before she licks it. "Hey."

"Hey." The house is eerily quiet. "Where's Luna? Actually, where's our whole family?"

"Josh has her. They're visiting his grandparents at their

retirement home tonight. And Mom and Dad are out with Peter's parents."

I open the drawer and find a spoon of my own to dip into the jar. "It's so weird. They're BFFs all of a sudden."

"I know!" Tabby exclaims, holding out the jar for me. "I guess that's how it used to be, but I barely remember it."

"Right, because you were *so young* back then."

Tabby rolls her eyes. "Wait, you're older than me? I had no idea."

"What are you doing tonight? Besides this," I say as I take another spoonful.

She lets out a long sigh. "I switched shifts at the diner so I could go to the movies with Mia and Steph, but they had late rehearsals for *Sweeney Todd*. I mean, it's fine. I don't even like *Sweeney Todd* that much anyway. Well, the movie was awful, but some of the songs are okay. . . ."

What she doesn't say: If Luna hadn't happened, she'd be rehearsing for *Sweeney Todd* too.

"You would have been an awesome Mrs. Lovett," I tell her.

"I totally would have," she says with a sniff. "So. Now I have a thrilling night of homework ahead of me."

She's trying to snark about this to make it better, but it can't have been easy for her to give up theater.

"Do you, um . . . want to do something instead?"

She taps her fingers on the table. "Depends. Make me an offer. Bonus points if I don't have to change out of sweatpants."

I snort. Then it comes to me. "Let's have a sleepover."

"What?" She laughs, this high-pitched sound that's nothing like my own laugh. When I used to watch my sister onstage, I was amazed by how she could morph into a completely different person. Sometimes it made me wonder if I knew her at all.

"Let's have a sleepover here. We could play with makeup and watch TV and eat terrible, wonderful food."

"That actually sounds really fun. I haven't done anything like that in forever."

And I guess I haven't either. Or, well, ever. Sleepovers with Peter—which are now Forbidden—were usually spent playing board games or watching movies. I didn't even care that one time Peter wet the bed. There was nothing Peter could do that would disgust me. His body was working against him. I couldn't judge something he couldn't control.

So we order pizza, find a recipe for homemade face masks, and line up our entire nail polish collection on the bathroom counter. Then we sit on the floor with our face masks on, show tunes playing from Tabby's phone. I don't complain, though there are about a million other songs I'd rather listen to, even Peter's mopey piano music.

"I've missed things like this," Tabby says wistfully, and though this isn't something the two of us have ever really done, I'm sure she's missed doing it with her friends. It makes me think about everything else she's probably missed since having Luna, which, admittedly, isn't something I think about very often.

"I could watch Luna for you," I say, thinking back to what Josh said on Halloween. "If that would help."

"Really? You'd do that?"

"Why are you so surprised?"

She shrugs. "You've never expressed any interest."

"She's my niece. I want to get to know her."

"She's a cool little person."

"That's arrogant, considering she came from you."

She elbows me, and a timer goes off, indicating it's time to rinse off the masks.

Afterward, we make our way into the living room with the intention of watching some bad TV, but my sister's in a talkative mood.

"Tell me things about your life," she urges as we flop onto the couch. "Please?"

Before Luna, on Friday nights Tabby would be getting ready for dates with Josh or going to a theater-kid party. I'd be listening to Peter play the piano, hoping he'd look at me differently from how he'd looked at me for the past few years.

If I was ever jealous of Tabby's friends or her relationship, I haven't felt that way in a while. I tell her about dance team and Montana and Liz and Queens of Night. "Oh! I read the first one," she says.

And I tell her about Peter and the complete lack of anything happening there, our continued attempts at normal. Though she doesn't have any sage advice, she just listens, and it feels like enough.

"You could still audition for shows," I say. "When Luna's older?"

"Oh, I will. I'm not done with theater, but it's hard to see everyone else doing the same regular things and me . . . not. And don't give me some BS about how this is what I chose and I should—"

"I wouldn't," I say quickly, because I've never thought that. "I would never say that. You're allowed to be sad about it and still be a good mom."

"Thanks," she says, and I can tell she means it.

When Josh gets home later, he and Tabby do their nighttime routine with Luna. It's strange how suddenly lonely I feel after having my sister to myself the whole night. But it's there, once the bubbly warmth of our evening together wears off.

My parents don't get back until after midnight.

"Out this late on a *school night*?" I ask them incredulously when they walk in the door.

"We had *such* a great time," my mom slurs. "Sophie, sweetheart, would you believe how delicious rum is?"

"Oh my God, did Peter's parents get you drunk?"

"They all got drunk," Dad says on his way to the kitchen. "I was the designated driver. We went to a jazz club, and the drinks were much stronger than any of us thought." He pours Mom a glass of water. "Drink this."

"I haven't been drunk like this since . . ." She giggles at my dad. "Our honeymoon. Remember that night in Hawaii?"

"File this under information your daughter did not need to know," I say with a groan. But I'm glad they can still have fun like this.

I imagine that three very drunk people was a bit much for my dad to manage tonight, though, so I wait in the living room while he helps my mom get in bed.

"Out like a light," he says after shutting the door to their bedroom.

"You're not tired after a night of debauchery with Ben and Holly?"

"A little, but I was planning to wind down with a podcast."

"What is it?"

At this his entire face lights up. "One of those true crime podcasts. This one's about a body that disappeared on a cruise ship."

"Creepy."

"You want to listen with me? I can pull up episode one."

I shrug. "Sure. Why not?"

He retrieves a headphone splitter and another pair of noise-canceling headphones. There's no shortage of audio equipment in our house. As we listen, my dad watches my reactions and as a result totally gives away what's about to happen next.

"You never wanted to do anything like this?" I ask when the episode ends with ominous music. I'm totally hooked now. Curse you, true crime podcasts, you got me. "Make your own podcast?"

He shakes his head. "I'm much better suited to work behind the scenes. You, on the other hand . . . You've always been onstage."

"Doesn't mean I'm not scared to death every time I'm about to go on." People think performers are all alike. That anyone who goes onstage must be a naturally outgoing, extroverted person. But that's not true. When we perform, it takes all my brainpower to focus. It took me the longest time to be able to forget about the audience, to focus solely on the art.

"There's something I've been wanting to talk to you about." I tell him about the choreography workshop in San Francisco, the one with the rapidly approaching application deadline. "Do you think I should apply?"

What I really want to ask is something along the lines of this: What will Peter do without me here? Will he grow even closer to his bandmates?

Will he be glad to see me when I come back?

"When I went to Israel," Dad starts, which is not at all where I thought this conversation was going, "I was terrified. I hated flying, hated not having control over plans. I threw up on the plane and was convinced it would be a horrible trip."

"But then you met Mom, and it turned out to be the best decision of your life?"

"Actually, that wasn't what I was going to say. I mean yes, of course, I met your mother, and that was, as you know, quite life-changing. But before that, what I loved was the independence. It was the first time I'd been away from my family, from my home, for any extended period of time. I had close friends, and I didn't know how I'd live without them. But . . . I did it. And by the end I was proud of myself." He laughs. "Until your mom and I got lost. But that clearly turned out all right too."

"So what you're saying is that I should try it."

He steeples his fingertips. "Eight weeks is a long time."

"Two months."

"You're worried about Peter."

Slowly I nod.

"Peter's going to be okay without you," my dad says.

What I don't tell him is that sometimes I'm not sure I want him to be.

CHAPTER 20

PETER

EVERY TIME I'VE BEEN IN A WAITING ROOM, IT FELT like we were only waiting for bad news. Bracing ourselves for it with white-knuckled grips on uncomfortable chairs.

These days my parents are considerably more relaxed. My mom taps at her phone with glossy lavender talons, and my dad squints at a crossword puzzle in the back of an ancient parenting magazine.

I brought a book, a memoir by Patti Smith, but I leave it closed on my lap. I take this opportunity—my parents at ease—to mention something I'm not sure they're going to love.

"I've been doing some research about Israel," I say, which makes them glance up.

"Israel?" my mom repeats, like I've told her I was doing some research about cooking meth. "What kind of research?"

"Um." I fiddle with my bracelet. "I was looking into Birthright, actually. The trip Sophie's parents met on?"

"With what money?" my mom asks. My medical expenses have not been cheap. We're lucky to have good insurance, lucky my parents have good jobs.

"Birthright is free," my dad says.

"Is it . . . safe?"

Of course that's what she'd ask. Of course she'd assume that, simply because Israel's in the Middle East, it's unsafe, despite the thousands of Americans who travel there each year.

It makes me wish, not for the first time, that my mom were Jewish too.

"Very safe." My dad shuts the magazine. "They have a security guard travel with the group, don't they?"

I nod. "And members of the IDF, too."

My mom's eyebrows climb up her forehead.

"Israel Defense Forces," I supply. "That's the military there. Everyone has to do mandatory—"

"I know that," my mom snaps. *Snaps*. It's unlike her.

"You can't go until you're eighteen, but I could apply this summer." It's not even that I want to go that soon necessarily. For the past couple months, this combative itch has been building beneath my skin, a desire to push my parents.

To see how much they'll fight back.

"Why the rush?" My mom crosses her arms. "You're just starting to feel better, Peter. Why risk it?"

Why not take full advantage of everything my body can do now? I want to ask.

"What if you missed a dose of your immunosuppressants?" my dad says. "Or something happens with the donor kidney?"

"How will you be able to keep up with your medications if you're traveling on your own?"

They're so focused on the "what if." They always have been.

"I wouldn't be on my own. I'd be with a whole group of people. And I'll be in college in a year and a half. How will you trust me to keep up with them then?"

"College!" She says it so loudly that an older couple across the waiting room looks over at us. I hope they're not waiting for bad news. "Whoa, whoa, whoa. We haven't even gotten there yet. Let's focus on what's in front of us now. One day at a time."

It's fire in my veins now, this urge to bite back at them. Before, I never had the energy. Being sheltered was great if it meant another first edition on my bookshelf, another gift to buy my complacency.

"But—what am I supposed to do?" I'm surprised when the words aren't filled with the anger I intended. Instead, they sound almost . . . hurt. "Stay here forever? I thought I'd finally be able to be more independent—"

"Peter." My mom clutches my arm. I try to wrest my jacket sleeve from her grasp. "I wish you could have a normal life, but it's always going to be different for you. You must understand that."

"You're the ones making it different for me!" I say. "Making it harder! There are so many things I should have been able to do, but you wouldn't let me. Do you know how much I didn't get to experience because of you?"

"Enough, Peter," my dad says.

But I haven't had enough. I'm tired. I'm tired of how repetitive my life has become, an infinite *DC al fine* that sounds the same every fucking time. Is it really so awful of me to want *more*?

"Could I—could I at least take driver's ed?" My voice is small now. I'm ten years old, asking my parents why I can't go to the Oregon Coast with Sophie's family. Why I can't go on a field trip on Seattle's Underground Tour. Why I can't take PE.

"We'll discuss it later," my dad says.

"We could get you a new keyboard instead," my mom says. "You've had that Yamaha for a while."

I set my jaw. "I like the Yamaha."

"Peter?" calls the nurse, putting an end to our waiting but not to my frustration.

Inside the exam room, Dr. Paulson goes over my blood work and tells me exactly how well I'm doing. For one of the first times in my life, though, my parents aren't as easily impressed.

Sophie: Help me paaaaaaaaaack
    Sophie: I don't know what to briiiiiiing
    Peter: Okaaaaaaaaay
    Sophie: Are you making fun of me?
    Peter: Neverrrrrrrrrr

Sophie frowns at her open duffel bag. Articles of clothing are strewn across her room, and down the hall, Luna's crying, Tabby attempting to soothe her.

"Aren't you just going to be wearing what you usually wear for dance the whole time?" I ask, sliding into her desk chair and stretching my legs beneath me.

"Most of it, but . . ." She reaches for a pair of sweatpants, drops them into her bag. "I've never been on a trip by myself. I'm worried I'll forget something."

As subtly as she can, she kicks a blue bra out of my line of vision. I'm suddenly fascinated by the ceiling.

Between band practice and dance team, we've barely seen each other in the couple weeks since Halloween, with the exception of rides to school. I've missed two football games now because of band practice, but I've promised her I'll make the next one. It's hard to pass up spending time with Diamonds, whether we're playing or hanging out. The only time I've felt like myself lately was with the band. The terrible truth: Sophie is both a reminder of everything I went through and everything I can do now.

It's strange spending evenings and weekends apart, having things to tell her that she doesn't already know. Strangest, though, is that I haven't yet told her how I feel about Chase. Now that I've spent more time with people who are so open about the way they identify, I *want* to tell her I'm bi. I want to feel close to her again—no secrets. "I'm so nervous," she says.

"About the workshop?"

She waves her hand. "Not so much that . . . the rest of it. Being in a hotel with people I don't really know, mainly. It's a lot of people. What if I throw up on the bus or snore or make a fool of myself in any number of other ways?"

"You do know them, though," I say, trying to sound encouraging. I spin the desk chair in quarter circles, back and forth and back and forth.

"Only sort of." She balls up a faded pajama T-shirt I recognize from when the synagogue her family goes to twice a year participated in a city-wide kickball league a few summers ago. They called themselves the Matzah Ballers. Her dad played— and turned out to be shockingly good—and we all made fun of the T-shirt, which features yarmulke-wearing matzah pieces chasing after a ball.

I point at the shirt. "That reminds me. I was thinking about going to Friday-night services sometime."

"At Temple De Hirsch Sinai?"

"Considering it's the sole Reform synagogue within a fifteen-mile radius, yeah. Do you . . . want to go with me?" I'm not entirely sure why I ask. Maybe because in a perfect world, Sophie and I could explore our identities together, learn more about this thing that connects us in a way we've never really talked about.

Sophie snorts. "To services? Voluntarily?"

"I thought it would be, I don't know . . . fun? Interesting? Enlightening?"

"Or boring. I don't understand why you're suddenly so into

the Jewish thing. You've never been like that." At least she doesn't say: *But you're only half.* "Something's weird about you today."

"I'm not weird. This is just how I am."

She crosses her arms over her chest. "No. You're definitely weird."

I let out a long breath and dig my feet into the carpet to stop the chair from spinning. "There's something I've been wanting to tell you. For a while, actually."

"Okay . . ." She shoves a few shirts out of the way so she can sit on the bed next to her duffel. "You're scaring me."

"It's nothing bad!" I say quickly, but this does nothing to erase her concern. My heart picks up speed. "You know Chase? Cabrera? From the band?" I'm not sure why I add all these descriptors. Of course she knows who he is. She lifts her eyebrows as if to say exactly this. "Well. Uh. I sort of . . . like him." *Exhale.* There it is. God, saying it feels good. Immediately, my shoulders release a tension I didn't know they were carrying.

"I don't know why you'd be in a band with him if you didn't—*oh.*" The moment it dawns on her is clear. Her mouth forms an O, and her eyes go wider than I've ever seen them. "Are you . . . ?" She leaves it up to me to fill in the blank.

"I'm bisexual." I'm happy with the way it comes out: no stammering. Clear. Solid.

After a few quiet moments, she asks in a small voice, "How . . . long have you known?"

"A long time. Years."

"Do your parents know?"

209

"Yes."

More silence—she's processing. Her brows furrow and then unfurrow. "You like girls and guys. Is it . . . ? Is it equal? Is that a dumb question?"

"No. Not dumb. I doubt it's an exact percentage."

At this, she nods, then becomes very interested in the floral pattern of her comforter, as though she's seeing the roses and sunflowers for the first time. "You could have told me," she says softly. "If you'd wanted to. It wouldn't have changed anything between us. It *doesn't* change anything between us."

"I know. I appreciate that." I wasn't ready to tell her, though—not because I worried about how she'd react, but because it felt like one thing in the world that was entirely mine. Now it feels just as much a fact about me as my dark hair or my love for Rufus Wainwright. Part of who I am, but not the only thing I am.

"Does—does Chase like you too?" She twists her mouth to one side of her face. "Sorry, I have so many questions."

"No, no, it's okay." I can tell this conversation's weird for her. Not necessarily because I like a guy, but because we don't talk about this kind of thing. We only talk about it when it involves us. And those conversations never went past this point. I let myself say out loud what I've been hoping for weeks now: "I think so."

"Oh. Wow. Wow." She smiles, but it looks forced. "That's exciting, right? So what happens next?"

"Honestly? I have no clue." Though my imagination has

plenty of ideas, most of which involve an empty house or the back seat of a car.

"Me either. I've never been in a relationship . . . obviously." The way she says this—it makes me feel a twinge of *something* that isn't wholly pleasant. "Thank you. For telling me."

I nod, and an unusual silence cloaks us again. Once the newness of my declaration wears off, she'll get used to the idea of Chase and me. I just wish she could know how I feel when I'm around him. But it's something so electric, so *alive,* I'm not sure I could put it into words. It would be like trying to play the piano with a dripping paintbrush.

"The three of us should hang out sometime," she blurts.

"Yeah?" I grin. "I'd love that."

"You guys are friends, and maybe more than friends, and he has to be cool, right? Cool enough to hang out with me?"

"He is." I tap out a cheerful melody on her desk behind me. "And—Soph. I'll be at your next game. I promise." I tell her this to express my gratitude: for understanding, for being so eager to spend time with Chase.

Her brows crease again. "Only if you want to."

"Of course I want to."

"I'll look for you in the bleachers, then." She pats her duffel. "I should finish packing."

"You want more help? Or more matzah puns?"

A laugh. It's a relief to hear it. We'll be back to normal soon— we have to be. "I think I can manage," she says. "I'll see you seder."

"Okay. Challah if you need anything."

CHAPTER 21

SOPHIE

EVERYONE ON THE BUS IS SINGING. MONTANA'S IN front with Coach Carson, their heads bent together over the workshop schedule. Next to me, Liz pokes my arm.

"You have to know this one," she says as the group belts out the chorus of an old Bruno Mars song.

I do know it. In fact, I've sung it in the shower and danced to it in my room. But there's something about big groups like this that makes me feel even more alone. I've always been like that. I'd see people singing in public and I'd get intense second-hand embarrassment, even though I wasn't singing. I've been on teams and in groups my whole life, but I've never fully felt like an integral part of them. They always seem to be parading around their closeness. *Look how comfortable we are with each other. We don't even care how embarrassing this is.*

Maybe I never joined in because I already had a best friend, someone I could share inside jokes with and laugh at the top of my lungs with.

Someone who is, quite possibly, falling for someone else.

"I'm just tired," I tell Liz, yawning, and lean my head against the window. "Besides, I'm at a really good part in Queens."

"Fine, fine. I won't disturb you."

The team launches into another song, and I adjust my earbuds. The book is good, but my brain is buzzing too much about Peter's confession to let me enjoy it right now. Peter likes Chase Cabrera. Peter is bisexual. The latter does nothing to change my relationship with him, though I wish he'd told me earlier. But that's selfish. This was his to tell, his decision.

The thing is, I have never been able to picture Peter dating anyone who isn't me.

I should have told him I'd go with him to temple because now it's another thing he's doing without me. But religion isn't something you can partner up and figure out together. Even for my bat mitzvah, I was so focused on getting through it, surviving it, not what it meant. If I'm ever going to figure out what religion means to me—*if* it means anything to me—I'm pretty sure I'll have to do it on my own.

I hold my phone up to the window and snap a selfie.

Help, I'm trapped on a bus with 20 people singing "Uptown Funk," I caption it.

I'm not expecting a response right away.

But it still stings that I don't get one until I'm off the bus.

Spokane is on the other side of the state, close to the Idaho border, a four-hour drive that felt much longer. It's a college town mixed with a farm town mixed with a suburb. Dinner is an Italian buffet before we check in to the hotel, where Coach Carson passes out our room assignments. The university's dorms are full, so most of the dancers are staying at the nearest hotel.

"No loud noises, no alcohol, and lights out by ten thirty at the latest," she says, and we murmur our agreement.

We're sleeping four to a room, and I'm with Montana, Neeti, and Taylor. Once we unpack, spreading out all our various products along the bathroom counter, Neeti and Taylor go to the hotel gym, leaving me alone with Montana, who's watching old episodes of *Parks and Rec* on her tablet.

"I sent in my workshop application," I tell Montana after I finish brushing my teeth. She's in sweatpants, her black hair loose on her shoulders, and after she took out her contacts, she put on glasses. It's always strange seeing someone undone for the first time, the way they are at home or with people they're fully comfortable with. My own makeup's been blotted off, my hair pushed away from my face with a stretchy headband. And I'd never wear this Matzah Ballers T-shirt to dance team practice.

Montana glances up from *Parks* and grins. "I'll keep everything crossed for you! Seriously, you would love it."

Truthfully, I'm not sure yet what I want: if I'm hoping I get in or hoping I don't, so I don't have to stress about making the wrong decision. Sometimes it's easier when decisions are made for you. The application involved an essay and a one-minute clip of a dance you choreographed, which I filmed during practice a few weeks ago. I was hoping Peter would edit my essay, but when he said he was overwhelmed with homework, I asked my dad instead.

"You're a great captain." I unclasp my Star of David necklace and lay it on the nightstand before sitting climbing onto Neeti and Taylor's bed. "The best since I started on the team." Our captain before Montana, a guy named Lyle, put the least experienced dancers in the back and never explained difficult combinations for long enough for those dancers to actually get better.

Montana puts down her tablet. "Thanks, Soph."

"You danced as a kid, right?"

"Since I was three. It's what I've always done and what I've always wanted to do. My parents, they've both had terrible office jobs for as long as I can remember. They come home exhausted and upset, and I can't imagine doing that. I never want to sit in a cubicle for ten hours a day."

That certainty about her path in life—I wish I had that. I love dance and I love choreography, but why doesn't that translate into the certainty that a summer in San Francisco is the right choice?

"It must be wild living with your sister and the baby." Montana moves along the conversation with an effortlessness I've never had.

"Extremely. I spend most of my time with Peter anyway, though." It slides off my tongue as though it's still true.

"You talk about him a lot," Montana says. It's more of an

observation than an accusation. "Like, you rarely answer a question without including him somehow."

"I do?"

She nods. "That must be what it's like when you grow up together, though, right? Like, Liz is my best friend, but we only met freshman year. I can't imagine what it's like with someone you've known forever."

When I'm quiet, she must realize I'm not in the mood to talk about it, so she holds up her tablet. "You want to watch some *Parks*?"

So I scoot over to her bed, and we watch eternal optimist Leslie Knope save Pawnee over and over until someone knocks on the door.

"It's me!" Liz whisper-calls, and Montana hits pause on *Parks* and scrambles out of bed to let her in.

Only, it's not just Liz—it's Liz and the rest of the team and at least two bottles of liquor. The room immediately feels cramped and too warm, and my chest aches for the closeness I had with Montana fifteen seconds ago.

"It's almost ten," I say around a yawn, a little embarrassed by how old that makes me sound. I assumed we'd raid the vending machine, watch a couple more episodes, and then crash. I was not expecting a party.

"We're young. We'll be fine!" Liz ushers the others into the room like she's getting people onto life rafts while the *Titanic* sinks. "Hurry, hurry!"

Kunjal and Gabe flop onto the bed I was sharing with

Montana, and Neeti and Taylor, who've returned from the weight room, start handing out plastic cups. Liz uncaps a bottle of whiskey and begins passing it around. I must be watching the scene with horror, because Liz grabs my arm and wiggles it, trying to get me to loosen up.

"Sophie, Sophie, Sophie," she says. "You haven't been to a dance team sleepover."

And this is exactly why. At Montana's party, I was social only with the help of alcohol, and I'm not going to drink the night before the workshop. I've only just barely begun to feel comfortable teaching a dance in front of a group. I need a purpose, and I highly doubt we've gathered here to dance.

Montana drapes herself over an armchair near the window, taking dainty sips from her cup. "No one's having more than one drink," she says, ever the captain.

I stand awkwardly in the middle of the room before taking a seat on the edge of one of the beds.

"Monty," Liz says, and Montana groans as though she hates the nickname and has told Liz this numerous times. Liz nudges Montana with her hip to make room for her on the chair. "You're up first! Because that's how much I love you. And you're the captain, so you know, you have to set a good example and all that."

"Do your worst."

"Truth or dare?" Liz says, and I have to muffle a laugh. I am in a hotel room playing Truth or Dare, and it sort of sounds fun.

"Your dares are evil, so truth, definitely."

217

Liz pouts. "Fine. Have you ever had a sex dream about a teacher?"

"Ms. Lawler, and I'm not even embarrassed about it because she's gorgeous," Montana says breezily, and a chorus of catcalls and whoops erupts from the room.

"Pick the next victim," Liz says.

Montana dares Neeti to dance down the hall wearing only a bra and underwear. Neeti picks Kunjal, who picks Danica, who dares Liz to apply a full face of makeup without looking in a mirror.

"That wasn't too bad," Liz says when she finishes, and oddly enough, it isn't. Then she turns to me and quirks her mouth. "Sophie. Truth or dare?"

"Twenty bucks on truth," someone whispers. I can't see who it is, but I hear someone else snicker.

It makes sense, though: I am not a dare kind of person.

Maybe it's because I'm away from home or because I'm still reeling from Peter's announcement. Maybe it's that I'm sick of everyone pretending they know exactly who I am. But tonight I decide to be.

"Dare," I say, hoping it comes out confident but hearing a tinge of uncertainty in my voice anyway.

Liz raises an eyebrow. "Hmm, okay, gotta make it a good one, then." She taps her fingers on her chin, and then her face splits into a wicked smile. "Call room service and order something off each section of the menu."

"That's . . . too easy," I say carefully.

"While pretending you're having an orgasm."

The team howls. My face flares with heat.

"She's not gonna do it," Kunjal says to a sophomore named Corrie.

Before I can think about it too long, I lunge for the landline on the nightstand between the two beds and press the button for room service.

"Room service," says the male voice.

"H-hi," I start. "My name is Liz Hollenbeck"—I lift my eyebrows at her and she shrugs—"and I—I, mmm, I'm in room f-f-four ten." I inhale deeply, let it out slowly.

"What can I do for you this evening, Ms. Hollenbeck?" the poor guy asks.

"Probably a whole lot," I say, and in the armchair Montana explodes with laughter in a way I've never seen. It's good to see her letting go a little. Liz jumps up from the chair and shoves the room service menu at me. "But let's start with the—the—oh my God—the French onion soup."

"Is anyone filming this?" Neeti says.

Taylor gestures to her phone, which is pointed right at me, and flashes her a thumbs-up.

Instead of getting embarrassed, I let them urge me on.

"Of course, ma'am," the room service guy says.

"And then—oh. *Ohhhhhh.* Oh God, oh God, oh God. I'll have the macaroni and cheese. Right there. Yes. Right there."

"Right . . . where?"

"Just, um . . . on the plate," I say.

"Are you all right, ma'am?"

"I'm so good," I say, and heave out a long, contented sigh. "Mmm, so, *so* good."

"Can I get you anything else?"

"Hmm . . ." I drag my finger down to desserts. "The crème brûlée."

"Excellent choice. Is that going to be it for you, ma'am?"

"Yes!" I affirm, slapping the nightstand. "Yes! Yes! Yes!"

It's not until I hang up that I burst into giggles myself. Montana is nearly crying; she has to hold on to Liz for support.

"I'm dying," Kunjal says. "You are my hero."

My head is light, and I can't stop smiling. I could get high off this feeling. I love this team. I love this night. I love Truth or Dare.

"I didn't know you were capable of that," Corrie says.

The truth is that neither did I.

CHAPTER 22

PETER

I'VE ONLY WORN A YARMULKE TWICE: ONCE AT Sophie's bat mitzvah and a year later, at her sister's. "How does it stay on?" I asked my dad as I bopped my head around, hoping it wouldn't fall.

He reached into his pocket. "A very special magic called bobby pins."

Sophie couldn't stop laughing at the reception later, after she read her Torah portion. "Peter . . . in a yarmulke . . . oh my God."

"Can you say that in here?" I asked. She laughed harder. I didn't get what was so funny about it. Was it because I wasn't fully Jewish, like she was? Or I didn't have the kind of head made for hats?

Tonight I take one from the basket inside the synagogue entrance and place it on my head as easily as the other men do, my dad included. Like last time, he passes me a hairpin.

"Did you know," he says, "that 'yarmulke' is actually Yiddish? It comes from the Polish word for 'skullcap.' In Hebrew, it's called a kippah."

"I did not," I tell him. All around us, people trade hugs and handshakes. My dad and I stand apart, strangers in this sanctuary. I wish it weren't just the two of us, but my mom insisted she had a cold coming on. And even if Sophie were in town, she made it clear she had no interest in going.

We take seats near the back. "You don't want to sit closer to the front?" he asks.

I shake my head. Somehow it seems like a more sacred space up there, one that should be reserved for the more devout.

The Shabbat service isn't as long as Sophie made it seem. We stand up, we sit down, and we stand up again. Every so often, people sort of half bow, and I do my best to follow along, trying to figure out which words and phrases trigger a bow or a change from sitting to standing. Trying to keep up is exhausting in a fascinating kind of way.

My dad is reading the Hebrew, singing along. As best I can, I follow along with the English transliteration, but I don't know the tunes of any of the prayers. I like the way they sound, and though all of this is foreign to me, it feels *right* more than anything. Jewish is what I am; I'm convinced of that now. I'm not half.

Afterward, challah and hors d'oeuvres are served in the foyer. The sweet bread has never tasted better. The rabbi who led the service, a middle-aged man in a silver yarmulke, makes the rounds of the room. I'm positive he'll skip right over my dad and me until he stops in front of us and sticks out his hand for my dad to shake.

"I'm Rabbi Levi Edelstein," he says. "I don't believe I've seen you in our congregation before, so I wanted to introduce myself."

"Ben Rosenthal," my dad says. "And my son, Peter."

I become shy, as though meeting a rabbi is the equivalent of meeting a rock star. Still, I shake the rabbi's hand too.

"Welcome! New to the area?"

"Not exactly." My dad shrugs. "We're just . . . not the best Jews."

Rabbi Edelstein laughs heartily, like he genuinely finds this funny. I decide I like him.

"My mom isn't Jewish," I blurt.

"No matter," Rabbi Edelstein says. "You're more than welcome here. Do you by any chance play kickball? Our recreational team, the Matzah Ballers, is starting back up in a couple months, and we're pretty good, if I say so!"

"That might be fun, huh, Peter?" my dad says, and I can only imagine how Sophie would tease me if she knew I'd joined the Matzah Ballers.

"Sure," I say.

"I hope to see you both back here?"

"You will," I tell the rabbi.

It's nearly eight by the time we leave the temple.

"So, what's the verdict?" my dad asks as he starts the car.

"I really liked it. I wish I could have understood it."

He chuckles. "It's amazing what sticks with you. I haven't

read the Hebrew in a long time, but I guess it's still in there."

"Why didn't I have a bar mitzvah?"

He's quiet for a few moments. The wipers slash across the windshield, a duet with the *tickticktick* of the blinker.

"Did Mom not want me to—"

"*No*," he says emphatically. "Peter, no. I know your mother doesn't understand this. She had some bad experiences with religion growing up, so she's always been a little opposed to it. But I don't want you to blame her for any of this. We wanted you to find your own way. She and I were both forced into religion as kids. It wasn't a choice for us."

"You gave me the choice."

"Yes."

"I'm choosing this. This is what I want."

"I can see the family resemblance" is the first thing I blurt when Chase introduces me to his middle sister, Carlie, who's home from college, and his youngest sister, Chloe. His oldest sister, Catelyn, lives in Portland with a toddler and a newborn.

Carlie groans. She's wearing a gray WSU sweatshirt and has Chase's same golden-brown hair. "Oh, we know."

Chase's mom heads over from the kitchen in an apron that says in small letters, AS FAR AS ANYONE KNOWS, WE ARE A NICE, NORMAL FAMILY. "Peter! Welcome. I'm Jess. I've got homemade pizza in the oven. You like pizza, right? What kid doesn't like pizza? If not, I could also make you a sandwich, or some pasta, or—"

"Peter loves pizza!" Chase says, and I have to stifle a laugh, remembering the first day in English class.

"Pizza sounds great," I confirm.

She grins. "Perfect. Make yourself at home!"

I wasn't entirely sure what to expect when Chase invited me over for a game night at his house. When Chase told me his dad passed away, I guess I was expecting a fractured family. A grieving one. But the Cabreras are bright and full of energy.

"I, um, like your apron?" I say to Chase's mom.

"A Mother's Day gift from this one," she says, jabbing at Chase with the spatula. "He thinks he's so funny."

"I am. And you love it." Chase sweeps an arm through the air. "I'll give you the grand tour. This is the most cynical person to ever have lived." He pokes his sister.

Carlie swats his arm. "I'm part of the tour? Then this guy"—she runs a hand through his hair, messing it up—"is the nosiest little brother. He texts me basically every day asking about my classes, how the dorm food is, what music I'm listening to . . ."

"Sorry for caring," Chase says, but I love witnessing this interaction between them. It makes me wish again for a sibling, though I'm pretty sure the time for that has passed.

Chase leads me through the rest of his house, hardwood floors and patterned curtains, family photos and abstract paintings.

He pauses at the end of the second-floor hallway. "This is my room," he says quietly before he opens the door, letting me in first.

I thought my room was a music room, but *wow*. Album art covers every inch of the walls. There's zero white space, making the room feel like a music museum. I spot Led Zeppelin and Heart and Simon & Garfunkel, Depeche Mode and Fleetwood Mac and Queen.

"This is the coolest," I say as I marvel at all the album covers. It's a huge compliment, saying you like someone's room, the one cube of space they have in this world that's wholly theirs.

"Thanks. Carlie and I did it last summer. I spent months collecting CDs and records until I was sure I had everything I wanted. More than a hundred, at least."

"Wow. I love it."

Then I'm momentarily stunned into silence, distracted by the heat of his body behind mine, much closer than normal. His hand grazes my arm as he shifts so we're side by side.

"The band really likes you," he says, staring straight ahead at *The Dark Side of the Moon*. "I'm—we're—uh, glad you joined."

I have to bite back a smile. "I like them too."

"You guys ready?" Chase's mom calls from downstairs, and I snag one more glance around his room before we join the rest of his family in the living room, where his sisters are deliberating in front of a cabinet overflowing with games.

"What are we playing?" Chase asks, swiping a slice of pizza for me before taking some for himself.

"Taboo!" Chloe announces.

"You always want to play Taboo," Carlie says with a groan.

"Because it's the best."

"I've never played it," I say, and then even Carlie agrees that I must.

We settle onto the couch and chairs, eating our pizza over the coffee table. Chloe is clearly the most competitive, whining when our conversations distract us from the game. Chase and Carlie talk about a recent Marvel movie I haven't seen, and Jess is eager to regale me with Fun Facts about Chase.

"I like to think his musical talent is genetic," she says. "I played a little guitar growing up, and Chase's dad played the drums."

"Hey, I played flute!" Carlie says.

"In middle school," Chase says. "And you hated it."

Carlie shrugs. "I was good, though."

"Humble, too," Jess says.

"Our dad was *great*." Chase's eyes go dreamy, lost in memory. "He played in a band in Argentina when he was in college. Mom, do you have the tapes?"

"I have the tapes!" she says, rocketing out of her armchair. "And by tapes, we do mean literal tapes." She rummages through the cabinet unit, pulling out a tape and placing it into a sound system. "Oh—this was Ernesto's twelve-minute drum solo." She eyes Carlie. "That must be where you get your humility."

It feels almost like a betrayal, being so at home with this family that isn't mine and isn't Sophie's.

I can't help loving it.

"Who knew you were so good at Taboo?" Chase says.

"Beginner's luck?" We decided to go for a walk around his neighborhood after putting the game away because I wasn't ready to go home yet. And I don't think he was ready to let me. "I really like your family."

"They're a little too much."

"They're exactly the right amount," I say. "I . . . was sort of surprised by how much your dad came up."

"It was a long time ago. We all just thought we'd be miserable if we only cried when remembering him. We didn't want it to ever feel like we couldn't say his name in our house." A smile crosses his lips. "I remember bits and pieces of him. Mostly his drumming. He had a kit in the garage, and you heard him on the tape—he was *good*. He was the one who got me into music."

"I'm sure he'd have loved Diamonds."

Chase laughs. "He'd have a lot of constructive feedback."

We pass a bar. A restaurant. Another bar. Chase hums a song I don't know, a sound I've gotten used to. It's not at all grating. It's completely endearing.

"I can't wait until I'm twenty-one," Chase says. "We could get into so many more shows. It's not even nine o'clock and we can barely go anywhere."

I point. "That bookstore's open."

He smirks. "How convenient."

Inside, I inhale the musty scent of old books. The store's deserted except for a woman reading a fantasy novel behind the cash register and two orange cats curled in a plush bed next to a bin of bargain reads.

I find myself drifting toward the section marked PHILOSOPHY. I run a finger over the peeling-apart spines of the books. Aristotle, Aquinas, Bacon, Böhme, Comte. When I land on Descartes's *Meditations on First Philosophy*, I pull it out and open it.

"The ending in that one is kind of a letdown," Chase says from behind me. He brushes my arm with a few fingers.

"Descartes is considered the father of modern Western philosophy. Have you heard the phrase 'I think, therefore I am'? Or in Latin, *cogito, ergo sum*?"

"I have not. Explain it to me?"

His nearness makes my heart race. Staring down at the yellow-gray page, I say, "Descartes was trying to find a statement that couldn't be doubted. He'd already disproved everything he used to believe in, but the fact that he was able to think meant that he existed, and that couldn't be disproved."

"You're so cute geeking out over all this," he says. "You don't even know."

My heart leaps into my throat, making speaking a serious challenge. "When I first read that—*cogito, ergo sum*—I felt . . . reassured somehow. That no matter how terrible I felt, I existed. I could *think*. God, I probably thought way too much. I still do."

"Not a bad thing," Chase says. He backs up a bit, and my body misses his closeness already.

We continue to wander.

"I went to services last night," I tell him.

"Services?"

"At temple."

"Ah, so have you gone full Jew?"

Gently I shove his shoulder. I'm not entirely sure if non-Jews can say the word "Jew." It's something I've wondered myself. It's a weird word, one that sounds offensive depending on tone of voice, yet is merely a description, like "redhead" or "guitarist."

"I liked it a lot. Being there." After services, my dad and I talked about college and the band and how I do want to go to Israel one day. "What do you think you'll do after high school?"

"Oof. That's a real capital-Q question."

"Sorry. It's been on my mind lately."

Chase pauses in the middle of an aisle. "I'd love to go somewhere with a good music program. I might want to be a music teacher or something, but I don't know yet."

"I don't think I want to go to school in Washington." As soon as I say it out loud, I realize it's true. Out of this state, away from my parents: That's the only way I'll be truly independent. "Sometimes I worry I like too many things to narrow them down to one major."

He steeples his fingertips beneath his chin. Points them at me. "Ideal world: Where are you, and what are you doing?"

I ponder this for a moment. "I'm in another city, a quaint college town or a bustling metropolis with a university smack-dab in the middle of it. I'm studying music and literature and philosophy and history and *everything*. I imagine myself up late in this spectacular library that's an architectural marvel, and I'm surrounded by books, and I have so much homework to do but I don't even care because the library is so incredible."

"Where am I?" he asks. He inches nearer, his hand coming up to rest on my arm.

I draw in a breath. "You're . . . Maybe you're there too. Maybe we're studying together. Friday-night nerd club, college edition."

"And what are we, in this ideal world?"

"I—I don't know," I admit, my voice scratchy in a way I've never heard it before, distracted by the warmth of his hand through my jacket. "What are we now?"

He's so close that what happens next is both inevitable and somehow entirely unbelievable: We both lean in, lips meeting for the first time. His hand tangles in my hair, and I reach up to cup his face, pulling him toward me. He's not close enough. I wonder if he'll ever be close enough. His mouth opens against mine, and then there are tongues and teeth and his hips pushing me back against the bookshelf. It's the closest to delirium I've ever felt. I'd be convinced I was having an out-of-body experience if I weren't so aware of my body, at least every place he's pressed against it.

A first kiss in a bookstore has got to be the best kind of first kiss.

I move my hands from his face to his chest to the hem of his jacket. He sighs, and I might like the sound of it more than Rufus Wainwright's *Poses*. I could put it on loop and turn it into my favorite song.

"The band really likes me, huh?" I say when we take a breath.

"Shut up," he says, laughing, which is fine because I have no words left. All the books in the store have stolen them from me.

I'm not sure how long we stand there in the corner. The bookseller kicks us out at closing time—but she's smiling as she does it—and we each buy a book because we feel guilty about staying in there so long. We don't even look at the titles until we're outside in the dark, holding them up to streetlamps. *What to Expect When You're Expecting* for Chase, and *Bunnicula* for me. We laugh and we kiss and we laugh some more, and then we link our hands together. It's raining, but we don't care.

If this is life, I've missed out on so damn much. I've missed that being kissed beneath the earlobe is the most fantastic feeling in the world. I've missed that someone tugging you close, pressing their body against yours, turns your stomach inside out. It's like the world is saying, *Welcome to your new life, Peter. We have a surprise for you.* And suddenly I love surprises.

PART III

CHAPTER 23

SOPHIE

"I'VE NEVER SEEN SO MANY LEG WARMERS IN MY life," Liz says as we enter the college's performing arts building, and it's true. There's no shortage of leotards, leggings, and leg warmers here, most in shades of pink and black, with a few patterns thrown in. Everyone's stretching, comparing schedules, chattering about our upcoming classes.

We're split into groups: beginner, intermediate, advanced. Montana strides confidently toward the advanced group, while I eye the intermediates. Liz glances between the two groups before joining me.

Montana spins around, noticing we're not with her. "Seriously?"

"You're way better at technique than I am," Liz says with a shrug.

The performing arts building has a long hallway, multiple

studios, and a massive auditorium. There must be several hundred dancers here from high schools all around the state. In a way, it's a trial run for this summer's workshop—if I get in.

Saturday morning is devoted to technique classes, with the afternoon open for electives. I'm taking a choreo workshop and an experimental modern class, and then more choreography tomorrow morning.

My enjoyment of a technique class hinges on the teacher. Growing up, I had one teacher who rarely even played music in class because she wanted us to focus on keeping time with each other, not the music, and it frustrated me so much. Most classes, you warm up as a group, do a couple steps and phrases across the floor, with time for some choreography at the end. I was always waiting for the choreography. I wanted to master the steps, sure, but more than that, I wanted to string them together and create something new.

After my ballet and jazz technique classes and sandwiches in the college dining hall for lunch, it's time for choreography.

The teacher is a curvy woman with dark skin and a mass of black spiral curls, a professor of dance who introduces herself as Collette.

"Welcome, welcome," she says as we shuffle inside. Montana's in this one with me. "Let's start with a dance icebreaker, since we don't all know each other. I'd like us to stand in a circle and introduce ourselves along with the first style of dance we ever learned and a short phrase that represents that style."

My very first class was a toddler tap class, so when it's my turn, I do a shuffle-ball-change with my bare feet. I liked tap, but it's the kind of class, sadly, most dancers swap out for advanced ballet and jazz as they get older. That's what programs want to see when you're auditioning. Most other dancers say ballet, but some say jazz or modern, one hip-hop, and one who surprises us all with merengue. When it's Montana's turn, she executes a flawless double pirouette.

"Wonderful. So you're all here to learn about choreography," Collette says. "Choreography isn't just about being a technically good dancer. Not all the best dancers are the best choreographers. It's a very special skill set, and while a lot of us might start out imitating other choreographers, it's all about finding your voice as an artist.

"Who are some of your favorite choreographers?" Collette asks. "No need to raise your hands."

"Martha Graham," Montana says immediately. "Of course."

"Of course," Collette agrees with a smile. "But why?"

"She revolutionized modern American dance. She's an icon."

"Who else?"

Other dancers offer up names: Alvin Ailey, Merce Cunningham, Katherine Dunham, Bob Fosse.

"Twyla Tharp," I say softly, surprising myself. I never volunteer answers in groups like this, and definitely not without raising my hand. I am a new kind of Sophie this weekend.

"My favorite too," Collette says. "They all have a distinct style, yes? Their own voices. You could probably describe them using a single word or phrase. By the end of today's class, I want you to come up with a word or phrase for yourself. You're not married to this for the rest of your life, of course," she adds after a few nervous giggles pass over the group. "But I do want you to be thoughtful about it."

Collette breaks us into four-person groups, and at first I'm anxious that Montana and I are separated. We all get the same song, and each person is charged with choreographing sixteen counts. It's meant to test our teamwork abilities with people we've just met and our cohesion as a group. Collette circles the room, offering advice.

At the end we perform our pieces, and she asks us to write on a whiteboard a word or phrase we'd use to describe our voice.

Unexpected, I write.

This workshop makes me want the summer program so much more, a want that scares me a little. I am so accustomed to not getting what I want that it's terrifying to think it could actually happen.

Maybe my onstage and offstage selves aren't as different as I thought—because right now I feel like the best version of me.

When we pile back onto the bus on Sunday, my muscles are sore but happy. I throw my head back and sing along with everyone else. I don't care that I can't carry a tune. I know this song and this is my team and right now I love all of them.

I open Instagram to post some photos from this weekend, but first my thumb lands on a post from Peter.

It's a photo of his band, all of them sitting in a booth at the Early Bird Diner. It's Peter and Chase and four people I've never seen before, and all of them look extremely *cool*. That's the only word for it. It's not even a recent picture, thanks to Instagram's bonkers algorithms. That's even stranger, that Peter was in this picture a couple weeks ago and I didn't even know about it.

The hashtags, though. The hashtags are what kill me.

Diners Are Forever

#diamondsarefornever   #latergram   #dinersofinstagram #grease #bandbffs #amidoinghashtagsright

I have to stare at them for a while, waiting for my mind to unscramble the letters. My stomach rolls over. This weekend I've been so consumed by the workshop and these people I didn't think liked me but really do that I've barely thought about him. Suddenly, though, I wish I could reach into the screen and grab him and hold him close. These strangers—that's what they are to me even if he's hashtagging them #bandbffs—don't know him, cannot possibly *know him*.

The photo makes this very separate part of Peter's life feel so official. It summons back the ugly thoughts, the ones that make me wonder why he doesn't feel the tug of the invisible thread between us, whether he's with them right now, and whether he's having more fun with them than he ever has with me.

I hate myself for thinking that, but I can't make myself stop.

Liz gives me a ride home after I hug everyone in the school parking lot where the bus dropped us off, and they tell me for the hundredth time that my phone call was the funniest thing they'd ever seen. I'm not sure if that Sophie followed me home.

My phone lights up with a text from Peter while I'm kicking off my shoes.

Peter: Something happened last night. With Chase.

Peter: Are you home? Can you come over? I've been dying to tell you.

Not now. I want to linger in my weekend a while longer.

Sophie: I'm wiped. Tell me tomorrow on the way to school?

Peter: Sure. Okay.

A lamp is on in the living room, and my dad has his headphones on.

"Hey, kiddo," he says quietly, so as not to wake anyone up. "How was your weekend?"

"Exhausting, but good. How's the murder podcast?"

"Murdery."

"Can I sit and listen with you again?" I'm not sure I'm ready to be fully alone, and I love that my dad and I can sit in silence.

"Of course." He pats the couch next to him. "You've been with people all weekend. Was it too much?"

"Too much social. Sophie on overload," I say robotically.

"We can just listen," my dad says, as though understanding I don't feel like talking right now.

But my mind wanders. *Something happened with Chase.* They

declared their love for each other. They kissed, and it was much better than either of the two questionable-circumstance kisses Peter and I have shared. My kidney stopped working and Chase offered up one of his own.

Surely it was something good, something that made Peter happy. After my dad goes to sleep, I leave my still-packed bag on my bed and turn on my computer. My curiosity is stronger than my exhaustion.

Chase and I aren't friends on any social media platforms, but most of his pages are public. There are photos with his family, a trio of sisters. They're posed with their arms around each other, grinning, and it's jarring partially because I can't imagine Tabby and me posing like that. There are photos of him with friends at football games, concerts, school dances. There are photos of his band, a couple with Peter but most without, including a very dramatic photo of them on a playground. Chase is on a tire swing, one of the girls is on a rocking hippo, and the other girl and guy are perched on a slide. They all look extremely serious.

There's a news article that comes up too—an obituary from years ago. His dad passed away, and oh God, I can't imagine.

Then I find his YouTube channel, which is also public. There are a handful of poorly filmed concert videos, but most of the videos are Chase in his room playing guitar. It should be self-indulgent, but it isn't. He's charming and funny, a skilled musician, though these acoustic covers aren't really my thing.

None of the videos have more than forty-two views, which somehow makes me like him more.

It's not that I'm cursing his existence, wondering what Peter sees in him.

It's that I can tell exactly what Peter sees in him.

CHAPTER 24

PETER

"SOPHIE, CHASE. CHASE, SOPHIE. I GUESS YOU guys already sort of know each other?" The three of us stand at the ice rink entrance, hands jammed into our coat pockets as I make this awkward introduction. Chase beat us there; Tabby took the shared Orenstein car today, so Sophie and I bused it.

"In the way you know someone you've been in school with for a few years without actually having spoken, yes," Chase says. "Hey, Sophie. I've heard a lot about you."

She blushes. "Hi. I, um . . . same."

In the week since our bookstore kiss, Chase and I have seen each other a few times outside of school, but we've stuck to our own friend groups during lunch. So this really is the first official meeting of my boyfriend and my best friend.

"The dance team is great this year," Chase says. His mouth bends into an easy smile.

Sophie tugs on a few strands of hair that have escaped her slouchy gray beanie. She's had that hat for years, and I've always thought she looked so cute in it. (No, of course I never said anything.) "Thanks. Peter said you play guitar?"

"Peter is correct. You'll have to see us play." He bumps my shoulder with his. "Your friend here has some real skills."

"I know that," Sophie says, her voice tinged with a sharpness I'm not used to hearing.

I'm not clueless. If Sophie felt anything for me beyond friendship around the time of the party kiss, this can't be easy for her. While I don't want to make her uncomfortable, Chase is my boyfriend now. When I told her about him, she smiled and squealed and told me how happy she was. All I want is for the three of us to be able to spend time together. I don't want to live a life in segments.

"Should we go inside?" Chase says. His cheeks are red with cold. "It's freezing out here."

"I'm not sure inside will be any better, but yes," I say, opening the door for the three of us.

It's late November, the weeks between Thanksgiving and Christmas, when everyone decides ice-skating sounds like fun before realizing no one is actually very good at ice-skating. As a result, the rink is packed.

"Are you any good at this?" I ask Chase as we wait in line for skates. Ahead of us, Sophie tells the person at the counter both our sizes, six for her and ten for me.

"No idea. I haven't been since I was a kid."

Sophie hands me the skates. They're musty and damp and I have no desire to wear them, but I sit down, take off my shoes, and roll up my socks as high as they go to eliminate any accidental contact between the skates and my skin.

When I stand up, I'm immediately off-balance. The skates are too heavy on my feet, the blades awkward. Sophie grabs my arm, saving me from falling.

"You suggested skating so you could make fun of me," I tell her.

She holds a hand to her heart. "I would never do a thing like that."

Chase turns out to be so bad he wobbles like a baby giraffe still getting used to its feet, and I try hard not to laugh. Mostly because if I did, I'd want to cover my mouth, and I need my hands to cling to the wall.

A kid in the middle of the rink gracefully lands a double axel.

"He's mocking us," Chase says. "What a little asshole."

Sophie glides around effortlessly. Forward. Backward.

"You're making us look bad!" Chase calls to her.

She scuffs up some ice as she stops near where we're holding on to the wall. "Come on," she says to me, holding out her hands. The freckled tip of her nose is apple-red. "I'll help you."

I grip her mittens tight. She skates backward, which makes me feel even worse about my inability to skate a few inches forward.

"We'll start slow," she says.

"What about me makes you think I'm graceful at all?"

She bites her lip to avoid smiling. "Bend your knees. You're too stiff. And lean forward a bit."

I do, and it feels a little easier. A little less like I'm going to fall and break a leg at any instant. I throw a look over my shoulder at Chase, who's still against the wall, but the backward glance messes with my balance. My skate wobbles, and I slip, but Sophie holds me upright, a feat, given her size.

"I'm going to make us both fall," I say.

"No. I have you." Her gaze is solid, steady on mine, and it makes me believe her. "You won't fall. One foot, then the other. Good! Nice job."

She's definitely lying, but we manage one lap around the rink like this.

"You're getting better," Sophie says as we skate over to Chase. I half expect her to swap us out and help him around the rink, but why would she? She barely knows him. Instead, she tries tugging me along for lap two, but I pull my hands from her grasp.

"You go," I tell her. Her gaze flicks between Chase and me, her expression unreadable. I feel my face get hot, despite how arctic it is in here.

Chase shakes his head as he watches her skate away.

"What?" I ask, positive he'll say something about her skating skills. "I'm sorry this isn't as fun as Sophie thought it would be."

"Nah," he says. "It's not that. It's the two of you. Don't take this the wrong way, but . . . it's strange seeing you together. You guys are really different. If you lined up everyone at school and asked me to pick out your best friend, I can't imagine choosing her and going, 'Yes, you two are definitely best friends.'"

"Oh." I'm not entirely sure how to respond to this. "Well, we've been friends for a long time. We grew up together, right across the street." Suddenly I'm overwhelmed with the need to defend her.

"I'm sorry. I shouldn't even say anything, especially after what she did." He stares down at the ice. "I'm—I don't want you to think I'm jealous or anything. I swear that's not it."

"No, I get it." I watch her go past again. "Maybe we had more in common when we were younger."

It's not something I've allowed myself to say out loud, but as soon as I do, I regret it. *Gratitude*. That's how I should feel about Sophie. Our connection isn't obvious to an outsider—which, in a way, is what Chase is—but it's real to me, and to her.

There's something else, though, something that takes me a few moments to identify—a pang of *missing*. Like I miss Sophie even though she's right here, gliding along the ice in her gray beanie, fiery hair peeking out from beneath it.

We last another half hour before clomping off the ice and heading to a nearby coffee shop, where we snag a few chairs near the fireplace.

"How exactly did you guys become friends?" Sophie asks, holding her hands next to the fire to warm them up.

"English class." Chase takes a sip of a drink that's probably more chocolate than coffee. "Peter helped me with medieval literature. And then I heard him play piano, was mesmerized, and somehow talked him into playing with the band."

"Right, you really had to twist my arm."

"It was all an elaborate scheme to get you to go out with me." Chase slings an arm across the back of my chair, fingertips grazing my sweater. "You'll never know." All I want is to move closer to him—and it's not that I'm shy about displays of affection in public, given our first kiss was in a bookstore—but something in the way Sophie glances at Chase's arm on my chair and then very pointedly away turns my body to stone. I don't want to act like we're rubbing it in her face that we're together, not when she's looking at me like that. We all need more time to figure out how to navigate this.

"What kind of music is it, exactly?" Sophie asks.

"Hmm. Sort of like the Clash meets Death Cab with the voice of Debbie Harry," he says. Sophie gives a small shrug as though indicating she doesn't know them. "With a little Rufus Wainwright thrown in. I take it you're not as much of a Music Person as Peter?"

"Um, no, I definitely am," she says with an odd laugh. There's probably no greater insult than someone saying your taste in music isn't great or you don't know enough about it. "I'm not sure if Peter told you, but we used to have a band. Well. Kind of."

She puts an odd emphasis on the "we." I wonder if Chase hears it, or if I imagined it. *We* used to have a band.

Chase furrows his brow. "You did?" He looks almost hurt, like *you didn't tell me?* "What do you play?"

"It wasn't really a band," I say quickly.

"Peter played the piano while I choreographed dances," Sophie says. "So . . . not a traditional kind of band."

"Oh," Chase says. "Still. That sounds cool."

"It is," Sophie says, keeping it in present tense, though we haven't played together in months.

For a few moments, we sip in silence.

"Do you guys do anything for Christmas?" Chase asks.

"I'm Jewish," Sophie says.

"Oh—I'm sorry." Chase flushes. "I guess I meant Peter, since your mom's not Jewish. . . ."

"We have a tree," I say. I helped my mom decorate it last weekend. "And we do the present thing." When is my family not doing a present thing? "But it doesn't really have any religious significance."

That's true of all holidays, essentially: We celebrate everything, but nothing means very much. Though I'm hopeful going to temple will change that.

Sophie's still frowning, fidgeting with her hair.

"I don't like it when people assume," she says quietly. "Look around us." There are stockings dangling from the ceiling, our cups are printed with green and red patterns, and "All I Want for Christmas Is You" is playing from the speakers. "It's impossible not to be bombarded with it in December. I can't help feeling excluded all the freaking time."

"You didn't even want to go to temple with me," I say.

Her eyes cut to mine. "Not going to temple doesn't make me less Jewish. It doesn't mean I can't be offended by the assumption that because I live in America, of course I celebrate Christmas."

My stomach rolls over, and I stare down into my cup so I don't have to make eye contact with either of them. Sophie's never combative like this, and I'm not sure if it's because Chase struck a nerve or because this whole situation is new for us. I'm certain Chase didn't mean to offend her, but I also can't imagine how she feels this time of year. She's always talked about how even in liberal Seattle, everything is Christmas this time of year. While I've never minded it, part of me wonders if the proliferation of it subconsciously worked to make me forget about my Jewish side, to erase it. Until recently, at least.

"I'm so sorry," Chase says again, his cheeks pink with embarrassment. "I seriously didn't mean to assume."

"It's fine," she says with a wave of her hand.

"I guess this is why everyone says you shouldn't discuss religion," I joke, trying to lighten the mood. All I get are two tight-lipped smiles and more silent sipping.

"I should probably head home soon." Sophie checks the time on her phone. "I have dance team practice later." She swipes over to the bus app and sighs. "The next one isn't for forty-five minutes."

"I could give you a ride," Chase offers, his expression soft, as though he's trying to smooth things over with her.

"Are you sure? We're going to the same place, so I guess that would make it easier for you." Sophie softens, as though accepting Chase's olive branch. "Thanks. Peter, is that okay with you?"

I pick up my empty coffee cup and nod. Sophie and Chase's

first meeting was bound to be awkward. At least it wasn't a disaster.

In the parking lot, the three of us stand in front of Chase's car for a few moments.

"I'll ride in back with you," I say to Sophie.

"No, no, that's ridiculous," she says. "You both sit in the front. I don't want Chase to feel like he's chauffeuring us around."

"I don't mind!" he chirps as he unlocks it, sliding into the driver's seat.

I make a move to open the back door, but Sophie puts her hand over mine. "Peter. Seriously. Go up front."

"Or you could go up front."

She groans. "Oh my God, just go."

Fortunately, the car ride proves much less uncomfortable than skating or drinking coffee. As soon as Chase starts the car, an electronica song I've never heard starts playing, but Sophie yelps from the back, "I *love* this song," and Chase turns it up and they both belt out the lyrics. The entire exchange shocks me— Sophie's not the kind of person to sing in front of a stranger, much less *with* a stranger. But when I peer back at her, she's grinning.

The conversation flows a little easier after that. Chase apologizes once again about the Christmas faux pas, and Sophie wishes him a very happy Hanukkah.

When he pulls to a stop in our neighborhood, Sophie pops off her seat belt.

"Are you coming?" she asks me.

I glance over at Chase. "I, um, I think Chase and I might keep hanging out."

He nods.

"Oh." She fiddles with the strap of her bag. "Sure. Okay. That makes sense."

"I'll see you tomorrow, though? First night of Hanukkah at your house?"

"Right. Yes." She takes a moment, seems to collect herself. "Have a great time!" she says, much too enthusiastically. "I mean—not too great a time. Like, an average time. But still good?" Her face is red now. "Just . . . have fun."

"We'll try," I tell her. I'm not sure why it feels like the wrong answer.

I watch her in the rearview mirror until she becomes a best-friend-shaped dot, then disappears.

CHAPTER 25

SOPHIE

THE FIRST FEW MONTHS AFTER LUNA WAS BORN, she terrified me. She was so small, so delicate. I was afraid to even hold her. Tabby and Josh had enough help, anyway, with Luna's four grandparents. It was easy for me to fade into the background, slip across the street to Peter's whenever Luna tested the strength of her lungs.

It's an entire year and a half after she was born that I'm alone with her for the first time. Thursday night after winter break, Luna and I stare each other down for a solid couple minutes after Tabby and Josh leave. She's only just begun to string words into phrases, so it's not yet possible to have a real conversation with her, to ask her what she wants to do. I peek outside. No rain, and it's been a mild winter so far. We only get flurries and slush every other year, and every time, the entire city panics.

"How do you feel about going to the park?" I ask, careful to keep my voice from sliding into baby talk. Tabby and Josh are careful not to talk to her in that high-pitched voice people reserve solely for infants and puppies. Tabby told me normal speech is easier to understand and helps language development.

"Yes, please!" Luna says. At least she's a very polite eighteen-month-old.

I button her into a tiny coat and throw on my dance sweatshirt and a chunky scarf. On our way to Meridian Playground, she walks on her own, babbling to herself.

We play together on the slide until exhaustion from dance catches up with me, and I let her run around on her own while I park myself on a bench nearby. When I pull out my phone, I have a message from Montana. It's a link to a video, the final project she choreographed last year. I hit play and turn the volume down, watching the dancers move in a way that's both graceful and athletic, like most of the pieces Montana choreographs. *You can make this too*, she writes.

I mull over a few different responses before sending back I hope so with a dancer emoji. When I look up, Luna's got her fists buried in some bark—and it looks like she's chewing on something.

I spring to my feet, dropping my phone on the bench. "Luna? What are you eating?"

She turns to me, showing off a mouth smeared with blue. In her hand is a chunk of sidewalk chalk.

"Luna, no! You can't eat that!" I lunge toward her, but not

before she smashes the rest of the chalk into her mouth, swallows it, and offers me a very blue grin.

I drop to my knees in the bark and place a hand on each of her little shoulders. I only glanced away for a few seconds. A minute, tops. I pick her up—God, she's heavier than she looks—and plunk her onto the bench next to me. Grabbing my phone, I ask Google, "Can you eat chalk?" A list of potential symptoms freaks me out enough to call Poison Control. I find the number online and, thank God, someone picks up after the first ring.

"Poison Control."

"Hi, um, my niece ate a piece of chalk?"

"What's your name, ma'am?"

"Sophie."

"Sophie, calm down. We'll get through this, okay? I'm Diane."

"Okay. Diane. Thanks. Hi." *Breathe*. I wrap my free arm around Luna to keep her from squirming off the bench.

"How old is your niece?"

"One—one and a half."

"And she ate a piece of chalk?"

"Yeah. Sidewalk chalk. It's, um, blue." I let out another shuddery breath. I'm sure she doesn't need this last piece of information, but I feel compelled to add it.

"Fortunately, a small amount of chalk is nontoxic," Diane says.

"What exactly is a small amount?"

"Even if she ate an entire piece of it, she should be fine. Can you give her some water?"

"Um—" I didn't bring any with me. "I can, yeah."

"Great. Then what you want to do is watch her closely for any signs of lethargy or tummy troubles, like vomiting or diarrhea. If she exhibits any of those symptoms, you take her to the ER for further evaluation, okay?"

"God, I feel like such a fucking idiot. Sorry. Sorry for swearing."

"It's okay. I've heard worse. And this happens more often than you might think. Little kids are incredibly good at getting into things they're not supposed to. Your niece is going to be okay, Sophie."

"Thank you. Thank you so much."

I practically sprint home, tugging Luna alongside me. I watch her drink an entire sippy cup full of water. Then she grabs her favorite picture book and holds it up for me to read.

We settle into a living room armchair with the book. I'll only call my sister if she starts showing any of the symptoms Diane mentioned. If Luna's completely fine, there's no sense in worrying her. She deserves a night off.

"Again," Luna says when we finish the book for the third time. She doesn't mind my slow reading, and by this point I've nearly got it memorized. She's obsessed with this one; one night Tabby read it to her twelve times. But my voice is trembling, and I can't stop staring at her, as though something disastrous is about to happen.

It's only been twenty minutes. How long did Diane want me to wait? Why didn't I ask? God, I'm not sure I can handle this on my own. With shaking fingers, I call the only person who could calm my nerves.

"Hey. Are you home?" I ask, peering out our front window at his house. The shades in his room are drawn.

"Yeah, why?"

"Can you come over? It's kind of an emergency."

He must hear the panic in my voice. "I'll be right there."

And just like that, he is, in his REI jacket and thermal T-shirt and constancy.

It's strange, sometimes, that we still ring each other's doorbells, but I guess it's more out of habit than anything else. When Peter and I first started going to each other's houses, our parents would say, "Make sure you ask if Peter wants something to drink!" or "Did you ask if Sophie wants a snack?" Training us to be polite, even though we'd been friends for so long. We grew out of that, eventually stopped asking because the other person knew they could grab a water glass or an apple and it didn't matter.

"Did I interrupt you?" I ask, closing the front door behind him.

"I was just doing homework."

"Fun homework?" I examine his face—there's a brightness in his eyes I don't entirely recognize. "You look happy." I don't mean it as an accusation, but somehow it sounds like one.

It's been a couple weeks since the ice rink and the coffee shop and the awkward drop-off. A couple weeks of band practices and daylong weekend dates with Chase. This past week we saw each other only on morning rides to school.

I don't dislike Chase. Really, I don't. Jealousy—at least in the romantic sense—is part of it, of course. I can admit that. What's worse, though, is the fear that I'm losing Peter to Chase, to the band, to a world that doesn't have me in it. I've been slow to let Montana and Liz into my life, but Peter threw the door wide open for Chase and his band. He has been solely mine for so long, and now I am terrified he'll realize there are far more interesting people out there than the girl across the street.

"Homework is always fun, Soph." Without undoing the laces, he kicks off his shoes, then shrugs out of his jacket and hangs it on a hook in the hallway. He can't possibly feel that comfortable at Chase's house. I'm positive he wouldn't stride into Chase's kitchen and pour himself a glass of water. "What's wrong? You said it was an emergency?"

I gesture to where Luna's curled up in the armchair, focused on the pictures in her book. "Luna ate a piece of chalk, and I called Poison Control, and they told me she should be okay but that I should keep an eye on her. And I don't know if I can sit here and quietly freak out alone."

"You don't want to call Tabby?"

Again I consider it, tangling my fingers in the chain of my Star of David necklace. Then I shake my head. "I can't. This is my first time babysitting her, and I can't have fucked up like this, and . . . I really need everything to be okay."

He places his hands on my shoulders, the universal you-need-to-calm-down gesture. "I'll wait with you. You don't have to be alone."

Peter heads over to Luna, scooping her up and placing her in his lap. Obviously he's spent less time around her than I have, but there's an ease to his interactions with her that I can't help envying. Maybe he's naturally good with kids and we've never been around enough kids for me to realize it. When he reads to her, he's animated and all smiles, and I am putty on the couch next to them.

Eventually Luna's eyelids start to flutter, and we take her upstairs.

"Thank you so much for doing this," I whisper to Peter after we close the door to her room. We head down to the kitchen, where I place the baby monitor on the counter.

Peter leans against the counter next to the stove. "You don't have to thank me. This is . . . This is what we do."

"Do you want some pasta or something?"

"I could eat."

The next few moments happen in perfect tandem: Peter filling a pot with water, me fumbling in the cabinet for which of four different varieties of noodles I want. I decide on bow ties. I know they don't actually taste different from other pasta shapes, but they've always been my favorite.

There is something so effortless about him in my house like this, a time machine yanking me back a few years. When we attempted to make s'mores and we set off the smoke alarm. When the power went out and we ate organic knock-off SpaghettiOs out of a can and pretended it was a gourmet meal. When I got my first period and we were home alone and he was so terrified when I yelled from the bathroom that I was bleeding that he called 911.

Every space in my house has a Peter-memory attached to it, and I have ached for him in every one of those spaces.

"You're sure you don't have to get back to studying?" I ask, desperate for reassurance. What I'm hoping to hear: that he wants to be here with me, especially after the past few weeks have carved an odd distance between us.

"Eh, the excitement of it has worn off a little for me."

I mock-gasp. "Wait, are you saying you're not in love with school anymore? Are you realizing, like the rest of us, that it's not the most fantastic place in the world?"

"Shut up," he says, laughing. He flicks a salt granule at me.

Here we are: best friends bouncing back again.

It doesn't feel like enough.

When the water starts boiling, I drop bow ties into the pot. "Things have been weird between us," I say quietly, taking a chance. "It's like—it's almost like I'm not allowed to touch you anymore."

"What?" His eyebrows furrow, and he bites down on his bottom lip for a second. "Why wouldn't you be allowed?"

"Because of"—I wave my hand—"what . . . happened at the party. And because of—of Chase."

"Just because I'm dating someone doesn't mean we're not allowed to touch. We're best friends. Nothing can change that." He softens even more. "Soph. All of that's in the past. We've moved on."

I glance between the cloudy pasta water and his clear dark eyes.

"We're still us, right? Because—I miss you. I really, really miss you."

"I'm right here," he says, and with that, he leans in so I can hug him. It's such a relief to touch him that I nearly gasp as I place my head on his shoulder and press my nose into the softness of his sweater. I want to wrap it around me like a blanket so that all I see and breathe is Peter.

All of that's in the past.

We've moved on.

If friendship is the only way I can have him, then I should take it.

He probably doesn't know that he's holding me up. It's not just today with Luna that's sunk me underwater. It's realizing that this right here can't always happen, that he can't always be here for me. But today he is wholly mine. He wouldn't have let me deal with this on my own.

It is a fearless kind of hug. My legs tangle with his, and my heart hammers in my chest. Though it's probably been only a few weeks since we last hugged, I've missed this: our bodies pressed together like it doesn't matter that underneath these layers of fabric there are parts of him I desperately want to know. Even though I told myself we'd be friends and it would be fine.

I don't think I meant it.

"Maybe we can Terrible Twosome this weekend," I say to his shoulder.

"Yeah," he says. "Maybe."

"You really do seem so happy today." I drag my fingers along the back of his sweater. "I mean . . . I like it, I'm just . . . wondering if there's any particular reason."

I want him to tell me I make him happy. That he loves being here at my house doing something as basic as making pasta. That it's not Chase or the band—it's *me*.

"I'm alive," he says. "Isn't that the best reason?"

With my head on his chest, I close my eyes, satisfied with the answer for now. "It is," I whisper, feeling his heart beating against my cheek. *Tick, tick, tick.*

Steady as a bomb because of how dangerous he is.

CHAPTER 26

PETER

MY WEEKENDS CHANGE. THEY USED TO BE SOPHIE Time: the Terrible Twosome, a movie, a board game. Talking about insignificant things until they felt significant.

Now weekends are for the band, for Chase. I turn seventeen, and the band throws me a party at Aziza's house. Chase and I spend hours in used bookstores and coffee shops, and sometimes we find an all-ages show in the evening. We talk about music and about ourselves. We share secrets. We learn the geography of the back seat of his car.

Sophie and I talked about playing together, but I had band practice and she had dance team and we couldn't figure out a time that worked for both of us. And with our first show since I joined scheduled for next month, I'm busier than ever.

For the longest time, I wondered how I'd ever be able to be in a relationship with someone who knew so little about me. But the newness is what makes it exciting. It feels like I'll never stop learning about Chase, like how he's broken his right arm twice and unashamedly loves Maroon 5 and has a ring of freckles around his navel.

"How do you feel about boats?" he asks on a Saturday morning at the end of January.

I step onto my front porch to meet him but don't close the door behind me yet. "Good, I think?"

"There's this music store on Bainbridge Island with an incredible selection of vintage guitars. We'd have to take a ferry to get there."

I haven't been on a ferry in years, so I nod my agreement. "Before we go. Um." I peek into my house. "My parents want to meet you."

"I would love to meet your parents," he says, and they are suddenly at the door.

"This is Chase," I say, hoping my face isn't bright red. "Chase, my parents."

"Great to meet you," my dad says, enthusiastically pumping Chase's hand up and down. I silently beg him not to make a dad joke.

"Do you want to come in?" my mom says. "Can we get you a cup of coffee?"

"Actually," I say, "we were going to catch a ferry. So we should probably get going."

My parents trade a knowing smile.

"It's like you're worried we'll embarrass you," my dad says.

"Please. Embarrass him," Chases urges, eyes twinkling, and I groan.

"How long have you had your license?" my mom asks, and proceeds to ask a number of other questions about his driving record, despite the fact that I've been in a car with him before. I guess those times, he was a friend from school. Now he is my boyfriend.

Once Chase passes her test, we're on our way.

Even though it's cold, we climb up to the top deck of the ferry. The wind plays with our hair, and we tug our coats closer to our bodies before deciding tugging each other close is much better. Forty-five minutes later, we're back on land. Bainbridge Island is green and quaint, with mountains towering in the distance. In other words, it looks a lot like everywhere in the Pacific Northwest, but there's a comfort in that. There are always trees, always mountains, always water.

The music shop is at the end of the main drag.

Chase pauses in front of it. "My dad and I used to go here all the time," he says, and suddenly I understand, even more deeply, the appeal of this seemingly unremarkable music shop on an island an hour outside of Seattle. "It's where he got all his gear. And then, once I saved up, I got my first guitar here." He grins. "And, hopefully, my second guitar."

The Doors are playing inside, and it's not very busy.

"This is the one," Chase says, pointing at a stunning emerald-green Gibson Les Paul. "Gorgeous, right?"

"I'm almost afraid to touch it."

"Me too. Don't look at the price tag. It'll depress you."

We wander around the store for at least an hour, playing instruments we do and don't know how to play, browsing the massive record collection, talking, as usual, about the bands we love and how much they changed our lives.

Before we leave, Chase stops by the guitar again, grazing its lacquered surface with a few fingertips. "I'm coming back for you," he whispers to it.

We spend the rest of the afternoon exploring the island. The entire day feels like a page out of time. I want to bottle up these feelings, these carefree days with him. When was the last time I experienced anything like this, the pure bliss of not worrying about anything? There are no urgent doctor's appointments, no exhaustion, no exchanges, no specter of sickness.

It's then that I realize I've *never* felt anything like this, and so I tell him.

"You are a really great person to be around," I say as we stand together on a dock, gazing out at our city. "You know that?"

He moves his hands from behind my back to the sides of my face. "That's . . . wow. I think that's the nicest thing anyone's ever said to me."

I laugh. "I'm serious. Can we do this every Saturday?"

"Absolutely," he says, and kisses me.

On our drive back to Seattle, Chase drums on the steering wheel, humming along to the music.

During a lull in one of the songs, I tell him, "My parents went out with Sophie's tonight. So . . . no one's at my house."

"Huh," Chase says. "I'm not sure why I'd be interested in that."

"Yeah, I figured you wouldn't be."

"The Forty-Fifth Street exit and then a left on Latona?"

"A left on Latona," I echo.

His jaw drops when he sees the grand piano in the living room. "Fucking hell. It's *beautiful*. Play something?"

I sit down and start "Clocks," which makes him groan.

He sits down on the bench next to me facing the opposite direction. "I wanted to talk to you," he says, drawing circles on my knee with a fingertip, "about the Sophie stuff."

The Sophie stuff. It sounds almost trivial, the way he says it, and for a moment my stomach twists in annoyance.

"We don't—"

"No. We do. Or I do, at least." He takes a deep breath. "I need you to know that I haven't been weird about it because you're bi."

"Oh—okay," I say, but I'm glad he says it. "I . . . appreciate that. I told you I liked her once, but trust me, that's completely over. I'm with *you*."

"I believe you," he says. "I know you've been friends forever. And I don't want to feel like I'm competing with her. I probably just need to get to know her better."

The annoyance fades. He doesn't understand Sophie and me, it's true—but I love that he wants to try.

"That means a lot," I say quietly, pressing closer to him.

"You have always looked so good behind that thing." He leans his head on my shoulder. "I don't know if there's anything hotter than a guy who plays piano."

"A guy who plays guitar?"

He kisses my neck, and I have to adjust so that we're facing each other on the bench. Then I get up, beckoning for him to follow me down the hall.

"Is that Mark?" Chase asks when we get inside my room, pointing to the chinchilla cage.

"That's Mark. I always thought it would be funny to have a pet with, like, a super-basic white-guy name."

"Mark," Chase says again. "Mark the chinchilla."

"You want to hold him?" I ask, already unlatching his cage.

His eyes get huge behind his glasses as I pass over the little mound of fur that is Mark. "I can't believe how soft he is." He runs a hand along Mark's back. "Oh my God, I think I love him."

I head over to my music collection and record player. "What do you want to listen to?" I ask.

"Something good."

"I'm not sure I like the insinuation that I own anything bad."

I help Chase return Mark to his cage, and he joins me in front of my record collection. Eyes wide, he pulls one out. "The Carpenters? You don't strike me as a Carpenters fan."

"They're good," I say. "And what does a Carpenters fan look like?"

"They're kind of, like, easy listening, aren't they?"

Shaking my head, I extract their self-titled album from its sleeve. "Their music is just . . . beautiful. That's the best word for it. Heartbreaking, too. Incredible lyrics."

I watch him, waiting for his reaction to "Rainy Days and Mondays."

"It's good," he says, and I let out a sigh of relief.

I wrap my arms around him, liking him in my room while the Carpenters are playing way too much. My room isn't the prison I thought it was after all.

This time when we kiss, it feels more like a prelude to something else. It starts slowly, sweetly, but quickly grows more desperate as I guide him over to my bed. I need more of him to get my hands on. I start unbuttoning his shirt, his chest warm beneath my hands.

"Your room is so organized," he says. He gestures to his shirt. "Do you want me to hang this up?"

Laughing, I help him take it off and toss it to the floor. I throw mine off too, and we sit there for a few moments, taking each other in.

"I love your cheekbones," he says, skating his thumb up and down the planes of them. "Is that weird? I don't know. I just find them really sexy."

All this time, I've been living with clandestinely sexy cheekbones. "No. I'm glad you like them. I—I find all of you really sexy." I tap his glasses. "Including these."

He smiles, removing them and setting them on my nightstand. When he comes back to me, his eyes go to the scar on my abdomen. I've been so wrapped up in him that I've forgotten to feel self-conscious about my body. He touches the scar gently, gently, first with his fingertips, and then with a brush of his lips.

"Is this okay?" he asks. "It doesn't hurt or anything?"

"All of it is okay. More than okay."

We make a fantastic mess: belts, jeans, socks flung onto the floor. His fingers travel south from my hips, and I think I might pass out. Time becomes meaningless. I blink, and my boxers are off. Blink again and his are too. Blink, blink, blink because how— is—this—happening? How can it all feel so good?

I've never been fully naked in front of anyone like this before, my desire for him so obvious. Without moving his eyes from mine, he curls his hand around me and starts tugging up, down, *yes*. I reach for him too. Everything is too vivid: the way he feels in my hand, his moan into my ear, another new favorite sound.

"Every time I hear this song," he says between heavy breaths, "and I'm going to add it to all my playlists, so it's gonna be a lot—I'm going to think about this."

It's that that undoes me, and he isn't far behind.

Eventually the record stops, and I turn it over for "Superstar" before returning to him.

Chase sighs, content. "The band thought that was pretty great," he says.

We hold each other in my bed for a while, because there's no rush to leave this room. He drums a melody on my back while I play an accompaniment on his rib cage.

CHAPTER 27

SOPHIE

IN THE MIDDLE OF JANUARY, I GO WITH LIZ TO A Queens of Night signing at a big independent bookstore north of Seattle.

"I can't believe we're about to meet Emi Miyoshi," Liz says as we push open the doors, her cape swishing behind her. She went all out as Nadiya, the Queens of Night protagonist who may or may not die in book four: lavender wig, false lashes, cape, and a double-bladed knife, Nadiya's trademark weapon.

The YA section of the store has been decorated like the Queens court, with black and purple columns and a replica of the gazebo where Nadiya was forced to betray her beloved to save her people.

"I'm more nervous than I thought I'd be," I admit.

Liz hefts her tote bag, filled with the original hardcovers, to her other shoulder. She explained something to me about a midseries cover redesign that I didn't quite follow but apparently upset a lot of fans.

"Me too. How can I possibly explain to her that her books changed my life?" She gives me a black-lipsticked smile, which looks only slightly menacing. "I'm so glad you came. These kinds of things aren't nearly as fun alone, and Montana's not really into Queens. Which is fine," she adds quickly.

Most of the chairs are already filled, but Liz and I managed to snag two in the third-to-last row, next to a trio of girls dressed as Deathhawks, the evil creatures the villain Svetna tamed to do her bidding.

"You want to work in publishing?" I ask, remembering Montana having mentioned it earlier this year.

Liz nods and pushes some lavender wig-bangs out of her face. "What I really want is to find the next Queens. The next Emi Miyoshi. Not just a blockbuster series, but a game-changing one, something that's never been done before."

"It's so cool you have two things you're so passionate about: dance and books." Peter's always had multiple passions too: books and music and Mark. I've only had one.

Well, two: Peter . . . and dance. Dance was always the afterthought, the second choice—until this year, at least. I loved the Sophie I was in that Spokane hotel room. Not even Peter knows that version of me, and I sort of like that there's a part of me he doesn't know, that I can be a mystery too. Peter has his band, and I have my team. It's natural for us to be exploring new things.

Liz shrugs. "Honestly, I've danced for a long time, but I'm not as into it as I used to be. If Montana weren't on the team, I'd probably have quit by now. But *you* . . . I've got a good feeling about you and the summer workshop."

My stomach twists as I imagine checking Instagram every day for photos of Peter and Chase and #bandbffs hashtags. I remind myself I have a world he's not part of too. *Natural.* This is natural.

"Yeah." I swallow. "Fingers crossed."

"I want to hear all about it. You'll text me, right?"

Liz . . . wants me to text her this summer? I guess I assumed our friendship or whatever it is expires in June, when we graduate.

So I blurt it out: "Why are you guys friends with me? You and Montana?" When she raises her eyebrows, I backtrack. "I mean . . . what do you get out of it?" God, I'm sweating now. Why did I ask that? I don't need my insecurities validated, don't need Liz to tell me it's because they feel sorry for me. I've never done anything to indicate I'd be a decent friend. I don't crack jokes; I don't have insight to add to a conversation. I'm only like that around Peter.

Full of regret, I shrink back into my chair as Liz gapes at me.

"What do we get out of it?" Liz repeats. "We like you? We don't have to get anything out of it. It's not, like, a transaction."

My voice is small. "I thought you felt sorry for me? Or you wanted someone to come with you to this signing because Montana didn't want to?"

273

"Sophie!" Liz almost sounds offended. "No. You're our friend. You're interesting, okay? You're fun. That conversation we had in the car on the way over, about what Nadiya's life in exile might have been like? I've never been able to talk to anyone else about things like that. And what you did on the phone in the hotel? Hilarious. Montana thinks your routine is brilliant, and . . . Have I inflated your ego enough, or should I keep going?"

I laugh, not entirely used to the warmth spreading through me. I want so badly to believe her. "I—I think that's good. It feels pretty inflated."

She shakes my shoulder. "Seriously. I'm so glad we got to know you better this year. I couldn't handle being alone in my Queens fandom any longer."

And I want to be the best version of Sophie even when I'm not with Peter—someone as bright as the person he sees.

Emi Miyoshi's talk is spoiler-free and wonderfully tantalizing; by the end of it, I'm already dying to start the latest book on audio. She's dressed like Liz—well, like a lot of the girls and some of the guys here—in a floor-length dress, feathered cape, and purple-black lipstick. After reading a few pages from her upcoming book, the first in a new series, she takes questions from the audience. Liz raises her hand but doesn't get called on, and I can tell she's not letting on how disappointed she is.

We make our way into the signing line, Liz lugging her tote bag and a couple new paperbacks, though she already has the hardcovers. When it's our turn, Liz rolls up her sleeve and shows Emi the tattoo she got that represents the ruling family from the book.

Emi gasps and drags Liz's arm closer. "This is excellent. Are you serious? I've never seen anyone get ink from one of my books! Can I take a picture and tweet it out?"

"Um, *yes*," Liz squeals, beaming as Emi snaps a photo. They chat about some lingering questions at the end of the series, which I try to tune out since I'm not there yet, and Emi signs every one of Liz's books with a purple pen.

When I pass my book to her, I do so with an awkward hello. Emi is the most famous person I've ever met, and I'm suddenly much shyer than usual.

"Who should I make it out to?" she asks.

I'm about to say *Peter*—I'd planned to surprise him with an autographed copy. But after my conversation with Liz, I'm not so sure.

"Sophie," I say, and it feels right. "S-O-P-H-I-E. Thank you so much."

Afterward, Liz and I browse the aisles, cracking up at books in the humor section and talking about how nice Emi was— "She's so famous, she doesn't have to be that nice, but she *is*"— and how amazing she looked.

"This was so fun," Liz says as we get into her car. "Even though, you know, I didn't get anything out of it."

I whack her with my copy of *Queens*. "Oh my God, stop. I get it. You like me, for some inexplicable reason." Liz raises her eyebrows. I roll my eyes and lay on the sarcasm: "Fine, you like me because I am a source of never-ending joy."

She hugs me. "I do," she says, "and you are."

It's past ten when I get home. The light in Peter's room across the street was off, but my house hasn't gone to sleep yet. Tabby and Josh are in the kitchen yelling at each other. Luna's in her high chair, wailing, and Tabby's still in her waitress uniform, a syrup-and-ketchup-stained apron tied around her waist.

I'm frozen in the hallway for a few moments, wondering if I should disappear into my room or attempt to intervene. Old Sophie would have disappeared for sure. But now . . .

"What have you sacrificed, Josh?" Tabby's saying, sounding unlike I've ever heard her. Her tone of voice—the frantic desperation in it—cuts at something deep inside me.

"You think I haven't sacrificed anything?" Josh says. "I haven't exactly had a normal high school life either. I can always tell when someone's been talking about me. The room goes quiet as soon as I walk into it. You know how often that happens, Tab? Every single day."

Tabby scoffs. "I'm sorry being in school is *so* hard for you."

"You're the one who decided online classes were the better choice so you could have a more flexible schedule."

They don't fight like this. They *never* fight like this. Of course I didn't assume their relationship was perfect, but I never imagined either of them had lungs like this. I glance between the darkened staircase and the scene in the kitchen.

"And have you ever heard me complain?"

A squeaky floorboard makes my decision for me. Tabby's and Josh's heads whip my way.

"Sophie," Tabby says, and as I inch closer, I notice how red her face is. "We didn't hear you."

"Sorry. I just got back. Where are Mom and Dad?"

"Out with Peter's parents," Tabby says.

"I'm going to take a walk." Josh breezes right by me into the hallway, where he grabs his coat. "I gotta cool down."

"We're not done here." Tabby stalks toward him, Luna still crying. "Josh. *Josh*. Don't you dare leave right now."

It's only then, with Josh on his way out the door, that reality dawns: They could break up. Though I complain about Josh being here all the time, he's become as much a fixture in my life as Luna.

"Sophie," Tabby says, halfway into her own coat. "Can you put Luna to bed? I have to go talk to him."

"Yeah," I say, though I'm frozen in the kitchen. "Go. Go. Do what you need to do."

The front door slams once, twice, and then I'm left with my niece again. I make myself spring to life because this small human needs me.

"Hey, baby girl," I say, slightly more at ease with her now. When I told Tabby that Luna had eaten a piece of chalk, she was much calmer than I expected. She said I did exactly what she would have done, that it could have happened to anyone, and to call her next time. I take Luna upstairs to her room, where we read her favorite book over and over. My parents come home, but Tabby and Josh don't. I rock her for a while and then gently lay her in her crib and turn on the baby monitor, which I take into my room.

My phone lights up with an event invite as I collapse into bed. Montana's having a dance team sleepover next weekend—on the same night as Peter's band's first show.

It hits me hard that I'd much rather go to Montana's.

If I went to the party, would Peter be upset I missed his first show? He'll have other shows, right? And . . . it's not like he'd be able to see me in the audience. I can barely pick people out of a crowd when I'm performing.

I've got to figure out how to stop this. How to fall out of love with him, how to unbind us when what I've done has connected us for years to come. Because this is what part of me, an awful part, still hopes: that if I give him enough time, Peter will realize I'm worth a relationship, worth giving a chance. That he barely knows Chase and I am the one who's always been here for him. That the connection to him I feel, the one that vibrates beneath my skin when he's near me, isn't one-sided.

And I can't put that sliver of a chance in jeopardy.

There's no real choice to make. Peter comes first. That's how it's always been.

Peter is running toward the things he loves. I'm not sure why it sometimes feels like I'm running away from mine.

As I hit NO on the RSVP to Montana's sleepover, I lie back down on my bed. It takes a lot of energy to love someone this much without being loved back the way you want. It drains you.

I have never felt quite this drained before.

I'm putting on pajamas when I hear the front door open and shut, followed by footsteps coming up the stairs. Then there are the soft sounds of Tabby crying as she checks on her baby across the hall, then turns to face my door.

I've already opened it for her.

"Hey," she says, her voice cracking the word in two. "Can I—"

I wave her inside. In the light, her face is blotchy, and I can tell she's trying to hold it together.

"Tabby," I say, and wrap my arms around her. Her body relaxes into mine, shoulders heaving. I pull her onto the bed with me.

"I am such a mess." She inhales deeply, reaching around me for the box of tissues on my nightstand.

"Did you—did you guys—" I can't even get out the question.

"Did we what?" Her eyes grow large as she realizes what I meant. "Did we *break up*? No! No, we're okay. Or . . . we will be."

"Do you . . . want to talk about it?"

She shakes her head. "No. Not right now. Could we just . . . watch something stupid and mindless? Or talk about literally anything else?"

I bring my laptop onto the bed with us. "There's a new season of *The Bachelor*."

"Perfect."

We watch together for a while—an episode, then two, of contestants accusing each other of being there for the wrong reasons. I wish I could more easily slip into an older-sister role, give Tabby the comfort she needs.

But maybe this is exactly what she needs right now: some-one next to her.

Me next to her.

CHAPTER 28

PETER

"WHEN WE GET FAMOUS," KAT SAYS AS SHE DABS glitter onto her eyelids, "we should have ridiculous preshow requests."

Chase glances up from his guitar. "Like Van Halen and the brown M&M's?"

We're in the green room at the Blaze, a teen center converted from an old firehouse. Everyone has their own warm-up rituals: Dylan is tuning his bass, Chase is playing some warm-up exercises, Kat is applying meticulous makeup, and Aziza is in the corner, sharing earbuds with Bette. She gets terrible stage fright, and listening to thrash metal, somehow, is the only thing that calms her down.

Given that it's my first show, I'm not sure what my ritual is yet. Before piano recitals, I usually tinkered with my phone or attempted small talk with the other kids. But this is different.

There's a whole audience out there who paid five bucks to see us, not just parents waiting for their kids to bang out "Heart and Soul."

"Exactly like Van Halen and the brown M&M's," Kat says.

"Brown M&M's?" I repeat.

Kat stows her pot of glitter and reaches for a tube of lipstick. "Van Halen specified in their concert rider that they wanted a bowl of M&M's with all the brown ones removed."

"It was actually a smart business move," Chase continues, "because they had this elaborate stage setup. So if they got backstage and saw brown M&M's in the bowl, they knew the venue hadn't paid attention to the contract and would have to double-check all their lighting and everything."

"Does anyone *have* M&M's? I want some," Dylan says, and Kat rolls her eyes.

"Knock-knock," comes a quiet voice from the doorway. Sophie, wearing tight black pants, a black sweater, and a swipe of dark red lipstick. All dressed up for my first show. She holds up a water bottle. "Peter, I brought you this. In case you need it onstage?"

"Thanks," I say, accepting it.

There are no free chairs, so she leans against my keyboard amp. We rode over with Chase. When we got here and I explained to the band that Sophie had known me forever, Kat asked immediately if she had any embarrassing stories about me as a kid. Sophie blushed. "So many," she said, and it made me happy, seeing her gain a bit of confidence with my new friends, "but my allegiance is to Peter. I'm sorry." My bandmates groaned, and I grinned at her, liking her here with us so, so much and unsure why it took so long for this to happen.

Worlds colliding.

Kat drops her lipstick into her bag. "What kind of music are you into, Sophie?"

"Mostly modern stuff," Sophie says. "I listen to a lot of remixes, I guess?"

"Have you heard the Manic Pixie Dreamboats? Or Chekhov's Toothbrush?"

Sophie gives her a blank look. "Guess not," she mutters. Suddenly her face pinches—it lasts only a split second, but it's long enough for me to notice.

"Soph?"

"What?"

I lift my eyebrows at her. "What was that, just now?"

"Nothing," she says quickly, right before it happens again. This time, she slides along my keyboard amp to the floor, clutching her abdomen.

All her life, Sophie's never complained about illness or injury. Ankle sprains, common colds, stomachaches—she waves it all off. It's why I'm convinced whatever is going on right now is something more serious.

"Shit, are you okay?" Dylan says.

"Fine," she squeaks, but her eyes are squeezed shut.

Everything around me dims as I focus solely on her, my mind spinning.

"We're on in ten," someone says. Chase? Dylan? I'm not sure.

"Sophie?" I lower myself to the floor next to her as she tucks her knees to her chest and shakes her head.

"What's going on?" Aziza.

"Is it cramps?" Kat.

I need everyone to be quiet for a moment so I can understand what's happening.

"Is it—" I ask Sophie, unsure how to finish the question. *Is it the transplant? Is it me?* Slowly, almost imperceptibly, she nods. It's a boulder shoved into my chest. The lowest A on a piano. "Has this happened before?"

"A . . . few times."

Five worried faces peer down at us. Chase is the only one who knows about the transplant, and I'm not sure I want to get into my—*our*—entire medical history right now with the rest of the band.

"Should we call an ambulance?" he says.

"No!" Sophie cries out, a little too loudly. Then, more softly: "No. I don't want to freak out my parents."

But she looks so tiny curled up against the amp, hair falling in her face as she clings to her knees.

I did this to her, and I've never felt so helpless.

Is this how Sophie felt with me for all those years?

"Why didn't you tell me?" I ask, gently brushing her knee. *Because she's too good. Because she didn't want me to feel the way I do now.*

"It doesn't happen very often, and the pain—I can usually take a few ibuprofen and it'll go away."

"Usually," I repeat, running my hands over my face.

"I have some," Kat volunteers, rummaging through her messenger bag and passing Sophie a blue bottle. I hand her the water bottle she gave me so she can swallow them.

"Let's give her some space," Dylan says, and everyone but me backs up a few paces in the small green room.

But Sophie—she scoots closer to me, her body crumpling against mine, and I stretch an arm around her to rub her back. I've always liked the way her body fits against mine, that I'm able to hold her like this. Chase's eyes meet mine, a frown tugging at his mouth. *Don't look at me like that*, I want to tell him. This isn't anything but one best friend comforting another.

"It happens sometimes, right after a transplant?" I say, more to convince myself that this is normal. *Right after*. It's been more than six months. I have no idea if this is normal.

"Sometimes," she says. "Sometimes later. Sometimes it lasts a long time. That's what they said. There haven't been a ton of studies done about chronic pain in organ donors yet."

"A long time as in the rest of your life?"

She doesn't say anything.

Someone knocks on the green room door. "Diamonds Are Forever?"

"For *Never*," Dylan corrects.

"Right. You guys are up in five."

"We should head out there," Aziza says, but I don't budge. To me, she adds: "You . . . want me to help you with your amp?" Her kit's already assembled behind the stage. Everyone else grabs their instruments.

Sophie is not okay, and it's *my fucking fault*. How can I go out there and play "Precipitation" and "Bad Ideas" knowing she's back here suffering?

"Peter," Sophie says softly, as though reading my mind. "You have to go."

"Give me a couple minutes," I tell the band.

"Okay." Kat offers Sophie a sympathetic smile. "I hope you feel better."

Everyone leaves but Chase, Sophie, and me. Three statues in a tiny room. Chase is still standing, guitar slung low across his chest, staring down at us as he turns a pick over and over in one hand.

Sophie breaks the silence. "I—I think I'll take an Uber home." The pain makes her stammer. Twists my heart. "I really want to hear you guys, but—"

"We'll have other shows," I say, but my voice sounds distant, like it belongs to someone else. "I'll come home right after."

"She's going to be fine," Chase says, and maybe it's meant to be reassuring, gentle, but I detect an undeniable thread of annoyance. "We're only going to be out there for half an hour, tops."

Half an hour, and then I can rush home to her. Okay.

I stand and hold out my hands to help her up. As I pull her to her feet, she gasps, collapsing against me, and I only just barely manage to keep her from falling to the floor.

"Sophie!"

"It's—fine," she grits out, grabbing at her abdomen, but it's so clearly not. She doesn't have to put on a mask with me. She needs someone to help her outside, to sit in the car with her, to make sure she gets home okay.

I can't leave her. And despite that my band is waiting for me, I don't *want* to leave her either.

Over the top of her head, I flick my gaze over to Chase. "I can't go. Onstage, I mean. You're"—I swallow—"you're going to have to play without me."

Chase's shoulders rise and fall. His eyes move between Sophie and me, and then he nods once, as though suddenly understanding something. It makes my stomach drop to my toes because that is *not* what this is. He can't even see it. Can't tell the difference between what this is and what it isn't.

"We played without a keyboard before," Chase says. "I guess we can do it again."

Then he's gone, leaving Sophie and me alone in the green room, pressed up against my keyboard amp that won't be amplifying any keyboards tonight.

"I'm sorry," Sophie's saying as she slides back down to the floor, and I join her there. "I'm so sorry."

"Hey." I touch her knee. "There's nothing to be sorry about."

The sounds of stage setup echo back to us: the beats of a bass drum, a guitar lick from Chase. I can't hear them introduce

287

themselves, but I imagine it: *We're Diamonds Are for Never, and we were always meant to have only four people!*

Then the opening chords of our cover of "This Is Radio Clash." *Their* cover. My chest aches with longing, though I'm confident I made the right choice. I'm here with Sophie, who gave me more than anyone ever could.

"I'll get an Uber," I say. "If you think you can make it out there?"

"I might need a few minutes." She pauses, and then: "Could you maybe just call my dad? That way you could stay here, and I don't have to ruin your entire night."

"Sophie," I start, intent on telling her she isn't—of course she isn't—but she just raises her eyebrows, and I relent.

He and Sophie's mom are at a restaurant, but he says they'll be here in fifteen minutes.

"My parents are obsessed with yours now," I say to Sophie, trying to lighten the mood. To distract her.

"The feeling seems to be mutual."

Her makeup is smeared, and as though compelled by instinct, I reach up to swipe off the black streaks beneath her eyes.

"What are you doing?" she asks, a laugh in her voice.

"I . . . don't know," I say, laughing now too. "Your makeup looked so nice earlier."

"Is that a compliment?"

"Yeah. Yeah, I guess it is."

We're quiet for a few moments, Sophie's mascara tattooed on my thumb. Her knees are still pulled up to her stomach, and while I'm sitting close to her, we're not quite touching. Together we listen to the applause after one song and then another.

"I'm so sorry," she says to her knees for the twelfth time. "I feel shitty about all of this. I didn't want you to miss the show, I swear. I know you guys have been practicing so much, and—"

"Hey. *Stop*." I scoot closer, placing a hand on her shoulder, trying to get her to look at me. "This is exactly where I want to be right now. Obviously it would be better if you were feeling okay, though."

She lifts her head, and something about her expression, the pureness of it, kills me a little. It's gratitude and pain and still, I think, *love*. I'm not sure what kind—only that I'm lucky to have it, something I wonder if I forgot or at least pushed to the back of my mind over the past few months. I'm lucky to have this girl in my life, this girl who changed my life.

"Thank you," she whispers.

"Is there anything I can do for you right now? Before your parents get here?"

She shakes her head. "Maybe—you could just hold me?"

"I can absolutely do that."

I put one arm around her shoulders and one around her legs, and she leans into me, settling one of her palms against my chest. Tonight she smells like some foreign perfume mixed with something achingly familiar. I rest my chin in her hair, and although it tickles, I don't dare move.

We stay nearly frozen like that for a while, breathing each other in.

When Sophie's parents arrive, promising to call the doctor on Monday, I load my keyboard and amp into their car but decline a ride home. Instead I hide in the back of the crowd during the next two bands' sets and then wait in the loading zone behind the venue for Chase. Regardless of how worried I am about Sophie, she'll be fine with her parents, and Chase and I left too many words unsaid between us.

It's colder than it usually is in February in Seattle, and my hands are frozen. If I tried to play piano now, it would be slow and stilted.

Chase is the last one out, after I've traded awkward, sympathetic good-byes with the rest of the band. At first he says nothing as he loads his guitar case into his car. Then he shuts the trunk and walks right over to me.

"I'm not going to pretend I'm not angry about this," he says, hands jammed in his pockets, breath meeting the air in white puffs. "But I also want to make sure she's okay."

"Her parents picked her up. They'll go to the doctor next week."

"Okay." He's quiet for a few moments.

"I'd hope someone's health would be more important than some show." It's not the nicest thing to say, I realize that. But his coldness toward Sophie is a little maddening.

"Did I not just ask how she was?"

"Not before informing me how pissed you were. So I could

tell you really cared." I cross my arms, unsure where this com-
bativeness is coming from, this protectiveness of Sophie.

"Seriously?" he says. "You *bailed* on us!"

"Because the girl who gave me a kidney was in pain! I'm
sorry if that takes precedence."

"And you're a doctor? You staying with her made that much
of a difference?"

That hits a nerve. "Yeah. It did."

Chase scuffs the frozen ground with his shoe. "Is she always
going to come first?" he asks, his brows drawn in a way that
makes him look more hurt than angry. It's not an accusation. It's
an honest question, and it makes me think.

"I—don't know." I bite down on the inside of my cheek.
Tonight she came first. She had to. Will she come first for a few
more months? Years? As long as her kidney is functioning in my
body?

He's shaking his head. "Peter. Sophie loves you, and not just
as a friend. It's . . . frankly pretty obvious."

My first instinct is to deny it—but nothing comes out of my
mouth. If it's true, there's something undeniably flattering about
it. Something that ignites a dormant part of my heart.

Something I felt when I was holding her earlier.

"I really like you," he continues. "But . . . I don't want to get
in the middle of whatever you have with Sophie, and it's becoming clear that I am."

"You're not," I insist, not fully believing myself.

"I felt it when we were ice-skating. And then you and me, at your house . . ." He blushes. "I thought it was going to be fine. I thought I would be able to ignore the deep connection you two have because you and I were building something of our own. When it's only the two of us, Peter, it's perfect. But I don't want to be constantly competing. Because you know what? She's always going to win. She's known you longer, and she made a sacrifice that, to be honest, I'm not sure I ever could."

"Sophie is my best friend. I've known her practically my entire life."

"I'm not asking you to stop being friends with her. I know there's plenty of stuff I'm not going to understand."

"I'm not asking you to understand! Just to *try*." I throw up my hands. "She—the entire reason I can even do this with the band is because of her."

"And what she did was *amazing*," Chase says. "I won't ever deny that. I don't want to be jealous, but I am, and I know part of that is my fault. I'm jealous of your best friend who gave you a kidney—because she gave you that and now she wants more from you, more than you want to give, maybe, and you won't tell her no. You won't tell her you need space. Maybe you feel like you owe her, or—"

"Don't use that word," I hiss at him. "Please. I don't—I can't go through life thinking I owe her."

A few late concertgoers make their way out of the venue, clutching their coats against the cold. Laughing.

"I think—" he starts when they're out of earshot, and then immediately stops. Brings a fist to his mouth, as though quite literally preventing himself from saying whatever he's about to say next. "I think we don't have a real chance until you figure things out with Sophie first."

A strange sound tumbles out of my mouth. "What are you talking about?" There's nothing to figure out with Sophie.

"Come on. You can't be that naive." There's a harshness in his tone that wasn't there a second ago, as though my perceived naivete offends him.

I take a few breaths, a few steps back. "I don't get why you'd even *say* something like that."

"Peter—Jesus Christ. You're so fucking smart. How do you not get it?" He holds out his arms as though reaching peak frustration. Chase probably curses more than I do, but there's something staggering about the way he wields it this time. "There's something there. I don't know if it's that you guys have been friends forever or what, but . . . there's something there."

There's something there.

Is there?

Sophie dancing on a football field.

Sophie kissing me at that party.

Sophie in the green room next to me, her body against mine.

My mind is like a scratchy old record, unable to play the track I thought I wanted. Instead it's skittering all over the place.

"I like *you*," I tell him.

"And I think some part of you might still like her, too." It's a tissue-paper theory, light as air.

I hold it in my hand, testing its weight.

Sophie with a scar to prove how much I mean to her.

Sophie. Sophie. Sophie.

It's entirely possible he sees something I don't. Something I haven't seen in a while.

"I don't—" I start, but I don't trust myself anymore. "Chase, *please*."

"Don't make this harder than it already is." He rakes a hand through his hair. "I'm giving you permission to pick her. Okay? She wins."

Those words cut deep. He says them so matter-of-factly. "I don't need your permission," I fire back.

Behind his glasses, his eyes blaze. "I *know* that. I was trying to be civil about all of this. But it doesn't seem like that's possible anymore."

My heart is racing. "Wait. Are we broken up? Is that what's happening?"

A beat. Then: "Yeah," he says, softly now. "Yeah. I guess we are."

Your first boyfriend is supposed to break your heart, Chase said all those weeks ago, and then shattered mine in a parking lot at midnight. A freaking premonition, that's what it was.

I don't respond. Can't. The cold has fused my jaw shut. I stand frozen in the parking lot as he gets in his car and pulls away. It's only after he's gone that I fumble on my phone for the bus schedule.

I'm going home, but not to my house. There's only one person I want to—*need* to—see after all this. The force of it is so strong, a buzzing beneath my skin. And it makes me wonder if Chase was right.

CHAPTER 29

SOPHIE

I NEED TO SEE YOU.

The text from Peter sends sparks through my body.

He *needs* me.

He needs *me*.

It's past midnight and the house is quiet. Tabby, Josh, and Luna are at his place, and my parents went to sleep downstairs shortly after they thought I did. I've been in bed, but I haven't been sleeping. For a while the pain kept me awake, but eventually it faded.

I missed Montana's dance sleepover because of Peter, and he missed his set because of me. There's an odd poetry to that. We've always been intertwined, our lives tangled. And now we are a great big knot.

Come over, I message Peter, and then I creep out of bed and into the bathroom across the hall, certain there's enough electricity in my body to make my hair stand on end. Quietly I brush my teeth. I put my hair up and then back down. I change out of pajamas and into cuter pajamas.

Peter messages me when he arrives, about twenty minutes later. My heart is thudding in my throat as I tiptoe downstairs and let him in, and then, as silently as possibly, lead him up to my room.

It's only when I close the door and switch on a small bedside lamp that I see he's a complete mess.

My Peter, falling apart.

He's trembling, crying, making an effort to do it softly so my parents don't hear him. He's never been shy about crying in front of me, or about crying in general. Not when we were kids, and not now.

He follows me into my bed without me even asking him to join me there. I prop the pillows against the headboard so we can lean against them. He's much taller than I am, but he feels limp, smaller than usual. And he is so cold. I run my hands over his ears and his cheeks, trying to warm him up. He's still wearing a coat, and I'm in shorts and a tank top. His skin chills mine, and I help him out of the coat so we can be even closer.

"Can you—hold me for a while?" he whispers, and my heart breaks in half. It's what I asked him to do for me earlier tonight.

It's all I want to do, but I have to know. "What happened?"

He's quiet for a few moments, making me think he's not actually going to tell me. Then: "Chase. We're . . . We broke up."

My breath catches. "Peter. I'm so sorry." But I don't want the details. Not now. Only him.

He nods. I tighten my arms around him, though it's the equivalent of a toddler hugging a tiger. He smells cold, if cold could be a smell.

"You're the only one I could talk to," he says, and I can't pretend it doesn't make me feel good. "You've never tried to make me be anything I wasn't. I was always enough for you, and you liked me because of that."

Loved you, I want to correct, but I don't.

He scrapes a hand over his face. "Fuck, I didn't even ask how you're feeling."

"I'm okay," I say. "My parents are freaked, but what else is new?"

"They must be taking pointers from mine." He holds my face in his hands, his eyes red and glassy. "Just us, right? That's all we need?"

I think about Montana and Liz and Emi Miyoshi and the entire dance team, about the potential of the summer workshop.

I think about Peter lying next to me.

"Just us." I touch my bracelet to his, metal to metal. I'd forgotten to take mine off.

He stares down at them. "God, why is this so hard? Why can't one fucking thing in our lives be easy?"

"I wish it could be easy too," I whisper.

He links his fingers with mine, brushing my knuckles. "Maybe you were right. About there being something between us."

My heart is a kick drum in my chest, my mind unable to fully process what I am hearing. "Y-yeah? Because, Peter, I—" And then I finally get the courage to say it, because I cannot bear to keep it inside any longer. With him in my bed, I am *so close* to getting what I have wanted for so long. "I don't know if I can be just your friend. I've tried. I've been trying . . . but it's too hard." He squeezes my hand, and I keep going: "I don't want to lose you, but—do you have any idea how hard it is to be this close to you without being together? Without—without touching you the way I want to?" I'm crying now too, salty tears dripping past my lips and onto my chin.

"Who said you were going to lose me?" he manages to say, eyes wide. "That can't happen."

"It feels like I've been losing you this entire year."

He shakes his head. He seems even smaller now, fragile. "Sophie. Sophie. You have me," he says, his hands coming up to grasp my back. "You'll always have me."

I press my face into his neck, where the exposed skin is starting to warm up. Slowly I brush my lips against the dip between his ear and shoulder. One small kiss. A reassurance, if anything else, that we will be okay after tonight. A curiosity. One turns into two, three, four—

"Sophie," he says again, my name a rumble in his throat.

I lift my face to look at him. There's something in his eyes besides sadness, something I haven't seen before. I feel so small in his arms. Like he could swallow me up, make me disappear.

His face is still a little cold, the tip of his nose a tiny iceberg as it bumps mine.

"Please don't cry." He brings a thumb to my cheeks, erasing a tear. "We're going to figure this out."

Suddenly Peter's mouth is on mine. *He* is kissing *me*, cold and then wet and then warm. He must taste the salt from my tears, because I taste it from his. There's an urgency in the way his lips move against mine, one that I have been craving for years.

I feel a tug, and his hand is wrapped around my necklace like when we kissed at Montana's party. I knew he felt it too—that connection we share—though I know it means something different to each of us.

It ignites a hunger in me. Suddenly, I need him closer. I roll myself on top of him, my legs on either side of his. I kiss his neck as I unbutton his shirt, wanting more, more, more. He slides down the thin straps of my tank top until we are skin to skin.

"God, I want you," I say. In my effort to be quiet, everything comes out as a breathy, desperate whisper.

His hands land on my hips, and when I rock against him, I can feel that he wants this too, and the realness of it makes my head spin. A hiss escapes his lips.

"Is this really happening?" he asks, a dazed look on his face.

Panic flashes through me for an instant. "Do you—want to stop?"

He shakes his head.

So we don't stop.

Soon we are in a puddle of sheets and clothing. In sixteen years of friendship, we have never been totally naked in front of each other, and tonight I drink him in. He's still skinny, though he's put on some weight since the transplant. And oh my God, he has hair *everywhere*.

His fingers go to my scar. "I did this to you. I can't believe I did this to you." His voice breaks.

I bring his hand to my mouth and kiss his fingertips. "You didn't do anything to me. It was my choice. It was the easiest choice I've ever made."

"Thank you," he says, then lets his gaze flick over my body. He nods. "You're so beautiful."

You are too, I think, but what comes out is, "I love you." I hope he knows how I mean it. A long time ago *I love you like a friend* turned into *I love you like I need to be close to you in every way imaginable*. "I love you so much."

Peter has always gotten what he wants. But this time—this is what both of us want.

He kisses me everywhere—my neck, my breasts, my scar, my navel, my hips. Gently I run my fingertips over his scar too. Then his hand is between my legs. "Can I?" he asks, breathless, and I sigh out a *yes*. "Tell me what to do. I want this . . . to be good for you."

Of course—if there is something Peter can get an A on, he won't settle for a B-plus. But at first I don't know how to verbalize it. How can you verbalize a need so deep it aches?

Somehow I find the words. It's tentative, like all my firsts with him, but soon it's deliberate, adventurous. *Good*. And then my body reaches that cliff so intensely that I can barely control myself as I shudder next to him, moaning into his shoulder.

"Did you—was that—"

"Uh-huh," I say, breathless.

"Oh," he says, but he's sort of grinning, like he's proud of himself. It is so fucking adorable that I pounce on him, pinning him down, kissing him with more ferocity than I ever have before.

"Are you sure you want to do this?" he asks, and it's then that I realize *this* is actually about to happen.

I want it more than I've ever wanted anything.

"Yes, yes," I say as I kiss him even harder, pressing myself against him in a way that conjures this magnificent groan. I can't help smiling at that.

A six-pack of condoms has lived in the back of my underwear drawer since I learned Tabby was pregnant, and I slip out of bed to retrieve it. It felt smart to have them. Just in case. When I bought them at the drugstore, I spent way too long debating whether to get a single condom or a three-pack or a twelve-pack or a thirty-six-pack. I couldn't tell which size meant I was being too presumptuous. If he wonders why I picked a six-pack, he says nothing. He simply tears the foil packet, but then struggles with the condom.

"Do you want me to help?"

"I got it," he says, and then it's on, and he's above me, my heart beating so hard he must be able to see it trying to crash through my chest.

There's an awkward few seconds where he stabs the inside of my thigh instead of *in* me, but then we figure it out. I bite the inside of my cheek, bracing myself for what society has warned me will be painful—but it's not. It's *different* more than anything else. There's a little discomfort as he pushes deeper, but then the discomfort is gone, and it starts to feel good. Odd and new, but good. The next time we do it, I'm sure it will feel even better.

In my fantasies, our bodies snapped together effortlessly, like this was the way we were always meant to fit. The reality is not at all like that. We don't know what to do with our hands, and I'm slightly worried about the expressions I'm making. Peter's socks are still on, and his stubble scratches my face, but I don't care. I don't care. None of that matters.

I'm so overwhelmed with how it feels to have Peter this way that I nearly start crying again.

Peter's face is serious, but I want to see him completely lose himself in this. I wrap my arms around his neck, pull at his hair. Again and again I say his name, the vowels and consonants blending, like I am begging for something only he can give me. Finally his concentration breaks, and exactly how good this feels is painted in the squint of his eyes, the O of his mouth.

"I don't know how much longer I can—" he says.

"It's okay," I reassure him, and then he lets himself go.

After he rolls off me, wiping the sweat from his brow, I

curl my body into his and lay my head on his chest.

"I love you," I say to his heartbeat. Suddenly I can't stop saying it. The words waterfall off my tongue, splash in the bed around us. I burrow closer to him. "I love you. I love you. I love you."

PART IV

CHAPTER 30

PETER

WE LIE THERE FOR A WHILE AFTERWARD. I RUN my fingers through her hair, liking the murmurs of satisfaction this elicits from her. In return, she peppers kisses all over my chest. My chin. My neck.

"I should probably go," I whisper, and she groans. "It's late. I—I don't want to wake anyone up."

"Noooo. I like this too much."

"Me too, but . . ." I glance down. "I don't know what to do. With that." I gesture to the condom, which I'm still wearing. Suddenly I want to throw a blanket over myself. My body looks too skinny, my legs like matchsticks.

"Oh," she says, regarding it strangely. Like it's no longer something sexual. Now it's something to throw in the garbage. "Right. Don't want my parents to . . ."

"Find it. Yeah."

As quietly as I can, I get dressed and tiptoe into the bathroom. I clean myself up, and mummy-wrap the condom in a dozen layers of toilet paper before burying it in the trash. I'm a strange combination of exhausted and on edge. Jittery, I splash water on my face, try to cool down. Blink at my reflection a few times, not sure what I'm expecting to see, because all I see is the same person who's always there.

When I get back into Sophie's room, she's sitting on the bed in a T-shirt and underwear, her legs bare. She smiles when she sees me. A kind of smile I haven't seen before. A smile that knows things about me it didn't know yesterday.

"Hey," she says quietly. Smiles again. "Hi."

"Hi." And then I'm not sure what else to say. What happens now is a complete mystery. Was this a one-time thing? Are we together now?

Sophie stretches, her T-shirt riding up and exposing her scar.

All of a sudden, my logic, which I must have left at the Blaze, comes rushing back. Every reason I thought a relationship with Sophie was doomed threatens to choke me. I can't feel like I constantly owe my girlfriend—if that's what Sophie were to become—my life. Can't have that debt between us. My body took over, asserting its independence, forgetting how easily this could lead to heartbreak for both of us.

No. Not just my body. I wanted to see what we had together, and what we had was frantic and sweet and maybe inevitable.

She had given me so much, and all I wanted was to make her—*us*—happy.

Slowly I sit back down on the bed next to her. She gets up on her knees to kiss me. "I love you," she says again.

"I—I love you too," I say, and at least right now, I must mean it in every possible way. *You and your big brain*, I want to add, to lighten this situation somehow. But I don't.

I don't want to break this girl.

And I don't want this girl to break me.

My body's heavy with exhaustion as I head across the street, my heart still calming down. Once I sneak inside my house and into my room, I shut the door and lean against it.

I'd never taken our pact seriously, mostly because I couldn't ever think that far ahead. We were so young. Babies.

The light in my own bathroom illuminates everything I didn't see in Sophie's. What we've done is tattooed all over my body. In the half-moons her nails left on my chest and back. My swollen lips. The red mark beneath my ear.

I crawl into bed, certain I won't be able to sleep.

Morning comes too soon. Winter sunlight peeks in through my blinds, and I groan, throwing an arm over my face. I let Mark run around my room for a while, but I don't leave my room until ten thirty.

My mom's at the kitchen table, frowning at her laptop behind her huge reading glasses.

"Where's Dad?" I ask, pouring myself a bowl of cereal.

"He got called in. Kid fell off his bike and chipped his entire front row of teeth."

"Ouch."

She types something on her computer, then deletes it. Then retypes it. "What are you up to today?"

"Probably homework."

"No plans with Sophie or with Chase?" She glances up, as though suddenly remembering. "Oh! How was your show last night? We must have been asleep when you got home."

I want to relish that my parents didn't wait up for me, that they trusted nothing horrible would happen to me. What they didn't bargain for: me doing something horrible to someone else.

"It was good," I say flatly. Desperate to change the subject, I slip into a chair across from her and point at her laptop with my spoon. "You must be getting close to 'the end' at this point, right?"

My mom barks out an unexpected laugh. "I wish. If only I weren't such a perfectionist."

"I'm not even sure I know what it's about at this point."

"Really? I must have told you years ago. . . ." She takes a deep breath before launching into an explanation: three generations of women, a family secret, a natural disaster . . . I can tell how much she loves it, despite the frustration it brings her.

This moment with my mom is oddly nice. It distracts me from the reality pounding against the inside of my brain: that I have no idea how to handle the aftermath of last night between Sophie and me. I'm terrified of doing the wrong thing, saying the wrong thing. Sophie's typically the one I'd ask for advice, and I definitely can't tell my mom, so I'm forced to deal with it alone.

In the past when our friendship flirted with romance, we were able to bounce back. But this time we went so far beyond friendship. I need more time to process it before I talk to her.

"Anyway," my mom says, "I'm sure you have better things to do than listen to me blather on about it!"

I shrug, and there must be something in the shrug that clues her in to the chaos in my mind.

"Baby," she says, dark brows furrowing. "You're okay, right?"

My heart leaps into my throat. There's something about your mom calling you "baby," even when you're seventeen, that's absolutely gutting.

"Just—a lot going on. The band, homework . . ." I trail off, realizing it's not "a lot" at all.

"We liked meeting Chase. You should invite him over for dinner."

I stiffen. "Maybe. Yeah." I get up, pushing in my chair. Another subject change. The two most important people in my life are off-limits. "You know, you could come to temple with us sometime. Dad and me."

"That's very sweet, Peter." She gives me a tight smile. "I'll . . . I'll think about it, okay?"

"Okay," I say as I finish my cereal. "I'll let you get back to it."

She returns to her book and I return to my room. Next to my bed, my phone flashes with a message from Chase.

I'm sorry about everything, it says.

CHAPTER 31

SOPHIE

MY EMOTIONS ARE TOO BIG FOR MY BODY.
After Peter leaves, I can't sleep. I am a live wire, pulsating and electric. Simply being in my bed is too much, the thoughts in my head too loud.

I snap on the small lamp near my bed and spring to my feet. There has to be a perfect song for these emotions. But when I scroll through my playlists, I land on Rufus Wainwright, Peter's all-time favorite, and so that's what I select.

I imagine Peter's hands on the piano keys and then on my skin.

I could make a dance to this song. One that's both vulnerable and joyful, full of longing and ending with satisfaction.

Just for Peter and me, the way we used to do.

By morning I feel well rested despite having barely slept. I'm a contradiction: desperate to see him, terrified of seeing him.

A hundred thoughts race through my mind. For anniversaries, will we celebrate our first kiss, or the first that happened on Saturday? Valentine's Day is next week. I imagine we'll have to make plans for that, maybe at one of the nicer restaurants in Capitol Hill. And I definitely want us to start playing as the Terrible Twosome again.

Peter is finally *mine*, and I'm not sure what that looks like. Will we kiss when we say hello the next time we see each other? When do we tell our parents?

I don't get a chance to find out—at least not today—because Peter texts that he's going to be buried under homework all day. And that's okay. Really, it is. Last night hasn't sunk in, but maybe by tomorrow I can convince myself it finally happened.

So I attempt some homework of my own before getting bored and texting Montana and Liz to see if they're free before remembering the party last night, and that they're probably still recovering. Sure enough, it's ten a.m. when Liz replies that she's still wiped, and a few minutes later Montana replies with the same thing.

Tabby's working the Sunday shift, so I drive down to the diner to see if I can get some free food.

"I'm swamped," Tabby says after I grab a stool at the counter, the only available seat. She's balancing several plates of waffles on her arms. "You had to pick Sunday brunch to visit me?"

"I'm sorry," I say, but she's already somehow across the restaurant, dropping off the plates.

I had sex last night, I want to tell my sister. *I'm like you now.*

314

A non-virgin. I'm in the club. Are there jackets? But despite whatever closeness we gained a couple weeks ago, I'm not about to announce this in a public setting. It'll have to wait for the right time.

Instead, I scarf down my free omelet and hash browns as quickly as I can. After I leave the diner, I stop at the outdoor mall, fight for a parking spot, and then spend thirty minutes in Sephora trying on forty-dollar lipsticks before deciding to buy none of them.

Home again. Restless, I meander into our backyard. My dad's wrapped up in a home-improvement project, cleaning out the old shed that's become a place to chuck things we can't bear to throw away but don't exactly want, either.

"You want to help me clean the shed?" he asks incredulously, and with a shrug, hands me a black trash bag.

I lean against the side of the shed. With a gasp, I pull my hand away, staring down at the splinter in my palm. My dad shakes his head. It's possible I'm not the home-improvement type.

After I fish out the splinter, I flop down on the couch in the living room and check my phone. Somehow it's only two p.m., and I have no idea how that's possible, unless I stepped into a time warp in Sephora earlier.

"Bored?" my mom asks, coming into the living room with Luna.

"No . . ." I toss my phone down on the couch and groan. "Fine, a little."

"Is your homework done?"

I groan louder.

"I was going to set Luna up with a coloring book. You're welcome to join us."

Because I haven't colored in forever, I shrug and follow the two of them into the kitchen, where my mom unloads all the art supplies Tabby and I accumulated over the years. Hand-me-down crayons.

It's calming, actually, to scribble across a magical forest. When I glance over at my mom's sheet, I drop my own crayon.

"Mom. Are you serious? That's, like, *good*."

She examines it, clearly proud. "I minored in art in college. I've always loved it."

"I didn't know that," I say, continuing to marvel at her creation.

Tabby comes home and Josh comes over, and they're as affectionate as they always are. We all have dinner together as a family, and it's unremarkable and uneventful and yet still really, really nice.

And later that evening I fall asleep easily this time, and with a smile on my face.

We have three big assemblies each year. There's the homecoming assembly in the fall, the winter spirit assembly, and the end-of-the-year assembly. This second one is mainly an excuse for shortened classes, to remind people they love their school and their sports teams, I guess.

They feel different from performing on the field at football games. In the gym, the lights are bright and everyone is there because it's mandatory, except for the kids who sneak joints behind the school.

I had to get to school early to go over our routine, so I missed giving Peter a ride. His mom said he was still asleep, which is unusual for him. Unusual for this version of him, at least. The post-transplant version. All morning, though, I've been thinking about Peter, Peter, Peter. Peter Rosenthal-Porter, the boy I gave my virginity to because I always knew, deep down, that I would.

The team's talking about the sleepover I missed on Saturday, but that's okay. I'll go to the next one, and Peter and I will go to the next house party together, too. As a couple. Peter and I are a couple, and I cannot stop smiling.

"Sophie, are you okay?" Montana says during a break.

"I'm happy," I call back.

She and Liz exchange a glance. "Did something happen with Peter?"

My face splits open, sunshine bursting through the clouds on a gloomy day. "Everything happened with Peter." Thirty-six hours was too long to keep this secret. Suddenly I want to tell everyone.

Liz clutches my arm. "I want to hear everything."

"She can keep it private if she wants to," Montana says. "Sophie, I don't need the details, but I'm really happy for you."

"After school?" I ask Liz, and she grins.

When it's time for the assembly, we paint Gs on one cheek and Os on the other, tie green ribbons in our hair. My piece is

317

part of our repertoire now. We dance it first, starting out with the hand claps, alternating between the old and the new, the vintage and the modern.

At the end, we rip the ribbons from our hair and stomp on them, and the crowd roars.

After the assembly, Principal Martinez gives us the rest of the day off. Montana asks us to hang back for a quick dance team meeting, during which she mentions a couple changes in our practice schedule now that it's basketball season. By the time we're done, everyone's cleared out of the gym.

Everyone except Peter.

He's standing near the locker room entrance, waiting for me. I grin even bigger when I see him because his hair is all messy, like he's been raking his hands through it. The light catches his bracelet, the one that matches mine.

My teammates retreat to the locker room, leaving Peter and me alone with the janitor, cleaning up the bleachers where people left scraps of paper and chip bags and silver and green confetti.

"Hi," I say when I get close to him. I am suddenly so, so nervous. Saturday night plays through my mind in flashes: skin against skin, the determined desperation in his eyes. It almost makes me blush now.

His smile is sheepish. "You guys were great. As always," he adds, though it's only the second time he's seen us.

"Thanks."

I expect him to reach for my hand, pull me in for a kiss. I let mine drop to my sides as though indicating to him that he can grab one at any time. But he seems as nervous as I am. Maybe he's not ready for public displays of affection quite yet. That's okay—we can learn that together.

I shouldn't be so anxious about touching him, so I inch closer. I reach my arms around his neck, which feels sort of awkward, like he wasn't expecting it and isn't sure how to make his body fit into mine. Then, as we hug, I brush my lips against his cheek, the corner of his mouth.

"This . . . is all really new to me," I say.

He nods.

"We can take this as slow as you want. Well. I guess it's already gone kind of fast. . . ." I trail off, laughing a little. Peter blushes. God, I love it when he does that. "But we don't have to tell our parents right away. I mean, I can't imagine they'd be anything but happy for us, but . . ."

He blinks at me a few times, like I am a piece of classic literature he is trying to interpret. A song he is trying to memorize. I have always admired Peter's passions. He's always had so many of them, and I wanted so badly to be one of them. Aren't I now? What we did Saturday night—what was that if not passion?

"Sophie," he says quietly, unable to meet my eyes now. "I— there are some things I need to say."

My sunshine smile slips right off my face. Slowly I back up, as though Peter is a wild, unpredictable animal. No. There's no way. Not after all these years, not after I finally got what I wanted.

"Say them, then." My voice is not my voice. It's chalky and shallow and belongs to someone whose heart is about to be broken.

But he can't. He glances between the floor and the banners of sports awards that hang from the ceiling, but not at me.

"Is everything okay? With the kidney?" I'm grasping here. There's something wrong with me that for a split second I hope that's what this is. That it's health-related, not heart-related.

The kidney. As though, even after all these months, it doesn't wholly belong to either of us.

"Yeah," he says quickly. "Yeah, I'm fine. The kidney . . . It's fine. This . . . It's obviously complicated. Especially after what happened on Saturday. I just—it kills me to say this, Soph, but we can't be together. Not the way you want to be. And I'm so, so sorry. I wish it could be different. I wish—"

We can't be together.

Except that's not it, not quite. It's that *he* can't be with *me*.

"You do?" I interrupt. "You really wish it could be different? We had a chance to make it different on Saturday night. We *made* it different. So don't apologize to me when you're the one, yet again, getting exactly what you want."

His face is pinched. Uncomfortable. He doesn't have control over this conversation.

Good.

"I told you before," he says, as though it's my fault for misunderstanding, for misinterpreting the signal that was his body on top of mine. "If we break up—or frankly, *when* we break up, because I'm seventeen and you're eighteen and let's be realistic, okay? When we break up, you either regret the transplant, or I'm left with a reminder of you breaking my heart. Either way, one of us gets destroyed." He wrings his hands. "There's—I can't see any good solution here."

I wouldn't break up with you, I want to say, though logically, it's not true. There's no way I can know that.

"God, I'm stupid," I say.

"Sophie, no," he says, reaching for my arm, as though I am the one who's in the wrong here and he needs to comfort me, reassure me that I made a mistake but it's okay. "No, you're not—"

I yank my arm away from him. "I am. I thought what we did—having sex—would connect us even more, that . . . I'd be more important to you."

I was so positive sex would make me feel closer than ever to Peter. Didn't he feel it too? That closeness? Our bodies were getting to know each other in a way they'd never known any others. It was something brand-new, and we would never experience it like this again.

"You *are* important to me."

"I thought we'd go to college together, and—"

"College?" Peter says. "Who said anything about college? Wait. Is that why you're going to community college? So you can—so you can wait for me?" When I don't reply, he has my answer. While I've never told him, I wasn't exactly keeping it a

secret. I always assumed winding up in the same place would be a happy coincidence. That he'd be *excited*. "Why would you do that? I've only just barely started to think about what happens after high school. You assume. You take me for granted, assume I'll be there."

"Because I want you there." I shake my head. "I've been so worried all year that you'd drop me when you found cooler, more interesting people. Like, I was the friend who was with you when shit was hard, but now you could upgrade."

His mouth falls open. "I've never thought that about you."

I run a hand through my hair, sliding the rubber band out of my ponytail. It occurs to me that I could agree with him. I could tell him whatever he needs to hear so we can go back to how we were before. I could tell him we're better as friends and we can erase Saturday from our collective memory.

But . . . I can't go back to what we were. I cannot be where I've been for so many years: clinging to him, drawing him back to me, trying to keep him from leaving. Constant agony—that's what it was.

"I don't get it," he's saying. "You have other friends too."

"I know, but—" *But they're not as important as you. They could never be.*

"Maybe we should both take some time to cool off."

I don't need time. I've had enough of it. I need to say all of this now. "Do you regret what we did on Saturday?" I ask, willing my voice not to quake. It does anyway.

He shakes his head, and when he speaks again, there's a

ribbon of frustration there. "No. I swear I don't. You mean so much to me. You do. It wasn't fair to you. I'm torn, and confused, and honestly, I still have feelings for Chase. We broke up because he thought I might still have feelings for you. Because of this codependent relationship we have, which probably isn't normal. Or healthy."

"Interesting word choice. 'Healthy.'"

Our tiny voices echo in the gym, his words bouncing off the walls and hitting me in the stomach. I cross my arms over my chest, suddenly feeling like I'm not wearing nearly enough clothes. My uniform barely covers me up. I shiver, running my hands over the goose bumps on my skin. It was hot when I was dancing, but now it is just me and Peter and the janitor, and I am too cold.

"There it is," Peter says, a snap to his voice that wasn't there a few minutes ago. He inches closer to me, dark brows slashed. "Is that what you want? To remind me that I owe you?"

"You don't—"

"I don't owe you? Then why do I feel that way all the fucking time?" He throws his hands up, the volume of his words shrinking me. Peter never yells, and definitely not at me. "It was your choice. I never asked you to do it. Is this why you did it, Sophie? So you'd have a reason to always keep me close to you?"

The way he touched me on Saturday, he was so gentle. This cannot be the same person.

I want to combat his words with harsh ones of my own, but my voice comes out meek. I wish it wouldn't. "*No,*" I insist,

323

putting more space between us, but deep down, in a place I've barely allowed myself to admit, he's not entirely wrong. There were a hundred reasons I did it, and there's no way it wasn't one of those hundred reasons. Maybe it was number one hundred, but it was still *there*. "I—I did it because you're the most important person in the world to me, Peter. You're my best friend, and I—I love you."

"Do you understand how much pressure that is for me? I can't love you the way you love me. I did once, when I was too young to know what it really meant. But now? I just . . . can't."

It stings, salt rubbed into a gaping wound, alcohol poured over a gash in my skin. This hurt—I want to turn it into anger. I want to hurt *him*, too. Because beneath all this hurt, I am furious. Furious at all the times he brushed my knee with his thumb and hugged me so fearlessly and slept next to me and acted like it was nothing when to me it was everything. If we were so close, how did he not know what his body was saying to mine?

There's a closet off the gym that's open, revealing a shelf of dodgeballs. I stalk toward it and snatch an orange one, bouncing it a few times on the floor.

"What, are you going to throw it at me?" Peter asks, a sour sarcasm in his tone.

I hurl the ball against the wall. "I have built my entire *life* around you," I snarl at him. "You've been everything to me, and what you're doing, breaking up with me before we even had a real chance? You make me feel like dirt." I grab another ball. "You don't text me back. Your new friends are more important than any of the traditions we ever had. You couldn't bring your-self to come to another one of my games. How many of your piano recitals did I go to, Peter?"

He mumbles something.

"What was that?"

"I said *a lot*." He pulls a hand through his hair. "I'm sorry. Those friends—I felt like they understood me in a different way. I wasn't the sick kid with them."

"You weren't the sick kid with me."

"But I was. That's all you've ever known me as."

The janitor is still watching us.

"Are we entertaining enough for you?" I ask him, and he turns around quickly, returns to dragging a broom across the gym floor. "Jesus fucking Christ."

Even as the words tumble out, I feel guilty for snapping at him, but this anger in my veins is too addictive. Peter looks stunned by it too. He is the one backing away from me now. I stare him down, this beautiful, tormented boy who let me con-vince myself he was the only one who mattered.

"Our relationship has always been about you," I say, trying to keep my voice level even as my eyes threaten to spill over. "And now I thought it could be about *us*."

"I'm not sure I understand."

I've never verbalized this before. But it's how I've felt, isn't it? "Growing up. It was always about what you wanted. We always played your games, watched your movies, listened to your music. You were the one with the shitty luck, so you deserved everything you wanted. I never had a say. I never complained."

He blinks at me like I've dug my fingers into his skin and ripped out what I gave him. "Of course you had a say."

"It didn't feel like it."

"I'm sorry we didn't get to listen to your fucking *music*, Sophie." A bitter laugh. "Is that what this is about? You can't possibly be that petty." He walks toward the closet and grabs a ball too. In an alternate universe, Peter and I are playing dodgeball and having an absolute blast.

"Oh yeah, that's exactly it," I tell him. I can lay on the sarcasm just as thickly. We're circling each other now, each clutching a ball. I know we don't actually mean to throw them at each other, but I can't help wondering if Peter wishes he could. Because, God, I do. "If we'd only listened to less Rufus Wainwright, we wouldn't be here right now!"

Peter's jaw goes slack, eyeing me like I'm feral. Like I will bite him and give him rabies. Then I will need a medical ID bracelet that says RABID ANIMAL. STAY AWAY!

Bounce. "I always forget that you're older than me," he says. "Probably because you can't seem to grow up."

How long has this venom been inside us? Snakes, both of us.

"You want to know what the most fucked-up part is?" I fire at him, feeling a tear roll down my cheek, then another. "The pain I'm in? It's worth it. I'd give you my other kidney if I could. I've seen you struggle my whole life, and I'd take all your pain away from you in a heartbeat. You're selfish, and you're spoiled, and you drain the energy from everyone around you, but I'd still do it again."

His face twists with hurt. "How was I selfish? I was *sick*! "

"That's not what I'm talking about." A shaky breath. Clenched teeth. "You said we can't be together? Fine. We're not together. We're not anything. I can't have you in my life any-more." I try to swallow, but the words are razor blades in my throat. "I just—I hate who I am when I'm with you."

And there it is: Aside from this preemptive breakup, it's not any single thing Peter did to me. No massive transgression, just a hundred little reminders that he's in charge of us. It's the walls slowly closing in on me, trapping me in my obsession. It's that I've clung to him so tightly that I've lost myself.

The ugly sentence lingers in the space between us, a poison-ous plume of smoke.

I don't take it back.

Because I meant for it to choke him.

"Sophie—"

"*No*. I am not letting you get the last fucking word."

I smash the ball right at his feet, and then I pivot and dash toward the door, my shoes squeaking across the gym floor. The janitor has either witnessed a dozen fights like this or is trying very hard not to act like he didn't just see us crumble to pieces.

Peter's shouting my name, or at least I think he is. I want to hope that he is, that the loss of our friendship means something to him. I fly out of the gym and down the hall, wiping at my damp face. The hallways are full of lockers slamming, everyone giddy with a surprise half day. Silver and green streamers and confetti are everywhere. I stomp on all of it, a streamer getting stuck to my shoe. With no energy to shake it off, I trail it all the way out to the parking lot, trying to rub away tears that keep coming.

Our lives have revolved around Peter always. He is the earth, and I am the moon. There was never enough I could do to get him to love me the way I wanted, to see me as more than just a moon.

I have never been enough, and he has always been too much.

CHAPTER 32

PETER

NUMBLY, I TRIED MY BEST TO CLEAN UP THE mess we made. I chased after the balls and shoved them back into the closet, but unlike Sophie, I couldn't race out of the gym. I walked slowly, with leaden feet, because I had no idea where I was going, nowhere I wanted to go, no one expecting me.

I hate who I am when I'm with you.

"Peter, school's out for the day," Mr. Lozano told me when our paths crossed in the hall. He chuckled. He'd become my favorite teacher, and I couldn't bear to let him see me like this. "We can't get rid of you, can we?"

I tried to laugh, but I might have growled instead. Then my feet remembered what to do, and they carried me out of the school and to the first bus stop I found, where I got on the first bus that arrived.

Now I'm headed south, past the Space Needle, into down-town.

I hate who I am when I'm with you.

It bangs around in my brain, warping the memories of our friendship. Every time she comforted me, was she secretly cursing me as well? For so long, she was my only person. I must have given in to her some of the time. I must have let her have her way. I can't have been the guy she described, not one hundred percent of the time—otherwise she wouldn't have loved me.

It's a selfishly heartening thought.

A message from Chase blinks on my phone. **Band practice?** is all it says. My mind was too all over the place to think to ask Chase about this on Saturday night. I wasn't sure if I'd be wel-come at band practice, or if our breakup was a Fleetwood Mac situation and I'm Lindsey Buckingham.

Can't today.

I shouldn't be having fun, playing music. But I feel bad about the brevity of the text, so I thumb out another one. **Can we talk later this week?**

A few minutes later, his **okay** comes back, but it doesn't lift the heaviness in my chest as much as I thought it might.

Hours later, after a half dozen more aimless bus rides through-out the city, I arrive home to find my parents getting dressed up. My mom's stabbing a pearl through her earlobe and my dad is straightening his tie. One of the nice ones, not one of the joke

330

ones with teeth on them that I imagine all dentists own. Yes, he has more than one.

"Where are you going?" I ask, dropping my backpack on the living room floor. I collapse onto the couch.

"We have reservations at the new Maria Hines restaurant," my mom says to her reflection in the foyer mirror. "It was supposed to be impossible to get a table, but one of your dad's patients knew the right people and got all of us in."

All of us.

"You and Sophie's parents?"

My dad holds up his hands. "Who else?"

"Can't you leave them alone for five seconds?"

"Peter," my mom says slowly as she turns to face me. "Is something going on?"

If I were a dog, the hair on my back would be sticking up. I'm sure I'm red-faced still, not yet recovered from the fight with Sophie.

No, "fight" isn't the right word.

Destruction.

Explosion.

Wreckage.

I scratch at the bracelet on my wrist. Suddenly it feels too tight. A shackle more than anything else. "You don't have to be indebted to Sophie's parents anymore."

My dad frowns. "Indebted? Peter, that's not what this—"

"You've been sucking up to them nonstop since the transplant! It's embarrassing."

"Peter. I think you should go to your room." My mom crosses her arms. "And frankly, I'm not sure if you should go out this weekend."

I choke out a laugh. "Wait—are you—are you grounding me? Wow. *Wow.*"

"It's our fault for being so lax with you lately," she says. "Honestly, we've spoiled you."

"You've *sheltered* me!"

"I don't know why this upsets you so much," my dad says, slightly calmer than my mom. "You love Sophie's parents."

"Sophie and I—" I shout, unsure where I'm going with that. I'm not about to tell them Sophie and I had sex. They used to know everything about me, but this is far too personal. Too private. It barely feels right to say her name out loud, not now. "We—"

Realization dawns on them at almost the exact same time. My dad's eyes get wide, and my mom brings a hand to her mouth.

Oh. Oh no.

They know. They can *tell.*

"Peter," she says slowly as she lowers herself onto the couch next to me.

"What? I'm fine." My throat is scratchy. Raw. I'm not fine. I'm a toxic, terrible friend. Some part of me thought I deserved all those things: the gifts from my parents, Sophie's attention. Her love, even. I can't get her words out of my head. I don't know how to apologize for all those years of taking so much from her, let alone this past year.

My dad sits down in a chair across from us. "So you and

Sophie . . ." He doesn't even need to finish the sentence.

I drop my head in my hands and nod. This is a thousand times worse than the sex talk.

"You used protection?" my mom asks. "You're such a smart kid, I shouldn't even have to ask, but . . . I need to know."

"Yes."

"And Sophie—she's okay?"

"I don't know." It's the truth. "Emotionally, I mean." I explain as much as I can without completely losing it: Chase, the breakup, the guilt I've felt for exploring a life that didn't always include Sophie. The horrible, horrible things I said to her in the gym. Things I wish I could take back. Things I couldn't have fully meant because I'm not a cruel person, am I? "I'm not sure we can get back what we used to have," I finish. And Sophie—Sophie doesn't want me back. At all.

I was a fucking idiot to think we could rewind. Go back to being friends, as though our relationship has ever been that simple.

"Peter," my mom says, turning sympathetic. "Oh, Peter." She shuffles closer to me on the couch, and I let her. All I want is a hug from my mom right now, so when she offers one, I lean into it.

I eye the front door. "Are you still going out with the Orensteins?"

"We should probably sit this one out," my dad says as he picks up his phone, making me wonder whether I've ended more than one relationship today.

The anger is back. The anger I had through most of my early teens, the blind fury I felt toward a world that had cheated me before I was born.

Later, when I'm not as mad at them and embarrassed they know about Sophie and me, I'll tell my parents I want to go back to therapy. That all three of us should go.

But for now I'm angriest at myself most of all.

I look around my room at all this stuff. That's what it is: stuff. Did I need the vintage record player? The Yamaha keyboard, when we already have the bajillion-dollar baby grand? The extra bookshelf space for my signed first editions? The chinchilla, because I couldn't have a hamster or a guinea pig—I had to have something exotic and expensive, something I knew my parents wouldn't say no to?

The truth of it is, all those things made me feel better when I was convinced nothing else would. Sophie can't possibly understand that. Sometimes I even craved the attention, the gifts. This is the real problem: My family never gave in, and I grew to expect it from Sophie, too. Deep down, I've always known the balance between us was skewed, and I never did a single fucking thing about it. The night we were together, I wanted so badly to even things out between us and only succeeded in making it all worse.

I fall onto my bed, running a hand under my shirt, tracing the line of scar that matches Sophie's, that will tie me to her for years and years to come.

If this is the point of no return with us, we can't ever erase ourselves from each other's lives.

CHAPTER 33

SOPHIE

I WASH MY SHEETS.

That's the first thing I do when I get home. I sit cross-legged on the floor in the laundry room, watching them spin and spin.

I make my bed, struggling with the fitted sheet. I either accidentally shrunk them or am totally inept. Both are also possible. Nothing fits the way it should, and I collapse in a heap on top of my unmade bed, breathing hard, tears backing up behind my eyes.

I'm still there hours later, when someone knocks on my door. I assume it's Tabby or my dad, so I'm shocked when my mom peeks inside.

"Peter's parents canceled dinner," she says. "Do you happen to know anything about that?"

That's all it takes for me to start crying again.

Her face breaks open, reveals a concerned mother underneath. One I wasn't sure I had.

"Sophie, Sophie, Sophie," my mom coos in this voice I've never heard from her before. "What's wrong?"

I can't pick one thing.

"Peter" is all I croak out. "I love him so much, Mom. And I wish I didn't. I hate that I feel this way."

"Oh, kiddo," she says as she rushes over to my unmade bed to hold me like she'd hold Luna. "I know."

I shake my head, tears dripping off my nose and onto my sheets below. "Not just as a friend. I *love* him. I've been in love with him for a long time, and he—he doesn't love me. Not like that."

I've always felt sort of intimidated by my mom the corporate executive, like we had nothing in common. But the coloring books with Luna showed me another side of her. And I'm starting to think there's so much more to my mom than I'll ever know.

Her face doesn't register surprise. Has she known this whole time? "It's the worst feeling when someone you love doesn't love you back."

"You—"

She nods. She gets what I'm trying to say. "In high school," she says. "Steve Rosso. He wasn't Jewish, so your grandparents never would have approved of him, but we sat next to each other in homeroom all four years. Rosso, Roth." Roth: my mom's maiden name, which she kept as a middle name when she got married.

I wipe my face with the back of my hand. "Was he cute?"

"The cutest. We talked every day, but we were in different circles. I was in the young business leaders group, and Model UN, and art club, and he played basketball and sang in choir. Our friend groups didn't overlap. But I thought about him constantly. I finally worked up the nerve to ask him to homecoming senior year, and I'll never forget what he said. 'As friends? Because I was sort of hoping to go with someone as a date.' As though it was so very clear I wasn't even in the datable category."

"Mom. Steve Rosso is an ass."

She cracks a smile. "That's very obvious now, but does that stop me from looking him up on Facebook every so often?"

"What's he doing?"

"Seems to be happily married. Three kids. Works in tech." She shrugs.

Bonding with my mom like this—I'm surprised to find I like it.

"I don't know who I am without Peter," I say. "Probably because I've never *been* without Peter."

"Do you think it's time to try? I'm not saying you're done being friends or that you can't go back to him. Just that independence isn't a bad thing."

"You mean 'loneliness.'"

She frowns. "No. Independence. That's different. You with the dance team girls—you have fun, don't you?"

I nod.

"That's independence." She straightens out a rumpled part of my sheets. "You and Peter are nothing like me and Steve. You two have always been complicated, so wrapped up in each other. Your dad and I worried so much about you when you were younger. We didn't know if he'd get better and what that would mean for you if he didn't. . . . It makes us sound like awful people, but we were so concerned. For him, and for you."

"I know."

"He's a wonderful boy, Soph. Don't get me wrong. But . . . is it possible—not intentionally—that he's holding you back?"

I think again about how I am with Montana and Liz. How I want more nights like that one in the hotel, more book signings with Liz and more choreography with Montana. Those moments are when I've felt fully myself.

With Peter this year, I've been chasing something I can never quite catch.

"I don't want to lose him completely," I say finally.

For a moment I'm worried she'll reassure me. She'll tell me I won't lose him, that he'll come back to me eventually. That the two of us will be okay.

But I'm not sure we will be, not now, and I'm relieved by her response.

"You *are* going to stop feeling this way. I can promise you that. I wish I could tell you when, but this kind of unrequited love doesn't last forever, kiddo. It just can't." She smiles sadly, running a hand through my hair. "Our hearts wouldn't be able to take it."

CHAPTER 34

PETER

THE REST OF THE WORLD SHOULD STOP OR AT least slow down after Sophie and I shatter, but of course it doesn't. It goes on, in the most infuriating way.

On Tuesday—how is it only Tuesday?—I bus to school and stay quiet in class and eat lunch alone in the band room. In English, Chase and I exchange pleasantries and awkward silence, but I can't bear to talk to him outside of school. Not yet, not until the hurricane in my brain has calmed down. Eleanor Kang has succumbed to the flu, but I can't even bring myself to enjoy playing piano in band. It suddenly feels like a massive responsibility to be in charge of an instrument like that.

Wednesday is the same robotic pattern, and it's not until I get home Thursday that I realize I can't keep feeling sorry for myself. I need to *do* something.

The first task is my room. There's so much in here I haven't used in years. I make a stack of books to donate, and after significant deliberation, part with a few of my records, too. Mark stays, of course. I love that little guy too much, and he's the only one who isn't mad at me right now.

Summer's only a few months away. I was anticipating a lazy, languid one, but it turns out there are a lot of transplant organizations that could use volunteers. I send a few e-mails, along with an extremely sparse résumé. The most impressive accomplishment on it is my GPA. I've got to fill that up. Maybe a job, too—make some money of my own.

After I send one last e-mail, I close my laptop and migrate over to my Yamaha. All day I've had a melody stuck in my head, and I've got to play it out. I might even write some lyrics.

It takes all my courage to meet Chase on Friday. The place I picked, a coffee-slash-chocolate shop along Green Lake, is nearly empty on a Friday night after services, except for a couple college students huddled over textbooks.

I grab a corner table and stare down at our message history. Yesterday I texted him a location and a time and he responded with k. That single letter kills me a little. There's no worse letter in the English language than *k*.

When Chase arrives a few minutes past eight thirty—the time we agreed on—he's wearing a gray jacket I've never seen before. Probably because I've only known him in winter. It makes me ache for other seasons we haven't spent together. I imagine the two of us on the beach in West Seattle, daring each other to dip a toe into the chilly water. Bonfires, ice cream, sunsets.

I was hoping—expecting—he'd look wrecked by the past week, but he looks as good as ever, no bags beneath his eyes, no lost expression on his face.

I used to love the newness and novelty of him, but what strikes me now is his familiarity. Though we were only officially together for a few months, it's easy to picture him draping an arm around the back of my chair or me sliding my hand into his, tracing his knuckles with my thumb.

"Hi," I say as he takes a seat across from me.

"Hi." He sips his coffee, but it must be too hot because he makes a face and sets it back down right away, so forcefully that some of it splashes the table. He didn't get a napkin, but I got two, so I hand him one. "Thanks," he says as he mops up the spill.

"Thanks for meeting me."

A brusque nod. Then: "Have you listened to the new Tarts album? It just came out."

"Oh—no. I haven't yet."

"Oh. It's good."

My tea has cooled down, so I take a sip. He tries his coffee again. "How . . . are you?" I ask.

"Honestly, not great," he says, bringing his eyes up to mine and stretching a hand across the table to graze my sleeve. "Peter, I'm so sorry about what I said on Saturday. I wasn't thinking clearly, and I get why you've been so upset with me."

It takes a second for it to sink in: He thought I needed space because I was *upset with him*.

"Stop. Stop. I have to say something first." I take a deep breath, trying to find the right words. There's only the truth. We can't move forward unless he knows it. "The night we broke up, after we fought . . . I went to Sophie's."

A muscle in his jaw ripples, as though he's clenching his teeth.

"I was really distraught," I continue. "A total mess. I told her what happened, and she was comforting me, and there were all these emotions, and . . . and we slept together." I expect to feel lighter after I confess it, but I'm only more keyed up, waiting for his reaction.

He closes his eyes for a moment, and when he opens them, he can't look at me. He's quiet for what feels like the length of an entire song.

"I—wow, a lot of thoughts right now." With a sigh, he scrubs a hand down his face. "I guess I'm glad you told me. Are you . . . together now?"

"No," I say quickly. Emphatically. "We're not. I've never been more certain Sophie and I aren't meant to be together that way." I pause for a few moments. Explaining Sophie and me to someone else has never been easy, and what happened Saturday didn't exactly change that. "I know Sophie and I have a weird relationship, and the transplant complicated it a million times over. I've been feeling like I owed her for what she did and guilty that our relationship wasn't what it used to be."

"Is that why you did it?"

It would be so simple to say yes. But that's only half the truth. "That was part of it, but I think another part was that I was curious. Like you said, maybe I needed the time to figure it out. I used to like her, years ago, and the closeness of our friendship messed with my mind. I thought those feelings were still there underneath. But . . . they're not there now. Earlier this week, Sophie and I had this massive fight, and even if we manage to come back from it, I'm pretty positive we're never going to be as close as we used to be."

"Shit. Wow." He doesn't exactly look heartbroken for me, but shocked, definitely. "I'm . . . sorry." He grimaces. "That was hard to say, if I'm being totally honest."

"I appreciate that. But you don't have to apologize. I messed up. The timing was really not great. I know that."

He goes quiet again. And then: "I'm not going to pretend this isn't extremely hard for me to wrap my mind around," he says. "But—you and I weren't together. I wanted you to figure this shit out with her. I know that with you, I stepped into something more complicated than I could imagine, but . . ." A long sigh. "I was sure you were worth it."

My heart picks up speed. "And now?"

"Now . . . I need some time to process all of this."

Time. Okay. Time is doable. Time doesn't mean "the end."

"Of course. Of course. I get it." I pause, debating whether I should say what I want to. I have to get it out. "I do still like you. A lot. I'm not saying that to make you process this faster or anything. I swear. I just wanted you to know that I've never felt better than when I'm with you, or with the band."

These words clearly affect him, though, twisting his mouth into a sad smile. "Like ninety percent of me is telling me I like you too much not to try this again." Before I can get excited about that, he continues: "And the band misses you. I know it's only been a week, but they get attached quickly, I guess. So . . . if you want to come back to practice tomorrow afternoon, I think it would make them really happy."

"I'd hate to disappoint them."

"Yeah," he says, his eyes hopeful behind his old-man glasses. "It's not the same without you. I mean—that's what they say."

Peter
10:21 p.m.
You don't need to respond, but I wanted to
tell you that I'm so sorry, Sophie.
For so many things.

Sophie
10:37 p.m.
Thank you for saying that.

10:38 p.m.
Oh. Hey. You're there. I wasn't expecting
that.

10:40 p.m.
What can I say? I'm full of surprises.

10:44 p.m.

You don't owe me an answer to this, either, but . . . did you mean what you said? About . . . not liking who you are when you're around me?

11:19 p.m.

I still need some time to figure it out.

11:25 p.m.

Okay.

CHAPTER 35

SOPHIE

THIS IS WHAT HAPPENS AFTER YOU BREAK UP with your best friend, the person you loved more than anyone in the world. You stop giving them rides to school. You avoid them in the halls. Your parents, who were also best friends, drift away from each other again. At doctor's appointments, you don't learn anything you didn't already know. Sometimes you hurt, and sometimes you ache, but the worst pain is one you can't put a name to and can't swallow a pill to fix.

The weekend after *that weekend*, Tabby drags me to the Early Bird for free waffles and a mountain of French fries.

"You've been mopey," she says, pointing her fork at me. "You needed this."

"Mopey. Yeah." I dip a chunk of waffle into syrup. Dipping is a much more satisfying—though less economical—use of syrup.

Regarding my mopiness, I'm not even sure where to begin. "Everything with Peter is a complete mess."

"That can't be true. I can't imagine anything could happen between you two to cause that."

"Well . . . we slept together." It's a relief to tell her.

"Holy shit. *What?*"

"Last weekend. And . . . I thought we were finally together, but we're not, and when we tried to talk about it, we just *exploded* at each other. What you said, about being friends with him knowing we can never be together? I couldn't do it. Too much of my life has revolved around him. It needs to fucking stop." My voice hitches, and Tabby reaches across the table to squeeze my hand.

"Soph," she says quietly, but I shake my head to indicate I'm not done.

"Whatever happens, it's going to be impossible for me to ever forget him because of *this*." I gesture toward the scar beneath my shirt. "All I want to do is stop loving him, but he's been part of my life for so long that I don't know how."

"What do you love about him?" she asks, grabbing a handful of fries.

The question throws me. "I—" I start, another piece of waffle halfway to my mouth. No one's ever really asked me that. *Because he's Peter. Because those are the feelings I have for Peter.* "He's smart, and sweet, and funny, and . . ." I trail off, realizing those are totally vague traits that could apply to just about anyone.

347

But Peter is not a vague person. I shake that away. Loving Peter has become as natural as my own heartbeat. "His music, that's a big one. We have this deep respect for each other as artists, and I've always loved that. Like we understand each other on a completely different level from people who don't get music. And he just knows me. Better than anyone."

Tabby nods. "Okay. I can see that. I was always sort of jealous of you two growing up. You bonded so immediately. You had each other and I . . . didn't have you. My older sister."

"Tab," I say, her words a blow to my heart. "You and I aren't that far apart from each other, are we?"

"No, but we've never been best friends or anything. And now with Luna . . ."

"That doesn't mean you and I can't be close."

"I guess it doesn't."

We chew in silence for a couple minutes, until I realize this entire conversation has been focused on my problems. "How—how are you and Josh?" Lately, they've seemed okay, and Josh is back to spending most of his time at our house. I'm not sure why I ever resented that. These days, I like that there's always someone around.

"We're good," she says. "Josh and I have disagreements. That's normal. But having a baby makes those about a hundred times more intense."

"Why did you decide to do your GED online?"

"Honestly? I knew it would be weird at school. It was bad enough when I was pregnant. Everyone knew, I mean, obviously. It was the worst from the teachers, though. They'd give me these judgmental looks, like they thought I'd ruined my life." She shakes her head. "But did Josh get any of that? Nope. He didn't get lingering stares or subtly offensive comments. Some people didn't even know he was the father or that we were dating. But for me, it was impossible to hide. It's hard having total strangers know something so private about you."

"I guess that's sort of what pregnancy is. Like carrying around a sign that says I HAD SEX."

Tabby snort-laughs at this. "I never thought of it that way."

"You have your friends, though."

"My high school friends?" She raises her faint auburn brows, which are the same shape as mine. "Soph, I haven't seen any of them in months. It feels like I don't have anything in common with them anymore, and it's hard to make mom friends because most of them are so much older. . . ."

"I had no idea. I'm sorry."

"I lost a lot. My classes and my friends and a good chunk of my independence. It was a sacrifice. I knew that going into it. But we also felt like we could raise a baby, with help, of course. I just never want it to feel like 'mother' or 'teen mom' is the only piece of my identity."

"That makes sense. You're my annoying little sister before you're a teen mom, that's for sure," I say, and she laughs again. I'm learning that laughing with my sister is one of the very best things. "What I don't get is how Mom and Dad were so against the transplant but so on board with your pregnancy."

"Sophie. You have selective memory or something. They were furious at first. I was fifteen. That wasn't supposed to happen. Telling them I was pregnant was the hardest thing I've ever done. But . . . we got through it. They love Luna. I'm sure they wish this were happening ten years from now, but this is our life. And I think we're dealing with it okay." She tows a fry through ketchup, drawing a red heart on her plate. "I'm not naive enough to assume Josh and I will get married. I love Josh an absolutely ridiculous amount, even when it's hard. We'll see how we feel after college. We don't want to feel pressured to rush into it, even though we have a kid."

Tabby's more mature than I could have imagined. "That's good."

"Maybe it's my maternal instinct, but God, I feel so weirdly protective of you now. Like, I want to go fight Peter!"

"Please don't. And we're only a year apart. Maybe we're supposed to protect each other."

"I like that."

"Sometimes I feel like you've left me behind. You're growing up, and I'm stunted. Like, you and Josh started having sex when you were fifteen."

"We'd been together for a while at that point, and we'd discussed it, and we felt ready."

"Do you guys still . . . ?"

"Yeah. We're super careful. Obviously. After I got pregnant, I was anxious about it, but Josh has always been the sweetest."

I can hear the love in her voice.

"He's a good one," I say, and she smiles.

"I want us to be able to talk like this," she says. "You and me. It's a total waste of a sister if we don't."

"I—I know," I admit. "I want to."

And then we fight over the last French fry.

When we pull into the driveway at home, my phone buzzes. I've spent so much time this year waiting on messages from Peter that for a moment I think it must be him.

But when I unlock my phone, it's not a text. It's an e-mail.

It starts with "Congratulations."

Which might be even better.

It takes me the entire weekend to go through my room and get rid of anything that reminds me of Peter. Scraps of sheet music from our Terrible Twosome days, which are almost assuredly over now. A used *Philosophy for Dummies* book he gave me as a joke for my sixteenth birthday. I never told him, but I actually read the whole book because I wanted so badly to understand the thing he loved so much, even though it took me forever and I loathed every minute of it. Into a trash bag it goes. Notes we sent back and forth in elementary school, most of them making zero sense to me now. Homemade cards, from his calligraphy phase in middle school, for various Jewish holidays. All of them go into the trash, even the one that just says, HAPPY DAY! He gave it to me on a completely random day, one that meant nothing to either of us.

351

Then I reach down to the medical ID bracelet, with the charms I thought were so sweet. I thought they meant Peter understood me on some deep level, but it's no big revelation that I love to dance.

So I dig my fingernails into the wire.

And I rip them off the bracelet, the ballet slipper and the music note.

I need to be away from all this, figure out who I am on my own. I'm hoping the workshop will help. No one will know me in San Francisco. I won't be quiet Sophie or Peter's best friend Sophie or kidney donor Sophie. I won't be Sophie, hopelessly in love with someone who does not love her back. I can be anyone, and I like the sound of that.

I gave Peter a piece of me—but maybe I also gave him the freedom to figure out who he was without me. And I should have realized much sooner that I'd given myself the exact same thing.

As I'm taking the last trash bag outside, I freeze when I see him across the street. He and his parents are getting out of the car. When he spots me, he pauses too, lingering in the driveway while his parents go inside.

I lift my hand in a wave. He watches me for moment, like he's weighing what he wants to do.

Then he waves back. It's not even a full wave; he just lifts his hand and then brings it back down.

He didn't owe me his love, and I didn't deserve it because of the sacrifices I made. Truthfully, Peter and I were unbalanced for a long time.

A friendship breakup has got to be worse than a relationship breakup. With a relationship, you can go back to being friends. There's at least the possibility of it. But after a friendship ends, what do you go back to? Do you simply become nothing to each other? Fade away until you barely recognize each other anymore?

He shuts himself inside his house, and I return to mine, a sense of calm spreading through me. I thought the fight and fall-out would turn my love for him to ashes. The flame is still there, though, a soft flicker. Every day I love him less, and one day I will love only our memories.

CHAPTER 36

PETER

MY FIRST PRACTICE BACK WITH DIAMONDS ARE for Never is awkward, but by my third, everything feels almost normal.

"I wrote a song for us," I announce during my fourth practice.

Everyone turns to face me. Over the past few weeks, Chase and I have started sitting together at lunch again, and he gave me a ride to practice today.

"You did?" Dylan says.

"Yeah—I mean, I've always kind of written music." I pause. It's hard to think about the Terrible Twosome without my chest aching just a little. "But I wrote this one with the band in mind."

"The floor is yours," Aziza says, motioning with a drumstick.

I adjust the mic in front of me, the one I've used to sing backup until now. My lyrics have hopefully improved significantly since "Dancing through My Heart." The song isn't about

Chase or Sophie, not explicitly. I love subtext too much for that. But my emotions from this past year are all over it. It's a mix of melancholy and hopeful, quiet until the final, crashing chorus.

"I love your voice," Kat says when I finish. "What were those lyrics in the second verse? 'At night the stars are jealous of/the wishes people make on us'?"

Staring at the keys, I nod. My lyrics in someone else's voice— that's trippy.

"That's fucking beautiful."

"You want to sing backup for me?" I ask.

"Absolutely."

"Can you play that opening again?" Chase asks. I've been most anxious to hear his reaction, but his tone is hard to interpret. "I want to try something."

"Sure," I say, gliding my fingers back into position.

Chase plays some harmonics, and combined with my soft piano notes, it sounds wistful and bright and amazing all at once.

"Keep going," I say as we slide into the chorus.

Together, we play the rest of the song. He experiments with chords, and I sing around a smile, and the rest of the band watches us.

"Did you guys just get back together?" Dylan says, and Chase flushes. Aziza plays a rim shot.

I cough, unable to look at him. "Um. Should we try it with all of us?"

We work on my song for the next hour, creating something whole and cohesive from my notes, my lyrics. The entire process still astounds me. We have a few shows booked this summer, and Kat and Dylan want to do a Pacific Northwest mini-tour next year if we're all still together.

We're not fantastic, but we're getting better, and we are a *we*. I'm part of a *we* that doesn't include Sophie, and I'm not going to feel guilty about that anymore.

The sun hasn't set quite yet when practice is over. It's the end of April, the weather teasing us with a summer that won't arrive for a few more months.

"My parents are letting me take driver's ed this summer," I say when Chase and I get in his car. We've started therapy, too. "So you won't have to chauffeur me everywhere."

"And if I like chauffeuring you everywhere?"

"I mean . . ." That's not the response I was expecting. "I guess . . . you could still do that from time to time."

The sun catches the gold in his hair. The Ramones are playing, but neither of us is singing along.

"I feel like we should enjoy the weather before the next sixty-five days of gloom," he says, taking an exit that leads to neither of our houses.

"You're such a Seattleite. Everyone here always feels guilty for not enjoying the sun when it's out."

"Because we get so little of it!"

I'm teasing, but my heart is racing. *We* should enjoy it, he said. "What did you have in mind?" I ask.

We wind up at a park overlooking the lake, and even after

we get out of the car, I'm not entirely sure what Chase's motivation is. If this means he's forgiven me.

"The band . . . really missed you," Chase says as we walk through the trees. Spring blooms are just beginning to come to life.

"Oh, did they?"

He stops in his tracks and taps my shoe with his. "Yeah. And—I did too. I missed you. Not just in the band. And playing that song with you today . . . I felt something incredible?"

"I did too." I try to disguise the hopefulness in my voice and fail. Slowly I inch closer to him.

With a deep breath, he rakes a hand through his hair. "Nothing feels as good as when I'm around you," he blurts. "Not playing music, not listening to music, not doing English homework. When I'm alone, listening in my car, I'm imagining you with some snarky comment or cool fact, or admitting you haven't heard a certain artist, and I'd tell you all about it. Or you'd find something new for me."

My heart is in my throat now. "I have a whole collection of songs saved up," I admit. "For if-slash-when you'd want to, you know . . . Be friends again."

"That's not what I want," he says, linking his fingers through mine. He tugs me close to him, and his other hand tilts my face until we're a breath apart.

"Oh" is all I have time to say before our lips meet.

CHAPTER 37

SOPHIE

WHEN THEY FIND OUT I MADE IT INTO THE workshop, Montana and Liz take me to their favorite café and insist on buying me a gooey piece of chocolate cake to celebrate. I might adore them.

"You're going to love it," Montana gushes. "And it'll be good for you to get away from everything here."

They know what happened with Peter, though I haven't talked about him as much I did with my sister. In an ideal world, I would've run to them and mourned the breakup. They would've watched bad movies with me, eaten ice cream. But I'm still trying to figure out this whole friendship thing.

"Yeah," I say. "I think it will be." Something tugs at my chest. High school and dance team—they're both almost over. "I'm going to miss you both next year."

"You'll have to come visit us," Montana says. "If you want to visit any colleges in NYC, you could totally stay with us."

A pressure builds behind my eyes. "I would love that."

"Don't cry!" Liz says, and they leap out of their chairs to squeeze me into a hug, which makes me really lose it.

"I just—I feel like you guys are kind of my people?" I say. "Is that weird?"

"Liz, we're *people*," Montana says, and I hug them tighter.

The closer it gets, the harder it is for me to believe this workshop is actually happening. I've gotten a roommate assignment and a packing list, along with a few choreographers to study before I go.

I browse Seattle Central's course catalog and I take my finals and I make it through graduation. I'm no longer planning to transfer wherever Peter goes, but I missed all the application deadlines, so for now, I'm a Seattle Central student. I'm already researching universities with good dance programs, though, and hopefully I'll be at one of them next fall. At first I'm not sure how I get through everything without Peter. But I have more than Peter now: I have my sister, and Montana, and Liz, and a closeness with my parents, even, that I didn't have before.

But I still don't want to feel like I've lost him completely. We've been tied together for so long that it doesn't feel right to leave for the summer without saying good-bye.

Sophie

5:12 p.m.

I got into the workshop.

Peter

5:17 p.m.

That's amazing!!! Congratulations!

5:19 p.m.

☺

Thanks. I'm terrified and excited.

5:20 p.m.

When do you leave?

5:24 p.m.

In three days.

5:30 p.m.

Wow.

5:48 p.m.

So . . . I was hoping we could talk before

then.

Before I go.

5:50 p.m.

I'd like that.

5:55 p.m.

Okay. Me too.

We agree to meet that night in the woods behind Peter's house. We don't walk there together, and he gets there first.

He turns when he hears me approaching, lifts his hand in

a wave. We wave now, like our parents used to do after they drifted apart the first time.

"I'm glad you texted," he says. "It would have been weird for you to leave and for us not to . . . talk. Just talking. No yelling this time."

"Thank God," I say, laughing a little, though it's not exactly funny.

"Congratulations again. About the workshop."

"Thanks."

"And you've been feeling okay?"

"For the most part." Which is true.

"Good."

More silence.

The wind plays with Peter's hair, and I shiver when the breeze hits my arms. Another gray-skied June.

He scuffs his shoe in the dirt. "Is this—what we did—is it the kind of thing we can never come back from? The kind of thing that ruins people like us?"

"I've sort of been hoping not." I let my shoulders sag. "What actually happened. The, um, act itself. It wasn't terrible for you, was it?"

He flushes. Laughs. "In the moment, no. Definitely not terrible."

I laugh too, nervously. "I'm glad my first time was with you. I think I would have always wondered, always wished it had been you. You don't—you don't wish we hadn't?"

"No. No. It was . . . nice. Being that close to you." He's entirely red now, focused on fiddling with the bracelet on his wrist.

"Good," I say, exhaling deeper than I expected to.

"It wasn't just sex, though. That . . . changed us, I mean."

"No. It wasn't. It was a lot of things."

"You were completely right about this friendship revolving around me," he says, "and that was not fair at all."

I nod. "And I can't do that anymore."

"I get it. You shouldn't have to."

He drags his hand through the leaves of a nearby tree, and I remember a time when we were convinced the sound of the wind rustling through the branches was actually the trees communicating with each other. This spot—this entire city—has too many memories.

"It's strange," I start. "I—I don't know what our friendship looks like if I'm not always giving in to you. And that's really hard to admit."

He tugs some pine needles off the tree, lets them flutter to the ground. His eyes are wide, deep, sad. "I'm so sorry, Soph."

Bravery compels me forward. I am not done yet. "I've always been kind of defined by you. And for a while that seemed good— like, I was so in love with you that it didn't matter. But I have to figure out who I am on my own. And now that I'm about to really go out and do that, with the workshop . . . God. I am so fucking nervous." Anxiety turns my breaths shaky. "There will be so many new people, so many strangers . . ."

"They'll get to know you," he says, and it strikes me that in the past, whenever he reassured me, he'd touch me, even in some small way. "And once they do, they'll love you. And your big brain, too."

My heart swells at that old joke. Maybe I thought we were past jokes now, that whatever our new relationship is, inside jokes couldn't be part of it. Hearing one again is bittersweet.

We stand there in silence for a while. Our silences never used to be like this. Silences between real friends are supposed to be comfortable. My dad told me that once, that that's how you know your friendship is true: You can be quiet together. But this one is charged, not peaceful. Like even a cough or a breath could disturb it.

"I'm always going to be grateful," he says, puncturing the quiet between us. "You know that, right? I could say thank you a million times and it wouldn't be enough. I could utter it once a minute every day for the rest of my life, and it wouldn't be enough."

"I—I know." I sigh. "And I want you to know that you don't owe me anything. This was my choice. And I've never regretted it."

There's so much space between us, our bodies unsure how to navigate this distance. We are crossed arms and shifted weight, elbow scratches and hand-wringing. "I really wanted to love you in that way at the same time you did," he says. "I hope you can believe that."

"But you didn't."

"No. I'm sorry." His brows knit together, and he looks pained for a moment. "We've had a lot of good times, though, right?

It wasn't always horrible, being my friend? Was it?" His voice cracks, and it nearly breaks me in half.

"No!" I say quickly. "God, no. Most of the time, our friendship was the best thing in my life."

"That's what I've been worried about. Like somehow this fight canceled out every good moment between us."

"It didn't. I swear."

He fidgets with his bracelet again. He hasn't said anything about my missing charms, but when we first got here, his gaze lingered on my wrist for a few moments before I tugged down my sleeve.

"You and the dance team, you've been getting closer, right? I see you in the cafeteria. You look . . . different with them than you used to."

"Yeah. We are. Montana and Liz are pretty great."

"I'm so glad."

"How's Chase?"

He gets this sunny expression on his face. "Good. Really good. We're back together, and it's going well. Slow, but good."

I echo him: "I'm glad."

We're all small talk now.

"Do you . . . have anywhere to be?" he asks.

I shake my head. "Why? Eager to leave already?"

"No"—and he looks a little shocked that I would assume this, even as a joke—"I—I have something for you." With that, he pulls out his phone.

"I already have a phone, but . . . thanks?"

A roll of his eyes. "Listen."

He taps the screen a few times, amps the volume. The piano notes are familiar at first, but I can't place them—

Until, suddenly, I do.

The song Peter wrote for me all those years ago.

When he loved me but I wasn't there yet.

The first time we fucked up the timing.

"Peter," I say, my voice breaking his name into three pieces. "You didn't have to do this."

"Shhh," he says, shushing me so we can hear the adorably juvenile lyrics he rerecorded just for me. "This is where it gets good. And when I say 'good,' I mean mortifying beyond words."

I'm crying now; I can't help it, and I'm not sure if I'm sad or happy or both.

Without worrying about what it means, I lean in and hug him tightly, his phone mashed between us, the song still pouring out of it. I inhale that good Peter scent like always, but it does not destroy me. It only aches a little, being this close to him. And when his arms come around me to pull me closer, I don't have to beg my heart to slow down.

I'm not sure who we'll be when I get back from San Francisco. I'm not sure if he'll still be half of Peter-and-Chase, or a fifth of his band. I'm not sure if I'll be able to hug him with this kind of ease or if he'll still want rides from me. I'm not sure if he'll text me in the middle of the night because he needs to play me a song he just discovered, or if I'll hear his melodies when I'm dancing.

But he will always be Peter and I will always be Sophie, and no matter who else we become, our history and our scars will always connect us.

"It's not that bad of a song," he says into my ear. "Is it?"

"No," I agree. "It really isn't."

And then I let go of him first, this boy who never belonged to me.

I

    let

        go

           first.

ACKNOWLEDGMENTS

My deepest gratitude to Jennifer Ung, who somehow did not run away screaming when I sent her my first draft. I'm perpetually awed by your brilliant insight and boundless enthusiasm. Thank you for helping me see what this book could be, for loving Sophie and Peter as much as I do. I could not be happier with this final product.

Sarah Creech: thank you, thank you for this stunning cover. You captured the book's wistfulness so perfectly! A million thanks too to Mara Anastas, Jodie Hockensmith, and the rest of the team at Simon Pulse. I'm forever grateful to my agent, Laura Bradford, for making all of this possible.

Thank you to everyone who read this book and offered feedback at various stages: Kelsey Rodkey, Kit Frick, Marisa Kanter, Sonia Hartl, Carlyn Greenwald, Gloria Chao, Rachel Griffin, Rachel Simon, Jennifer Hawkins, Jeanmarie Anaya, and Jonathan Goldhirsch. My dear Electric Eighteens and Class 2K18: thank you for helping make the debut experience (and beyond) such a positive one. I'm honored to know you all!

Thank you to the University of Washington Medical Center and in particular, Dr. Nicolae Leca, who so patiently answered my transplant questions.

As always, thank you to my parents for their excitement about every step of this process. As a kid, I asked them if it was okay if I added a swear word to one of the "books" I was writing. They told me I could even include *two* if I really wanted. I'm sorry to report this book has a few more than that. Ivan, my love and best friend, thank you for making me laugh every single day.

Finally, I'm so grateful for the booksellers, librarians, educators, bloggers, and fellow authors who championed my first book, *You'll Miss Me When I'm Gone*. Your support has meant the world to me. Thank you, thank you, thank you.

ABOUT THE AUTHOR

Rachel Lynn Solomon lives, writes, and tap-dances in Seattle, Washington. She is the author of two young adult novels, *You'll Miss Me When I'm Gone* and *Our Year of Maybe*. Once she helped set a Guinness World Record for the most natural redheads in one place. You can find her online at rachelsolomonbooks.com and on Twitter and Instagram @rlynn_solomon.